A mistake.

He was close. Too close. The moment was too familiar, as if no time had passed. As if he could bli

ye

wi

AUG   2012

BOOK YOUR PLACE ON OUR WEBSITE AND MAKE THE READING CONNECTION!

We've created a customized website just for our very special readers, where you can get the inside scoop on everything that's going on with Zebra, Pinnacle and Kensington books.

When you come online, you'll have the exciting opportunity to:

- View covers of upcoming books
- Read sample chapters
- Learn about our future publishing schedule (listed by publication month *and author*)
- Find out when your favorite authors will be visiting a city near you
- Search for and order backlist books from our online catalog
- Check out author bios and background information
- Send e-mail to your favorite authors
- Meet the Kensington staff online
- Join us in weekly chats with authors, readers and other guests
- Get writing guidelines
- AND MUCH MORE!

**Visit our website at
http://www.kensingtonbooks.com**

His
Woman

DIANA COSBY

ZEBRA BOOKS
Kensington Publishing Corp.
www.kensingtonbooks.com

ZEBRA BOOKS are published by

Kensington Publishing Corp.
850 Third Avenue
New York, NY 10022

All Kensington titles, imprints, and distributed lines are available at special quantity discounts for bulk purchases for sales promotion, premiums, fund-raising, educational, or institutional use.

Special book excerpts or customized printings can also be created to fit specific needs. For details, write or phone the office of the Kensington Special Sales Manager: Attn. Special Sales Department. Kensington Publishing Corp., 850 Third Avenue, New York, NY 10022. Phone: 1-800-221-2647.

Zebra and the Z logo Reg. U.S. Pat. & TM Off.

ISBN-13: 978-1-4201-0109-6
ISBN-10: 1-4201-0109-9

First Printing: December 2008
10 9 8 7 6 5 4 3 2 1

Printed in the United States of America

For Skip—

I love you

ACKNOWLEDGMENTS

My heartfelt thanks, respect, and love to Shirley Rogerson, Michelle Hancock, Karin Story Dearborn, and Mary J. Forbes.

Special thanks to my children and the Wild Writers for their continuous amazing support.

Chapter 1

He thought her a whore.

As if his opinion of her mattered now. But it did. Three years hadn't begun to diminish Lady Isabel Adair's love for Duncan MacGruder.

From the riverbank, she stared at the rush of water that cut through dense forest, the river a sanctuary she and Duncan had visited many times over. Where he'd drawn her into his arms and while his own hands had trembled with youthful nerves, he had claimed his first kiss.

Tears blurred her vision. No, Duncan hadn't forgiven her or forgotten. Fate hadn't been that kind. Except his loathing was but a pittance of what she had already served herself.

A stick cracked behind her.

Isabel whirled, her heart pounding. Had Frasyer followed her? Or had one of his knights? Shielding her hand over her eyes, she searched the tangle of elm, ash, and fir, straining to see through the strangled over-growth and the shadows for the faintest sign of anyone.

Nothing.

A gust of wind swirled around her, thick with the scent of the oncoming spring, tainted with the last dregs of winter. She willed herself to calm. The self-serving Earl of Frasyer could not have seen her leave Moncreiffe Castle. He had ridden off a short while ago with a contingent of knights to investigate a rumor that William Wallace, the Scottish rebel leader, had been sighted to the south.

A lie. One she had ensured reached his ears.

She needed this afternoon to meet in secret with her brother, Symon. By nightfall she would be snug within her bed and Frasyer none the wiser.

After making the sign of the cross, she spared one final glance toward the river of her dreams, then turned and hurried through the woods along an overgrown path. A thrill shot through her as she caught sight of the neglected crofter's hut, framed by the aged boughs of a fallen birch.

Fragments of pottery lay strewn near the door, tattered strips of cloth covered the sagging windows, and the nearby stable sat in shambles. Not even a wisp of smoke swirled from the hovel's half-fallen chimney. To anyone passing by, it would appear abandoned.

Isabel scanned her surroundings one last time before stepping past the ruins to enter the dim, candlelit room. Warmth and relief rushed her as she saw her brother standing facing her father, his back to her.

"Symon."

Steel hissed against leather, and Isabel found

herself with a tip of a claymore pressed against her neck.

The tall, weapon-clad man sporting a full beard had spun toward her in a trice, his stance fierce, made more so by the shadows carved upon his face.

A smile, as quick as it was tender, curved his mouth. His body relaxed. "Isabel." Symon Adair's red hair shifted on his shoulders as he slid his weapon into a leather sheath secured on his back. He stepped forward and caught her in a fierce hug.

"You should not have come. It is too dangerous."

"I had to see you." Isabel glanced at her father, who shifted uncomfortably several paces away. "When Da told me of your visit—"

Symon shot their father a harsh look. "You should not have mentioned my coming. It is risky enough for us to meet on my way to pick up coin for the rebels. You know well it is death for anyone caught within my presence."

Lord Angus Adair stiffened. "Blast it, lad, I—"

"I pestered him," Isabel interrupted, not wanting to spend their precious time together arguing, especially if Symon discovered that their father had been drunk again at the time of the telling.

"It is no excuse." Her brother caught her chin and scanned her face. "You have circles under your eyes. Is that bastard Frasyer treating you poorly?"

She winced. "Symon—"

"Is he?"

"No," she lied, afraid if she admitted the truth Symon would endanger himself defending her honor.

"You would be deserving better. Duncan would have—"

"Leave the lass be," Angus blustered as he stepped

forward, his bushy brows at odds with his balding head.

Symon scowled at his father. "Aye, it is not Isabel who is at fault, is it? But your gambling that is the cause of all this."

"Symon!"

At Isabel's sharp tone, her brother's eyes dulled with self-recrimination. "I know. I cannot change his losing our home to Frasyer on a bet any more than your decision to become Frasyer's mistress in place of payment."

"Nor would I be wanting you to." Liar. If she could, she would change everything. She would take back the three years of living a lie—a series of lies—and follow the abandoned dictates of her heart. But she may as well lie upon a faerie hill and cast wishes into the wind for all it would help her. She'd already lost Duncan's love. She refused to endanger the lives of her father and brother.

Symon brushed a strand of her hair behind her ear. "I had not meant to be badgering you. I love you, lass. My words are born of naught but worry."

"I know."

"If Frasyer treats you less than you are deserving, tell me, do you hear?"

"Aye, my bonny lad. You would be the first to know." With a lightness she didn't feel, Isabel gave him a sound kiss on his cheek, then walked over and hugged her father. "It is good to see you again, Da."

He returned the embrace, the tiredness in his brown eyes warming to pleasure. "And you, daughter."

She stepped away and dug out an aged leather sack from beneath her cloak. "It is the wild thyme and chamomile I promised you. Brew a tea with them in the morning. They will ease your headaches." Aches he wouldn't have to contend with if he drank less.

Aye, the drink brought on his pounding head, but his shame for her choice to become Frasyer's mistress to cover his gambling away their home had aged him a decade over the last three years.

Deep lines sagged his clean-shaven face. Too much worry stifled his once carefree expression. And his once thick, unruly whisky-colored hair, so like her own, now gave way to baldness with only fringes of a white halo gracing his head.

"Thanks, lass." With a nod, her father accepted the pouch and shoved the herbs in his pocket.

She glanced at her brother. Stern lines dug deep furrows across his handsome face. "You and the rest of the rebels will have moved from Selkirk Forest."

Symon stroked his fingers through his mustache, then down through his beard. "Aye. The bastard Longshanks is determined to have Wallace's head on a pike or any other who dares defy him in his bid to claim Scotland. We have moved into the bogs to the west." Devilment sparked his eyes. "I am not sure who are more hesitant to enter, the hounds or the bloody Sassenachs."

Isabel chuckled at her brother's use of the English king's nickname given to him for his height. She could easily imagine King Edward's knights' ear-blistering curses as they struggled to navigate through the soggy tract of land only to come up empty-handed.

"I bet you give them a fine run," she said. "If there is anything I can do—"

Blue eyes clouded with anger. "There is not."

On a broken sigh, she withdrew the gift she'd stowed within her cloak. She handed it to Symon.

"What is it?"

"Open it and you will see."

With nimble fingers, her brother unfolded the cloth. "Wallace's arms," he whispered in appreciation. He withdrew the delicate swath of fabric, smoothed it flat across his palm and traced a finger around the edge of the embroidered lion sewn in silver and complemented by a background of deep red.

Isabel touched the chain around her neck holding the finely crafted pendant hidden beneath. "The design matches my necklace."

His expression melted into pleasure. "It is a fine hand you have," he whispered, "like our mother."

Tears misted her eyes. No compliment could have touched her more. "I had meant to give it to you months ago. But this . . . this is the first I have seen you since I finished it."

With care, he folded the cloth over the delicate embroidery. "It is beautiful. And dangerous if you had been caught making it."

"You are worth any risk."

Symon drew her into a tender hug. "My thanks."

Isabel leaned into him, cherishing this moment.

The scuff of boots echoed from outside.

Stiffening in her brother's arms, Isabel whirled toward the entry. *Please, God, let me be wrong!*

The door crashed open. With their swords raised, knights charged the confines. Their leader stepped before his men.

Frasyer!

Symon withdrew his claymore and moved before Isabel.

With a curse, her father unsheathed his sword as well and moved beside his son.

The earl shoved his woolen hood away from his face. Brown hair tightly bound behind his neck accented gray eyes as caustic as a winter storm. He turned toward Symon and his nostrils flared with malignant satisfaction.

Isabel started forward. "No!"

Symon caught her arm and shoved her behind him. "Stay there!" He pointed his claymore toward the earl.

"How touching. It appears I have interrupted a family reunion," Frasyer drawled, as his knights spread out in the limited space behind him. His jaw tightened as he glared at Isabel. "And you. How dare you defy my orders to meet with this rebel!"

"Symon is family."

"Your brother is a traitor and will be dealt with accordingly." Frasyer nodded toward her father. "As will Lord Caelin."

"Let them go. Please." She fought for calm, but fear trembled through her voice.

Frasyer gestured toward the door. "Return to Moncreiffe Castle. I will deal with your betrayal later."

She'd seen him use this calm tone when his fury peaked. In the past, she'd always thanked God it was never directed at her. Except she doubted even God could help her now.

"And you," he said to Symon, his placid tone at odds with the fury burning in his eyes. "Tell me where Wallace is hiding and I may choose to spare your worthless life."

Symon spat on the floor. "I would die before I would tell anything to vermin such as yourself."

Outrage mottled Frasyer's cheeks. His gaze sliced toward Isabel. "Do not defy me. Leave!"

She swallowed hard. "And allow you to kill them?"

Frasyer's eyes narrowed on her. Comprehension flickered in his gaze, then a slow, mean smile edged his mouth. "You know where Wallace is hiding."

"Tell the bastard naught," Symon growled.

Her throat tightened. Why had her brother spoken? His claim had undermined any argument she might have used to deny her knowledge of the rebel leader's hideout.

Isabel touched the dagger hidden beneath the folds of her cloak. If she could move close enough to Frasyer, mayhap she could catch him by surprise and buy her brother and father time to make their escape.

"I wish to speak with you in private," Isabel said.

Frasyer arched a brow. "Speak."

She turned sideways and tried to step between her father and brother; they didn't budge. "Let me pass."

"Frasyer will not take you," Symon stated.

The earl's gaze flicked to where her hand had paused over her weapon. "Do not be a fool and challenge me, Isabel. I have twenty-two of my best knights in company." At her silence, the earl's lips curled into a nasty expression. "I see you have made your choice. An unwise one that your father will pay for as well. Not with his home, but with his life."

"No!" She shoved at Symon's shoulder; he blocked her as Frasyer and his men charged him.

Metal clanged as Symon intercepted a blow from Frasyer's master-at-arms. Two knights caught her father and slammed him against the wall. The knight closest to Lord Caelin bashed the hilt of his sword against her father's head.

Isabel withdrew her dagger as her father staggered, blood seeping from a narrow gash in his head. "Da!"

Symon's strangled curse caught her attention. Air exploded from her chest as Frasyer shoved his blade deeper in Symon's side. "Symon!"

With a rough pull, Frasyer freed his weapon.

Clutching his side, his face blanching, her brother crumpled to the floor. His claymore jangled to silence by his side.

The room spun. Isabel dropped next to her brother and gathered him into her arms. "Oh, Symon!"

"Isa—" A cough staggered from his lips.

"Stay quiet," she whispered, horrified at the bright red beginning to stain his side. *Oh, God, please don't let him die.* Not Symon. He was her only hold on sanity in her fractured life. No matter what, she could come to him. Always.

He couldn't die.

Frasyer caught her shoulders and hauled Isabel to her feet. "Where is Wallace?"

"Damn you!" She shoved against his chest and broke free. Isabel drove her dagger toward Frasyer.

The earl caught her wrist and squeezed. Pain ripped through her arm, and the knife clattered to the floor.

"You are a fool," the earl seethed.

A few feet away, Symon gasped for his every breath. Sprawled within his left hand lay the delicate embroidery of Wallace's arms.

"Let me go to him," she pleaded. "Symon needs me."

Frasyer's fingers bit deeper into her flesh. Cruel, determined lines scored his face. "Tell me."

"Do not," her father yelled.

Like a wolf sensing its prey, Frasyer's gaze settled on her father, pinned against the wall by two of his knights. "Mayhap he knows."

Fresh fear ripped through her veins. Isabel's entire body trembled. "No!" Frasyer's brand of questioning would cripple her father. And her brother, her dear brother, who lay dying, she had to protect him as well. "He knows nothing. I swear it."

Frasyer glanced at Lord Caelin with disdain.

She strained against his hold. "He is no threat to you."

"No?" Frasyer watched her with a calculating expression. "He had a rendezvous with a known outlaw."

The bastard. "He met his son!"

"As Earl of Frasyer and magistrate of these lands, I view his presence differently." He tugged her closer, his mouth curling into a sneer. "Give me what I want or I will charge your father with aiding the rebels and he will hang."

Stricken, she stared at the man to whom she'd already sold her soul, loathing him more than she'd ever thought possible to loathe another human being.

"He knows nothing," she whispered. "You know that. All that interests his mind is gambling and drink." Isabel cringed inwardly at the truth. If it would save him, she would admit anything.

"Is that so?" He leaned closer until their faces were inches apart. "I am not so sure. Lord Caelin is known for his, let us say, questionable associations."

Her brother's moans from several feet away,

dragged her gaze toward him. She needed to tend to Symon. "Please, do not do this."

"Whatever happens now is your decision. Will your father live or die?"

"My brother—"

"Too late for him. It is your father's life that we speak of."

Fear clawed at her chest. Desperately, she searched for another option to save her father and caught sight of her dagger on the floor. Isabel tore her hand free and dove for her weapon.

With a grunt of disgust, Frasyer planted his boot upon the blade. He stared down at her. "You may not be privy to the rebels' plans, but I would wager you know where they are hiding." He reached down and snatched the dagger. "It will take a fortnight to prepare and deliver the charges of your father's suspicious activity to King Edward's Scottish adviser, the Baron of Monceaux." His voice turned silky. "If you have not told me where Wallace's hideout is by then, your father will be found a traitor against England and hung. After, I will deal with you . . . in private."

Isabel opened her mouth to respond, unsure what to say.

"The Bible," Lord Caclin hissed between rough breaths.

Isabel crawled closer to her father so she could hear him.

Lord Caelin lifted his head nearer to her. "In your mother's Bible. Search for the answer there."

At the knowing smile creeping over Frasyer's lips, she froze. He'd overheard!

The earl gestured toward her father as he spoke

to his master-at-arms. "Take him to the Baron of Monceaux at Rothfield Castle. Notify him that Lord Caelin is to be charged with treason against the crown, and I will be sending a writ outlining the details of his offenses posthaste. King Edward will enjoy displaying his head on a pike for all to witness the penance if they dare to betray him."

"Yes, my lord." The master-at-arms motioned toward several knights. The men wrestled her father out the door.

"Da!" Isabel started to run after them, but Frasyer caught her.

Without taking his gaze from hers, the earl nodded toward another knight. "Travel to Lord Caelin's home and retrieve the family Bible. If anyone asks, tell them Isabel wishes to have it for prayers." He turned toward her with a smug look. "She will be needing each and every one."

The knight gave a brisk nod and left.

Her trembling legs threatened to buckle. How had everything gone so horribly wrong? She'd come here to see Symon and her father. Now, they were taking her father to England where his sentence of death would be certain. And Symon, dear Symon, her voice of sanity was dying. Pain fisted in her chest as her brother struggled to breathe.

Frasyer jerked her closer. "You know what you have to do to free your father."

So riveted on the sight of her brother crumpled upon the floor, she barely heard Frasyer's threat. Her brother was expiring.

"Is—Isabel," Symon rasped. He coughed, a rough, strangled sound.

Her heart was breaking as she watched her brother

fight for each breath, his pale face glistening with sweat.

"Please, help my brother," she begged.

Frasyer's eyes narrowed. "Tell me where Wallace is hiding."

The one thing he wanted was the one thing she couldn't give him. After Symon had sacrificed his life for Wallace's cause, she refused to betray him. Or the freedom hundreds of people—their people—had sacrificed their lives for.

Neither could she allow her father to die.

From the depths of her trauma grew a will so fierce, a determination so deep, she almost gasped. The strength, drive to succeed, overwhelmed her. She knew what she must do. While Frasyer attended his estate, she would find a way to slip from her chamber and retrieve the Bible. She prayed the heirloom held proof of her father's innocence against Frasyer's charges.

Then Lord Monceaux would make the prudent decision. She wanted to believe that as King Edward's adviser to the Scots, he would not hang a clansman when incontestable evidence of his innocence existed.

As her only hope, she had to try.

Isabel leveled her gaze on Frasyer. "I will tell you naught."

Disgust soured his face. "Then rot where you belong." Frasyer dragged her to her feet and shoved Isabel into a guard's arms. "Lock her in the dungeon."

"The dungeon!" Horrified, she fought to break free. She'd expected to be left guarded in her chamber as was common for gentry-held captives, not locked within the vile confines Frasyer had constructed below ground. To her knowledge, no one had ever escaped from there.

At least not alive.

"Frasyer!" Isabel pleaded.

He didn't turn or stop to listen as he headed outside. The clatter of hooves upon dirt and rock sounded as Frasyer, leading his men, rode past.

"Come." The guard dragged her toward the door. Frantic, she glanced toward her brother. "Symon!" She tried to jerk free of the knight's grip. He tightened his hold and hauled her outside.

As the fading shards of sunset greeted her, brilliant in their red-gold streaks across the sky, she caught one last glimpse of her brother's limp form.

A deep keening tore from her soul. Symon's blood stained the earthen floor in a crimson puddle. In his left hand, sprawled open, lay the delicate embroidery of Wallace's arms she'd gifted him with but moments before.

Leaning against the stone wall, Duncan Mac-Gruder stared at Alys haloed in the red-gold of the waning sunset. Her full mouth begged to be kissed, but her eyes were ripe with hesitation.

His body hardened nonetheless. Both knew why he was here. He'd tasted her charms many times before. Her ploy as an innocent was a game they both enjoyed.

A cloud slid over the fading sunlight, casting the woman in shadows. He blinked as her eyes grew more intense, her hair darkening to the spellbinding shade of aged whisky.

Isabel.

His breath caught in his throat at the wash of betrayal and longing her image evoked.

Sunlight spilled free as the cloud moved past and the image faded.

Bedamned. Why had he thought of Isabel now? The very memory of her threatened to destroy his mood. Would he ever forget her? In an agile move, he leaped to the ground before Alys. Aye, he'd bloody well erase every trace of Isabel from his body, mind, and soul.

"Just one kiss?" He allowed his smile to deepen into a dimpled curve.

"Me mum is expecting me." Alys made no move to leave.

"I will not keep you, but my heart would be breaking without a taste of your lips." He placed his hand over his heart. "You would not leave a man begging you for a wee kiss, would you now, lass?"

She hesitated a playful moment. "One then."

With his body thrumming with anticipation, he nuzzled her neck, savoring the silky skin of her throat. She shuddered, and he slid his hand up to slowly caress the back of her neck.

"Duncan?"

He nibbled his way along her jaw. "Aye?"

"I thought you were going to kiss me?"

"I am getting to that." When she wrapped her hands around his neck and drew him closer, he backed her farther into the cool shadows. He edged her against the stone wall until he could press the entire length of his body against hers.

At her moan, he cupped the swells of her breasts. Blessed simplicity. A soft, warm body to lose himself in without the complications of love.

Or betrayal.

Hoofbeats pounded in the distance.

He pulled away and whirled toward the sound. A rider was heading straight toward them. Friend or foe? With the English scouring the countryside for Wallace or any rebel supporters, one could never tell.

"Duncan?"

He glanced at Alys, the desire hazing her eyes made him curse the interruption more. Still, he had no choice.

"Be off with you now."

A pout formed on her lips. "But I thought—"

"I will be returning to your house later tonight. We will be finishing."

The echo of hoofbeats increased.

A frown touched Alys's forehead as she glanced toward the incoming rider. She faced Duncan. "I would be liking that." With a blush on her cheeks, she slipped around the stone wall and disappeared.

At the thud of hooves upon tufts of grass, with his body still raging its demand, Duncan glared at the incoming rider. He curled his hand on the hilt of his sword.

The lone man was slumped in the saddle. As he drew closer to Duncan, recognition dawned.

Symon?

He bolted toward his friend.

The horse cantered without guidance, its reins loose over the saddle and tossed about in the wind.

A dark red line stained Symon's left side.

Wild-eyed, the horse shied away at Duncan's approach.

"Steady there, lad." He snagged the bridle, the scent of blood strong. "Symon?"

His friend groaned and fell forward.

Duncan caught Symon and laid him on the ground as gently as possible. By God, the wound in his left side was an ugly, angry gash. It would take a needle and thread and a miracle to heal.

Why wasn't he hidden with Wallace in the bogs west of Selkirk Forest? What had occurred for Symon to risk exposing himself? Duncan tore a strip off his tunic and pressed it to Symon's side. "What has happened?"

Symon's eyes flickered open. "Frasyer."

Though whispered, the name exploded in Duncan's mind like oil tossed in a fire too hot. "The bastard. I will—"

Symon coughed and blood trickled from his mouth. "Save Isabel."

Isabel? His heart kicked for an entirely different reason. She was in danger? "Where is she?"

A shudder racked his friend's body. "Frasyer has locked her in his dungeon." He worked for his next words. "Get her out."

"I will," he said between clenched teeth, "after I murder him with my bare hands."

"No. With your ties to Wallace, Frasyer would gladly use any excuse to kill you. You must sneak in." Symon grasped Duncan's tunic, his body trembling with visible effort. The despair in Symon eyes chilled Duncan's blood further. "Promise me you will see her free."

He'd loved Isabel, and she'd betrayed him. Everything in him screamed to keep his distance from a woman who'd seemed so pure yet was poison to his soul.

"You need a healer," Duncan said.

Symon's breathing faltered. His hands fell limp to his sides. "It is too late for me."

'Twas true. His friend's voice had eroded to a harsh whisper, his skin decaying to a chalky sheen. "Symon—"

"Save my sister."

Duncan's heart tore apart. He loved this man like a brother and despised Symon's sister like Satan's curse.

Symon's gaze burned into him with fury. "Your vow!"

Duncan curled his hand into a fist and damned the words. Damned himself. He could do no less for a friend. "I swear it."

A flicker of peace touched Symon's face. "Give her this." His hand trembled as he slid a finely woven cloth stitched with Wallace's arms into Duncan's hand. "Tell Isabel . . . tell her I love her." He exhaled sharply. On a ragged breath, Symon sagged back, lifeless.

Chapter 2

With his body wedged against the cold stone walls of Moncreiffe Castle's latrine shaft, Duncan's muscles screamed their outrage. Bracing his boot in another slippery crevice, he pushed upward. With each step, he cursed the woman he'd come to rescue.

"You had better be appreciating this," he muttered to himself. He tugged the cloth secured around his nose tighter, then reached for his next hold. As if Isabel would. He needed wealth and status before she'd grant him her favor.

Such as she had done with Frasyer.

The thought curdled in his gut with the impact of the stench surrounding him.

The worn, worsted wool sack hanging from Duncan's shoulder snagged on a rough stone as he pulled himself up. He grumbled a curse under his breath as he untangled the bag holding the disguise for himself and Isabel.

Duncan wrapped his fingers tightly around the next stone. "And what did bedding an earl buy ye, lass?" His muscles bunched as he inched up. "The dungeon. And it is the why of it I will be learning when I reach you."

Above him, the dim flicker of light sifted through the portal. He wrinkled his nose in disgust. The insult of having to scale the latrine chute at dusk was humbling. With Frasyer's castle well guarded and after two attempts to sneak in having failed after his solemn vow to Symon two days past, Duncan had been left no choice but to slip inside using this dank entry.

As he stretched for the next indent, his fingers slid against the slimy surface. With a scowl, he wiped his hands on the thin cloth he'd wrapped around his waist to protect his trews. The stench was worse than fouled bog moss.

In the waning light, he searched for another hold. As much as he disliked Isabel, it would bring him no pleasure to inform her of her brother's death. His chest squeezed with a suffocating ache as he remembered his friend. At least he'd seen Symon properly buried.

So where was Symon's father, Lord Caelin? Of the many people Duncan had asked, no one seemed to know. He'd keep inquiring until he found him. As a close family friend, it was his duty to inform Symon's father of his son's death.

At the top of the latrine chute, he peered through the opening. A single torch lit the barren chamber. Mold clung on the lower walls. Rats squealed as they shot past, stirring dust motes. In the far corner near a poorly crafted bowl lay a pile of old rags. He scrunched his nose. The stench within rivaled that which clung to his garments.

"At least it is empty." With a grimace, Duncan squeezed through the hand-chiseled opening.

Men's voices echoed outside the door.

"Blast it." He hauled the bag up and dropped it to his side. Turning toward the door, he withdrew his sword.

Seconds passed.

Nearby, water dripped from a crack in the ceiling. Wind from the loch tunneled up the opening with an unsettling moan. Thankfully, the voices faded.

Relaxing, he secured his sword, tore off the protective cloth from his nose and garb and used both to wipe away any evidence from his climb.

Disgusted when he did no more than spread the brownish stains, he threw the soiled linen on top of the corner pile where it blended in. If his clothes reeked of dung, so be it. Without water to aid his efforts, he'd done all he could.

He tugged the priest's robe from the sack and shook his head at himself. "It is a sad day, lad, when you dress as a man of God for your enemy's mistress." But he'd made his promise—a promise he would keep before washing his hands of Isabel and her smoldering eyes and lying tongue once and for all.

He donned the garb, drew up the hood to cover his head, and headed down the corridor. At the entry to the stairs, voices echoed from below.

Duncan hurried down the spiral steps. As he moved into the shadows untouched by torchlight, two knights rounded the corner.

Nerves slammed home and Duncan slipped his hand inside his robe, clasping his hidden dagger as a precaution.

"Father," they greeted in unison.

He nodded. With his free hand, he made the sign of the cross. The knights moved aside in deference, and Duncan walked past, his grip easing on his dagger. He'd descended but a few steps when one of the knights called back.

"Father?"

Duncan halted, his senses on alert. Slowly, he turned to face them. "My son?"

One knight murmured something to the other, who then continued up the stairs. Once the other man had disappeared from view, the knight walked down and paused a foot away.

Relief edged through Duncan. If trouble started, at least the odds were even.

"It is about a lass," the knight said.

Duncan nodded, his grip upon his dagger firm. "We can speak of this in the chapel on the morrow if it serves you best." And by morning, he would be several leagues away with Isabel in tow.

The knight cleared his throat. "If you have time, Father, I would like to speak with you now. It will take but a trice."

"Of course." As if he had a choice. Trussed up as a man of God, it might raise suspicion if he turned the knight away.

A gust down the turret sent torchlight into a wild dance, exposing the man's cheeks flushed with embarrassment. "I have bedded two sisters and . . . they have each found out about the other." Guilt clung to his voice. "I am not sure what I should do? Or how to explain?"

Duncan almost laughed. Only a fool would bed sisters individually. Unless he was glib of tongue. Then he would bed them both at the same time.

"Father?"

He cleared his throat. "It is a serious sin you have committed. One not to be taken lightly."

The knight bowed his head with chagrin. "Aye. And that is why I have come. For my penance."

"You will be saying ten Our Father's and sweeping the chapel floors for the next fortnight," Duncan commanded. "The prayers will cleanse your soul of the sin and your labor will rid the church of the aged rushes."

"Thank you, Father."

Duncan made the sign of the cross. "Go then."

With a humble nod, the knight started to turn away, then paused. He sniffed. "Do you smell something foul?"

"Foul?" Duncan cursed silently, aware the hideous odor could only be a result of his climb from Hades. "Aye, it would be my cloak. One of the blasted dogs mistook it for a post and relieved himself on it." He shook his head with disgust. "I have aired it outside for the past three nights and still it reeks to the heavens."

The knight shrugged. "I have said myself the beasts should stay outside once the meals are over, but Lord Frasyer insists they remain within the keep."

"He is a stubborn man," Duncan agreed, "but one whom I serve through our Lord's guidance." He was surprised God didn't strike him down for that blatant lie. It'd take more than the Lord to achieve Duncan's forgiveness or acceptance for Frasyer luring Isabel away from him.

Or of Frasyer murdering Symon.

"Bless you, Father." The knight departed.

Duncan started down the steps. As he passed an arrow slit, he noted the sun had set and blackness was eroding the last fragments of the day. He had to hurry.

In the great hall, he avoided several more requests for his time with excuses of being needed at the chapel posthaste. At the dungeon's entrance, Duncan slipped past a guard busy charming a wench for a romp. With the castle secured for the night, the sentry had obviously dismissed any possible threat.

The trickle of water echoed from below as Duncan made his way down the steps Frasyer had shown him years ago, a time when they were friends. A lone torch impaled at the top of the steps illuminated the tufts of moss clinging in patches on the rough stone wall, lined with spider webs.

With quiet steps, Duncan rounded the last bend, only to collide with the ripe scent of the poorly kept cells. "God in heaven." Isabel lived in this? Had Symon known, he would have urged Duncan to kill Frasyer outright.

At the first door, he squinted through the tiny peephole.

Empty.

A tormented groan, he recognized as male, echoed from inside the next cell. Despite his assurance that Isabel meant nothing to him, his blood iced. *Please, God, let Isabel have been spared such brutality.*

Duncan moved on. Meager rays of light filtered through the small, narrowed windows. He couldn't make out if a prisoner was inside. After listening for several seconds, he concluded it was empty.

Frustrated, he hurried down the corridor. If possible, the stench grew worse. He almost heaved. Aye, he and his brothers had taken prisoners, a casualty of battle, but they'd ensured the men were treated with basic decency. This filth, that of rotting food and unkempt cells, wasn't fit for a maggot.

Whatever Isabel had done to upset Frasyer, she didn't deserve this.

"Where are you, lass?" His whisper melded with the echo of men's groans. Was Isabel hurt? Sick? Lying helpless and unable to yell for help?

If he didn't find her soon, with daylight fading, he might never be able to. With his mind steeped in emotions he'd rather not feel, Duncan moved to the next cell.

He peered inside. Wisps of the waning light embraced the profile of a woman standing near a pathetically small window. It outlined her slender body, the soft curve of her jaw, the paleness of her cheeks, and the lush whisky-colored tresses that settled over her shoulders like dying embers.

Isabel.

The years peeled away. Her laughter rushed over him, deep and warm. How her fingers had trembled as they'd skimmed across his chest with a nervous touch, and the need that had exploded between them as he'd stolen his first kiss.

Duncan smothered memories of their past, angry he could still be moved so deeply when it came to her. He removed the bar that bolted the thick wooden door and shoved it open.

Torchlight spilled into the dank chamber.

At the scrape of metal against wood, Isabel turned, her amber eyes wide and unsure. She frowned. "Father?"

Duncan glanced behind him, half expecting to

see a priest. He muttered a curse and shoved back his hood. "Nay."

Isabel paled. "Duncan?"

"Quiet, lass." He kept his voice soft. "The guards will be making their rounds soon, and you will be giving us both away." With one last glance toward the steps, he jumped into the cell and landed on the stiff bed of stale straw. "Hush."

"But—"

Duncan stepped forward and caught her arms.

A mistake.

He was close. Too close. The moment was too familiar, as if no time had passed. As if he could blink and make the nightmare of the last three years disappear.

Her full lips had parted in surprise, but wrapped within the soft luminescence of moonlight, all he could think of was her taste. Of how she had once responded to his touch. Except he'd never claimed what was rightfully his—that she'd given freely to his enemy. Nay, even worse, a false friend, as Frasyer had been during their youth.

Duncan released her as if burned. Isabel stumbled, then recovered.

"Why are you dressed like a priest? Or"—Isabel angled her chin—"has Frasyer sent you?"

"Frasyer? Nay. I came to help you escape."

She studied him as if trying to decide if he was telling the truth. "Why?"

His anger shoved up a notch. "Look around you, lass. You want to stay in this filth?"

She shook her head and slowly exhaled, drawing his attention to how her dress hung on her slender frame. The bastard was starving her. What other brutalities had Frasyer inflicted upon her?

"You should not be here," she said. "You are putting your life in danger."

He gave an indignant snort. "And you would be worrying about me?"

"Please leave."

He ignored her frantic warning. It didn't make sense. Unless . . . Duncan caught her wrists. "Is this a trap you helped Frasyer set up?"

Outrage spilled across her face. Isabel tried to yank her hands free. "I would never do such a thing."

"Like you would not break your betrothal with me to go to Frasyer's bed?" Bedamned! He hadn't meant to ask. He had no desire to relive the bitter betrayal of that time, but the words had already slipped from his mouth.

Isabel stiffened. "I would not see you harmed."

Oddly, he found himself believing her. In the scarred light, Duncan scanned the dismal cell. Except for a wooden bed piled with aged straw and a moth-eaten woolen blanket along with a half-empty bowl with contents he didn't wish to fathom, the chamber lay bare.

"I see Frasyer bestows his mistress with only the best of lodgings."

A blush scalded her cheeks, but she didn't turn away. "Why have you come?"

He released her. "Because Symon asked."

At the mention of her brother, her face lost any trace of color. Then, like the first rose of spring, her expression bloomed with hope.

"Symon?" A smile quivered on her lips. She stepped forward. "He is alive? Thank Mary, I thought he had died." She laid her hand on his forearm. "Where is he? I must—"

"Isabel." At his rough tone, her hand fell away. A dull pounding built in his head. He'd not wanted to tell Isabel like this, with her hopes soaring and her looking at him with such tender belief.

"Duncan?" Amber eyes watched him with fragile hope. At his silence, she clenched her hands into trembling fists. "Where is *Symon*?"

There would be no easy way to tell her. He handed her the embroidery. "He is dead."

"Dead?" Isabel's breath strangled in her throat as she clutched the delicate fabric. She'd allowed herself to hope, to believe the impossible. The cell blurred around her.

Symon.

Her brother, mentor, friend.

Dead.

Somewhere in the blackness, hands, strong and firm, caught her shoulders and brought her up against something warm. Something solid.

"I am sorry."

Duncan's whisper echoed in her mind. She'd foolishly allowed herself to believe the impossible— that her brother lived. All she wanted now was to cling to Duncan and allow him to protect her from this heartbreaking reality. To pretend the past three years had not happened. To imagine Symon healthy and happy, and Duncan's arms around her a common occurrence, not a gesture of borrowed support.

A yell from the courtyard startled her back to reality.

"We need to leave before the guards make their rounds," Duncan said.

Numb, she allowed him to lead her to the door. Steps echoed from the stairs.

With a curse, Duncan released her. He peered out the door. "Someone is coming. Stay here. I will return once they have left." For a second, he looked as if he wanted to say more, then he climbed from the cell. As he secured and then barred the door, blackness encased her. The soft echo of his footsteps faded.

Isabel sagged against the cold stone, wrapped her arms around her trembling body as she clutched the embroidery she'd given Symon, and tried to accept this twist of fate.

Duncan was here.

How she'd prayed for him to rescue her. Within that empty, forbidden world of her cell, she'd replayed the scene in her mind a thousand times. His smiling face framed by sun-bleached hair, the hair of a wayward faerie she'd always teased, laughing as his arrogant locks fell onto his shoulders in the haphazard tumble she so adored.

She would cry with joy as he swept her into his arms and claimed her mouth with possessive fierceness, that of the man who loved her, that of the man who could find it in his heart to forgive, and that of the man who understood she'd had no choice but to become Frasyer's mistress.

The rattle of keys down the corridor shattered her thoughts like pottery upon stone. They were naught but foolish dreams.

Symon would not rise from the grave.

And Duncan would never forgive her for becoming Frasyer's mistress as he believed. As much as she wanted to explain the circumstances leading to her role as Frasyer's mistress, she must not forget Frasyer's

threat to kill Duncan if she ever told him of her and
Frasyer's bargain.

She could only imagine Duncan's anger if he
learned the truth. There was no telling what he
would do. His knowing would only make a horrible
situation worse.

Aye, now Duncan was here. Not by choice, but
due to his loyalty to Symon.

Symon. Oh, God. She squeezed the embroidery
tight within her palm. Tears burned her throat.
Never again would she find comfort in her brother's
arms. In his strength. In his compassion. Or in the
sage advice of a brother who'd suffered his own personal misery when he'd learned of her decision to
become Frasyer's mistress.

By agreeing to Frasyer's demand, she'd thought
to protect her father and to save their home. Never
had she imagined her choice would one day play a
role in ending Symon's life.

But it had.

She shouldn't have gone to visit him that day, but
she had wanted to give Symon her embroidered gift.

Now he lay dead.

A sob racked her body. Then another. As tears
rolled down her cheeks, she turned to stare through
the window where the cold gray of the night stole
toward blackness.

She had to get out of here. To push past the pain,
to remember that more than her brother's life was
at stake. Her father depended on her.

Somehow, she must find the Bible.

Steps outside had her whirling to face the door. She
shoved the embroidery into her pocket as the slide of

a wooden bar clattered through the dungeon. Guards' voices murmured in the dank corridor.

A scuffle.

Terse voices shouted in argument.

Duncan! Isabel ran to the door. She pressed her ear against the cold wood and strained to hear.

Moments later, the voices stilled. Boots scraped to a stop outside her cell.

She stumbled back.

Wood grated as the bar to her door was lifted, then opened with a vicious shove. Yellowed torchlight raced through the blackness and one of the guards stepped into view.

"Here." He held out a half loaf of hard bread and a wedge of cheese.

She forced herself to step forward and accept the fare as if nothing was amiss. They hadn't seen Duncan. Another prisoner must have offered resistance.

"Move back," the guard ordered.

In silence, Isabel complied.

He jerked the door shut.

Darkness, cold and ugly, closed in around her. A cool breeze crawled over her skin. Outside, not even a star welcomed the oncoming night.

A shiver rippled through her as she laid the unappetizing food aside, her hunger having long since fled. She tracked the guards' movements by the slam of doors as they went from cell to cell to deliver the evening fare.

At last, except for the whistle of the wind and the moans of prisoners lost in their own misery, a morbid silence claimed the dungeon.

Like that of a living tomb.

Where was Duncan? With each passing second

that he didn't return, her fear grew. She'd lost Symon. Her father's life was in jeopardy. She couldn't lose him as well. "Where are you, Duncan?"

Seconds crawled past.

The passage of time building her fear with destructive intent.

When Isabel thought she'd go mad, the bar grated. She whirled as the door scraped open. Framed within the entry by the flicker of distant torchlight, Duncan appeared as if he were a defiant god challenging the world.

And as unreachable.

After a cautious glance into the corridor, he jumped down and shut the door. Darkness consumed them. "Isabel?"

The fear she'd harbored at his safe return vanished, the concern in his voice further weakening her resolve to remain aloof. She ran to him, and his arms wrapped around her without hesitation. His familiar touch unfurled an ache deep inside, a longing for Duncan that would never fade.

"Thank God you are safe. You were gone so long. I thought the guards might have caught you," she admitted, amazed she sounded so composed when she felt anything but.

He released her. "As if it would matter?"

"Yes," she breathed, wanting only to tell him how much. Or how she still loved him. And always would.

He gave a snort of disbelief. "Worry not, lass. I will help you escape. I have given my vow. I, unlike others, keep my word."

She flinched, grateful for the dark. Yet, she deserved his anger. But she couldn't change the past, nor, it seemed, the future. To explain the truth would not only expose her father's shame, but if Frasyer ever learned that Duncan knew her reason for leaving him, as he'd vowed on that fated day three years ago, he would use every bit of his power to hunt Duncan down and kill him. A vow she knew however ill achieved, Frasyer would keep.

"Believe what you will." She took a step back, too aware of him, of how her need for him had grown to a dangerous level.

"Aye, I will." His voice was grim. "Come."

Isabel followed him toward the door. If this was only about her, she might risk braving Frasyer's wrath. Now, her father, as well as the fate of the rebels, depended on her, too.

Once she'd retrieved her mother's Bible, she would bring it to Lord Monceaux, King Edward's Scottish adviser. A fair man her father had stated on many an occasion. Now she would entrust the English lord with the greatest of tests.

That of her father's life.

What would she do if the Bible wasn't in Frasyer's chamber? When she found the Bible, how would she deliver it to England? Stealing a horse was a crime punishable by hanging, but lack of time demanded desperation.

Not that it would change her fate. Once her father was freed, Frasyer still held documentation that would ruin her father. Frasyer would use this information to continue blackmailing her to remain as his mistress. Whether she lived within his chambers or his dungeon, the latter to prove his complete control over her, he would never allow Isabel her freedom.

Duncan opened the door and glanced back.

Torchlight spilled over Isabel. Her wide, expressive eyes, haunted by the loss of her brother, watched him. For one weak moment, he was tempted to hold her and promise he would protect her always, but he quelled the urge.

He gestured her forward. "Let us be gone." His tone was deliberately rough.

When she continued to stare at him, vulnerable and lost, he caught her hand. He silently cursed himself at the jolt of awareness that swept through him from a mere touch. A heat that betrayed logic. He didn't need to feel any connection with her or of how right it still felt to be in her presence.

Outside her cell, he led her to a dimly lit corner beneath the stairs subtly shielding a door to yet another chamber. From the lack of grating at the door, the cell beyond was designed to deprive prisoners of light. God knew what other atrocities to deliver pain lay within.

"Why are we stopping here?" she asked, clearly confused.

He retrieved the bag of clothes he'd hidden behind a barrel of water. "Put these on."

She opened the sack, removed the garments and glanced up at him with surprise. "Garb for a page?"

"You are needing a disguise. I doubt they will be allowing you to pass through the castle otherwise." He pointed to the darkened corner beneath the stairs where he'd hidden while the guards had made their rounds. "Change over there."

After a brief hesitation, she slipped into the blackened nook.

The rustle of her gown assured him she was stripping at a fast pace. As he waited, an errant gust of wind sent the torch in a wild jig. For a second, he caught a backlit view of the tempting curve of her bared breasts.

Duncan gritted his teeth and turned away, but he could all too easily envision her naked and stepping into the light. Her straight, whisky-colored hair cascading to frame full, taut breasts. How the flat stomach all but invited his gaze lower.

He wasn't sure which was worse, the emotional torment she had put him through, or the knowledge that his body still welcomed the sweet torture of her physically.

"Hurry up," he hissed.

"I am ready." She stepped into the light, her willowy body now hidden within the folds of a page's clothes and her hair concealed beneath the hood of the cloak.

"That should hide you well enough." He silently cursed the vision of her naked etched in his mind.

Isabel frowned. "What if they do not believe I am a lad?"

"For both our sakes, you had best pray they do." He drew up his own hood. What more could he say? Surely she knew the risks if they were caught. After living under Frasyer's roof and spending time in his dungeon, she should have become well acquainted with his cruelty. "This way."

At the landing, he was pleased to find the guard and the serving wench he'd passed earlier thoroughly immersed in their carnal act.

He motioned Isabel past the lovers. When she caught sight of their coupling, she lowered her gaze. Duncan frowned. With her role as mistress, he would have believed any innocence long past.

They approached the door to the great hall and Duncan paused. "Stay with me," he ordered under his breath. "Whatever happens, do not look around."

They'd barely entered the bottom floor of the keep when two guards heading toward the dungeon passed them. He increased his stride, the hard set of the men's faces prodding his unease.

With Isabel at his side, they crossed the large room. Appearing too tired to bother with comings and goings, the servants cleaning the trencher tables never looked up.

Once Duncan and Isabel had climbed the tower steps to where they were hidden from view, she halted. "Why are we going up?"

A faint smile curved his lips. Why indeed. He opened his mouth to inform her of their foul escape route when a shout arose from below.

"It is Lady Isabel," a man yelled. "She has escaped."

"Search the keep," another man's voice boomed.

Duncan grabbed her hand and started up the steps. "Run!"

Instead, she yanked her hand free. "You go. Escape while you can."

He whirled on her. Was she mad? Had Symon been wrong? Did she want to stay with Frasyer? "Blast it, lass. We have no time for this foolishness."

Isabel touched the embroidery shoved within her pocket. "No. I am not leaving."

Chapter 3

Duncan glared at Isabel, furious she'd argue about leaving. "It is not a debate." He caught her arm.

"Duncan—"

Ignoring her protests, he hauled her behind him as he hurried up the stairs. After a few tense moments, the abating pounding of footsteps below assured him they were safe for now. With their lord's fury driving them, the knights would search the lower floor. Then they would work upward.

Until Frasyer's men found Isabel, no space would be left unchecked.

They reached the latrine he'd used to enter the castle, and Duncan opened the door. A blast of fouled air greeted them. He started inside, but with her free hand, Isabel caught hold of the entry wall.

"Stop, Duncan."

He rounded on her. "If you have not noticed, the guards are scouring the castle for you!"

Amber eyes darkened with regret. "I cannot leave.

You have fulfilled your obligation to Symon. Go," she added when he opened his mouth to speak.

He gritted his teeth. Aye, he should leave her behind without a care. If she were caught and hauled to the dungeon, 'twas her decision.

Shouts of men boomed in the turret.

Her face paled. "They are coming up. Hurry." She twisted her hand free and backed into the corridor. "If I am caught, I will swear to them I escaped alone. They will not suspect your help. Go. You will be safe."

Why was she acting like this? Almost as if she cared about him? "I promised Symon I would see *you* safe."

"And you have done that."

"I do not remember giving you a choice." Duncan grabbed her hand and jerked her inside the latrine. She struggled to break free as he shut and barred the door.

"We will be caught if we stay here!"

He shot her a hard look. "Once you are away from Moncreiffe Castle, if you are foolish enough to return to the rat-infested haven of Frasyer's dungeons, it is your choice." Duncan started toward the round stone opening he'd crawled up earlier.

Isabel fought to break from his grip with his every step. "I told you, I cannot leave!"

He hauled her to him. "What is so blasted important that you would stay here at the risk of your life?"

"I—"

"Check the upper floors," a guard shouted nearby.

Duncan leaned toward her with menace. "Answer me!"

Isabel scraped her teeth across her lower lip as she

glanced at the door. Muted yells of men searching the keep echoed in the distance. Panic churned in her eyes as she faced him.

"My mother's Bible."

Of all the answers he'd expected, none were even close. "You will have to think of a better reason than that."

"I must take it with me."

Desperation battered her tone, but he refused to be swayed. "Procure yourself another Bible, or rather, if you are foolish enough to return, ask Frasyer to commission a scribe to pen you another copy. Regardless of the phenomenal cost, I am sure your lover will gratefully gift you with another." Hurt flashed in her eyes at his harsh words, but how did she think he'd feel at her breaking their betrothal a week before they were to wed to become Frasyer's mistress? He, at least, had loved her.

Frasyer was a man who Duncan had grown up with, a man he had once called his friend. But after the day Duncan had won a youthful joust between them, Frasyer's friendship had soured, his goal since, regardless of his title, was to win or take whatever Duncan desired.

Including Isabel.

He watched her now, as indecision flickered across her face and he couldn't help the twinge of regret that he no longer held the ability to surmise what she was thinking. Too much time had passed. The bond they'd once held was long lost.

"If I do not find the Bible," she said with an ominous softness, "my father will hang."

Stunned, Duncan straightened. "Lord Caelin is here?"

"No."

"Then where is he?"

"Please." Her tone held desperation. "We do not have time for this discussion."

"Aye, you are right there, lass. But I am not moving until I get answers. What does your mother's Bible have to do with your father's life?"

The guards' voices grew closer.

"I will say this once more," he warned into her panic-stricken gaze. "If I do not get the truth, I will truss you up and carry you, willing or not."

The words burst from her in a rush. "Frasyer has charged my father with giving the rebels money and sent him to the Baron of Monceaux in England for his crime. Before I was taken away, my father told me to search in the Bible. I believe proof of his innocence lies within." Her lower lip trembled. "Unless I find the Bible, my father is as good as dead."

Duncan scoffed. "Lord Caelin barely has enough coin to pay his servants, much less extra to give in support of Wallace."

"We both know that is true, but with King Edward's hatred toward Wallace, he would believe Frasyer's accusation. False or not."

Her reasoning made sense. "And go after Lord Caelin as if he were deemed a witch." The hard thud of boots below increased, and he flicked a glance toward the door. "Why would Frasyer accuse your father of a false charge? He is not a threat to him."

She lowered her eyes. "Nay, my father is a threat to no one but himself."

As her voice faltered, Duncan knew she referred to Lord Caelin's drunkenness, a shame she'd weathered since her mother's death when her father had succumbed to drowning his sorrows in drink. Aye, Isabel's pride was another strength that appealed to him, but her strength or any other attractive quality had naught to do with this moment.

"Just go," she whispered. "Do not ask me to leave here without the Bible. I will not."

As a man who valued family, Duncan understood, even admired her reason for staying and placing herself in danger. Though not wanting to, he couldn't help but respect her for her loyalty toward her father.

"So be it." He released her.

Relief swept over her face. "Hurry." Her fingers trembled as she gestured to the latrine opening, obviously surmising his planned route of escape. "The guards will soon reach this level."

He straightened, looking her square in the eyes. "I never said anything about my leaving."

Panic widened her amber eyes. She shook her head. "I refuse to allow you—"

Duncan caught her hand. "We both have stubborn streaks that could leave us here debating all night. Before the guards begin searching this floor, we need to hide."

"Did you not hear what I said?"

"After we retrieve the Bible," he continued as if she hadn't spoken, "then we will both escape. Once we are safe, you can do as you wish." He lifted the bar, opened the door, and nudged her through it.

"What if Frasyer catches us?"

"Then, lass," he said as he secured the door behind them, "we are headed straight to Hades."

Before she could reply, he led her down the corridor. She halted and tugged him back. "No, this way."

He glared at her, then followed. The brains of an

ass, that's what he had for agreeing to remain. When Isabel had refused to leave, he should have departed without her.

No hesitating.

No noble thoughts of protecting her.

No concerns for her life.

After turning her back on everyone after she became Frasyer's mistress, she didn't deserve his loyalty. Not that he was giving it now. Once they found proof to save Lord Caelin, he would leave.

"Start searching the floors above! She must be here somewhere."

Duncan stiffened as orders echoed from below. Steps pounded from the turret.

"They are coming." The fear in her voice underlined their precarious situation.

"I can hear that." Duncan scanned the doors lining the hallway, each as unfamiliar as the next. Although he'd trained with Frasyer during his youth, he'd never viewed more of the keep than the lower floors. "In here, quick." He yanked open the nearest door, hauled her inside and then snapped it shut.

The aroma of frankincense and myrrh enveloped them. An ornate rood hung centered upon the far wall behind an altar. Stained-glass windows, dulled by the night, served as if a shield from the dark. Several benches lay staggered within the room all facing the front.

A dry smile settled upon his mouth. How fitting. Of all the rooms he might have chosen, they'd entered Frasyer's private chapel.

"This room is too small," Isabel said. "They will find us."

"And where do you propose we hide? It is not as if you have offered any ideas."

"I had not expected you to stay."

"Your expectations matter not. I am here in deference to Symon," he said, irritation hardening his words. "And now it would seem I am needed to find proof to help save your father . . . if that is even the truth."

Isabel whirled, her face masked in outrage. "I would never lie about my father."

"Nay," he agreed, recalling how since her mother's death, she'd struggled to hold together a family led by a man who'd fallen apart and turned to drink. "That token you reserve for me."

He silently cursed himself for adding the last. He didn't want to reveal how much her leaving had hurt him, a pain that haunted him still.

Like a warrior, inch by admirable inch, her expression shielded off any sign of hurt.

How could she withdraw so completely, show indifference toward him when he battled a softening toward her with his every breath? Damn her.

And why hadn't Symon mentioned his father's imprisonment? Was he too weak to relay the information? Or had he known?

He glanced toward Isabel. His body hardened. Furious, he quelled his desire. This time he wasn't a green lad blinded by love. He was a man who knew her motive—greed.

A lesson he would well remember.

And heed.

Footsteps paused outside the door.

Duncan held a finger to his lips, waved Isabel forward and knelt at the altar. "Kneel beside me and follow my lead," he whispered. "If the guards come inside, keep your head bowed as if in prayer. And whatever happens, unless I tell you otherwise, do not turn around."

Isabel hesitated.

He saw her doubts. As if he didn't have enough of his own? "Now." He caught her and dragged her down to kneel beside him.

Hinges creaked, announcing the guard's entrance.

All too aware of Isabel trembling beside him, Duncan's nerves stretched to breaking.

The jangle of mail grew silent as the knight halted a few feet away. "Father?"

"Yes, my son," Duncan replied in a deep whisper.

"Forgive me for interrupting your prayers, but there has been an escape from the dungeon."

Duncan nodded his head in a show of concern. "Are we under attack from clansmen who are seeking to aid in a prisoner's escape?"

"Nay," the guard replied.

"Is the prisoner armed?"

The guard cleared his throat as if embarrassed. "Father, it is a woman we are seeking."

Isabel's tremors intensified.

Hold fast, he silently willed her. "So why interrupt my prayer?" he asked as if truly confused. "Has she been found dying, and I am needed to administer her last rites? Or has she given herself up and wishes to confess her sins?"

"Neither."

Duncan gave an annoyed sigh and prayed his irritation would be enough of a distraction.

"We think the woman is hidden somewhere within the keep."

Shielded by his cloaked hood, Duncan gave a slow nod. "What does she look like?"

The knight shuffled his feet as if hesitant to divulge the information. "It is Lady Isabel, Father. Lord Frasyer's mistress."

Isabel jerked.

The guard stepped forward, his boots scraping to a stop behind Isabel. "What is wrong with the lad?"

Duncan laid a hand on her robed shoulder and ignored the trickle of sweat creeping down his own spine. "The lad was caught ignoring his duties to care for his knight's horse. His knight flogged him for his crime."

Isabel trembled harder.

Duncan gently squeezed her shoulder and willed her to calm. "Part of his penance is to pray through the night for forgiveness from his sins."

The guard grunted with contempt. "The beating will help more than prayer."

"It is God's way to forgive those who sin," Duncan said with censure.

The knight remained silent, obviously having his own feelings about forgiveness in the case of a neglected steed.

"If I see Lady Isabel," Duncan said to move the guard on his way, "I will pass word to one of the knights immediately."

"Thank you, Father." The candles within the private chapel wavered as the guard exited the chamber, then steadied after he'd closed the door in his wake.

Duncan exhaled.

Isabel turned to him, her face taut with frustration.

"What have you done? They will soon discover that no lad ignored his duties to care for his knight's horse or was beaten this night. Then the guards will return, but now they will be looking for us both."

"Not until the morrow. They are too busy searching for you to be concerned with the fate of a foolish lad." He rose, hastened to the door and listened.

Muted footsteps and slamming doors echoed outside as the guards searched each chamber on their level. A man called. Another replied from farther away. After a long while, sounds of the search faded to muffled calls as the guards ceased their search in the upper levels of the keep.

Duncan sighed, relieved. "With the size of Frasyer's castle, the guards will re-search the lower floors and will not return to the upper level for a while."

"Mayhap, but rest assured, his men will continue in their quest until they find me."

Aware of how Frasyer guarded his own, Duncan realized she was right. "We can still leave now."

Her expression left no room for doubt. "I am not going. Not without my mother's Bible."

"Very well," he replied, having correctly anticipated her response. "Then I will ensure the guards do not return before we have had a chance to finish our search."

"How?"

"I will create a diversion. While they are distracted, it will give us time to find the Bible and escape."

"No," Isabel said. "With the guards swarming the keep, it is too dangerous. I know the layout, I could do—"

"Nothing."

She shot him a lethal glare. "My life is at stake as

well. If you think I will remain here while you are out risking your life, you know little of me."

He strode forward until a hand's width separated them. Duncan caught her chin with his fingers and lifted it until their eyes met, damning the jolt of awareness.

"Did I ever know you?" The words stormed out before he could halt them.

Her eyes softened. Her lips parted. "Duncan—"

He released her and stepped back, angry over his lapse of control. "Wait here. On this point I will not yield."

Isabel studied him, her stubborn look one he'd witnessed many times over. She didn't like obeying his order, wanted to argue, but from the resignation pooling in her eyes, he surmised she was thinking of her father.

"What will you do?" she finally asked.

"I will think of something." He relished the thought of causing the bastard Frasyer another troublesome blow. "Upon my return, we will retrieve your family heirloom."

At his reference to the Bible, her gaze slid to the floor.

Her evasive manner stopped him cold. A ludicrous thought popped into his mind. "You do know where the Bible is?"

Chapter 4

"Isabel, tell me you know where the Bible is!"

At Duncan's whispered demand, Isabel met his incredulous gaze, wishing she could offer him a different truth. She shook her head. "No."

Green eyes hardened to black. "You led me to believe you knew where it was."

She refused to feel guilty. She had given him many opportunities to leave. "I thought I could convince you to go without me."

"Even if I had left, with the guards scouring every nook of the castle to find you, are you daft enough to believe you would have time for more than a token search?"

"I still need to try."

The shouts of guards echoed from below.

"Do you have any idea where Frasyer has hidden it?" he demanded.

Isabel nodded, but the location was the last place she'd ever wish Duncan to see.

"Where?"

Isabel braced herself. "In Frasyer's private chambers."

Red stroked the hard angles of his cheeks. His eyes narrowed to slits.

Coldness swept through her. He would rid himself of her now. How could he not? A fact she should be thankful for, but a part of her still ached at his leaving.

"When I return, be ready to depart." He strode toward the door.

Return? No, he was supposed to be leaving! "Duncan?"

At the entry, he turned. "What?"

The hard expression on his face dared her to challenge his decision to remain. The stubborn, honorable fool. 'Twould seem he'd risk his life for her and her father due to his deathbed promise to Symon. Something she couldn't allow.

"Be careful," Isabel said, keeping her voice soft so as not to betray her intent.

A muscle worked in his jaw. "Careful? Nay, lass, I will take the risk. The last time I was careful, it was with you." He jerked open the door. "And you left me for Frasyer's bed." The seasoned wood settled behind him with a soft clunk.

She sagged back. His anger toward her would serve him well. More so when he returned to find her gone. Then he would quit Moncreiffe Castle.

Without her.

Breath heaving in his chest, Duncan glanced at the unconscious men with disgust. Only after he'd thrown the torch atop the pile of straw filling the wagon and the flames had begun to build had their outlines come into view. By then it was too late. The men had noticed him.

And charged.

Thankfully, both were poorly trained. Still, one of their blades had sliced his left arm. Keeping pressure on the wound to stop the bleeding, he sprinted across the bailey.

"The smithy's hut is catching fire!" a guard shouted from the wall walk. Several other guards located farther away echoed the alert.

Duncan bolted into the shadow cast by the keep as men raced past him toward the fire. Dragging in gulps of air, he braced himself against the cold stone wall.

He swiped the sweat from his brow. He was a knight. Not an inexperienced lad. He knew better than to let his guard down, but moments ago, caught up in thoughts of Isabel, he'd missed seeing the men standing near the smithy's hut.

At the clatter of steps, he flattened himself against the cold stone.

Torchlight outlined several guards as they rushed from the keep.

That a way, lad, keep thinking about the lass and you will have your bloody arse in the dungeon.

"Form a line," a man yelled from across the bailey. "Pass the buckets!"

Water sloshed from wooden buckets as they were quickly passed from man to man to be emptied onto the flames, then rushed back to the well.

The door beside Duncan creaked open wider. Two more guards ran past. After a quick glance around to ensure no one saw him, Duncan slipped inside the keep.

Servants hurried about, some grabbing empty cauldrons, others blankets to soak and beat at the flames.

"Put your backs into it and put out the fire!" a commanding voice roared from the bailey.

At the curt order, Duncan froze. He turned and looked out the stone exit. Outlined in the roar of flames stood Frasyer's familiar outline.

Bedamned! Isabel had said Frasyer was away. From the fear in her eyes, he'd believed her. Part of him marveled at how he seemed ready to accept her word at face value; the other part cursed his lingering naïveté, which had put him in this situation of wanting to help a woman who didn't deserve it.

A man ran past him and slammed the door to the keep, cutting off Frasyer's next words.

Holding his left arm tight against his chest, with the whir of activity, Duncan passed through the great hall unnoticed. When he reached the turret, he ran up.

As he passed the second-floor exit, his legs grew heavy. It took his entire concentration to push forward. When he reached the third floor, his vision began to blur.

Bracing himself against the wall, he lifted his cloak. Blood stained a wide swath of his undershirt and was seeping onto his robe. Grimacing, he tore a strip of cloth from the hem of his undershirt, then wrapped his arm tight to stop the flow of blood.

By the time he reached the chapel door, his legs trembled as if weighted by stones. He shoved the door open and entered. Embraced by the scent of frankincense and myrrh, he glanced around.

Candles flickered on a nearby wall, filling the chamber with a golden glow. The crucifix behind the altar lay haloed within the calm, its simple beauty lending to the surreal air.

But the room stood empty.

Where was she? He glanced toward the robes. "Isabel?" The garments hanging along the wall remained still.

"Isabel?"

Silence.

Another wave of dizziness swamped him. He gritted his teeth. Slowly, his mind cleared, and Isabel's words of caution echoed in his mind. Blast it. She'd told him to be careful, because she'd already decided to search for the Bible without him.

How could he have again given her his trust? He glared down the corridor toward the opposite end of the hallway to where the stairs spiraled up one more level. A forth floor, a novelty that only a man of great wealth could afford. And Frasyer's father's pride and joy.

Like father, like son.

His anger built. As Frasyer's mistress, Isabel had known the likelihood of the Bible being hidden on the elusive upper floor, but having planned on sneaking away, she'd kept him ignorant of where Frasyer's chamber lay.

Duncan started toward the steps. At the top, the corridor unfolded before him. Unlike the barren hallway below lit with several torches shoved within dreary wall sconces, a finely woven burgundy rug graced the entire length. Torches burned outside of each entry like polished sentinels, rigid within their ornate sconces.

Portraits of the current Earl of Frasyer preceded that of the majestic parade of his ancestors hanging prominently along the walls in gilded frames, each of their faces captured in an unyielding stance. The array of finely crafted swords hanging on each side of the portraits embellished the obvious.

Luxury. Wealth. Power.

A slight scrape of the door to his immediate left was Duncan's only warning someone was coming. He scanned the corridor. Bedamned, nowhere to hide!

He flattened himself against the wall, his dagger drawn.

A door creaked open.

Duncan lunged and slammed the person against the door, his dagger against the neck.

"Duncan, no!" Isabel gasped.

He blew out a deep breath and secured his weapon, all too aware of the soft press of her body wedged against his. "I told you to stay in the chamber below."

"I—"

"Never intended to remain and wait for me."

The flush on her cheeks betrayed her guilt. She glanced toward the window where outside, yellow flames from below in the bailey fragmented the night. Her mouth turned down.

"You risked going outside to start a fire?" Isabel asked. "I cannot believe that you—"

"Lass," he interrupted, irritated by the awe in her voice. He was far from a hero. More of a fool. "We face a greater risk than my going outside. Frasyer is here."

Her face paled. "He cannot be. It should have

taken him several days to ride to Lord Monceaux's with my father and deliver the charges."

The sincerity of her reaction was believable, but he'd learned his lesson. "Then why has he returned early? Or have you been lying to me about his leaving all along."

"I would never betray you like this."

His arm throbbed. Her image wavered before him. He steadied himself. "And what do you call breaking your vow to wed me for Frasyer's bed?"

For a long moment she stared at him, her face filled with sadness, then crumbling to regret. "The only decision I had."

"Decision?" Her explanation was naught but twisted words. He shook his head to silence whatever she was about to say. "There is little time for your prattle." With his arm hurting like the devil, he urged her forward. "Go."

The muted yells of men below supported his claim. Once safely away, then he would have his answers.

Isabel tried to pull free.

"What?" he demanded.

She shook her head. "I . . . It is nothing."

"For this once, spare me your lies."

Eyes filled with anguish met his. "Only one reason would cause Frasyer to return early. My father is injured. Or"—she swallowed hard, her voice thinning, her entire body beginning to shake—"he is dead."

"Isabel."

She ignored him. "Mayhap en route, Frasyer arranged for my father to have an accident? Nay,

Frasyer wouldn't kill him," she rambled. "He would never risk losing his control over me."

After her incarceration, the contempt in her voice didn't surprise Duncan, but her comment resurrected suspicions that she harbored a far darker secret.

"How long has Frasyer been gone?"

"Two days." She frantically searched his face. "But I need to know if my father is alive."

"Lord Caelin is not dim-witted," Duncan said. "With his poor health, he would not be foolish enough to challenge Frasyer or his guards." Unless he'd imbibed in one too many drinks, which wasn't likely under the earl's guard. "I believe he still lives."

Isabel seemed to find strength in his words. "Do you truly think so?"

"Aye." Duncan scanned the corridor, which was staggered by several doors. "Which room is Frasyer's?"

She didn't seem convinced. "Duncan—"

"Which one?" he pressed.

A loud cheer roared from the bailey.

"It sounds as if they have extinguished the fire. Hurry." Another wave of weakness struck him. He pushed forward. He refused to pass out until after they'd escaped.

Isabel shot him a nervous glance. "We may need to search more than Frasyer's private chamber."

"I thought you said that is where he would keep the Bible?"

"It could be."

"But you are not sure?" Duncan muttered, not liking where this conversation was heading or the anxious looks she kept sending him. "We will search every bloody room if need be."

Isabel opened her mouth to speak.

"If you know what is good for you, do not even ask me to leave."

Her eyes narrowed, but she remained silent.

Against the throbbing in his arm, he forced himself to walk by her side, her tantalizing scent doing nothing to improve his foul mood. Neither could he ignore the natural grace with which she walked, or how the fabric clung to her, revealing the soft swells of her breasts.

"And if the Bible is not in any of his rooms," he pressed, "where do you suggest we search next?"

"I am unsure." Isabel didn't look toward Duncan. He was furious, how could he not be, but he didn't understand how his mere presence was tearing her apart. All he could see was her betrayal.

God, she hated living this lie, how even now, with her father's life at risk, she couldn't tell Duncan the true reason she'd walked away from their betrothal. Or of Frayser's threat to Duncan's life if she revealed the truth.

She didn't doubt Duncan's abilities with a sword. Given a fair fight, he'd outmaneuver Frasyer as he had over and again throughout their youth. But she knew Frasyer. He wouldn't fight fair.

Over the years, she'd prayed to find a way to set things right, then she could tell Duncan everything. After three years, no answer had come.

Only the passage of time.

And regret.

Until this moment, it had not mattered that she'd never visited Frasyer's private room, that he'd not wanted her except as a reminder of what he'd taken from Duncan. She'd expected to conduct the search in private, her unfamiliarity of his personal living space going unnoticed. How could she fool Duncan? At least before he had arrived, she'd narrowed Frasyer's personal chamber down to one door.

"The one at the end."

"Of course," he muttered under his breath. "We would not want his chamber to be close."

In silence, she walked beside him and noticed he seemed to favor his left arm. "What is wrong with your arm?"

Not answering, he pulled his hand closer to his side as he continued forward. Then she noticed he winced.

"You are hurt!"

"It is naught but a wee scratch."

The stubborn fool, with an ego to match. "Try not to bleed to death before I can tend to the wound," she couldn't help but add, appeased when his mouth tightened.

"You would like that."

She didn't reply. She needed to keep her thoughts on finding her mother's Bible and escape. Not on Duncan or the love she'd lost. Though, with him so close, how could she not help but wonder how their life might have turned out if they'd wed?

Or not want him with her every breath.

A muted shout of a guard echoed from below.

Another, father away, replied.

Duncan opened the outer door and nodded for her to enter ahead of him. Thankful for any excuse to change the topic, Isabel hurried inside. She didn't miss his cool assessment of her, or the determination in his eyes to learn her secrets.

Why would he even care about her relationship with Frasyer? How could he after she'd broken their vows to wed and, from all outward appearances, willfully occupied Frasyer's bed?

What if by some twist of fate, Duncan still did have feelings for her?

Instead of joy, the possibility resurrected the old disappointment that had never quite faded. That of a home and children with Duncan.

That of love.

And of forever.

Her heart ached with the knowledge that such dreams never would be. Their time together would be limited to a few hours at most. Then they would go their separate ways.

Taking a steadying breath, Isabel halted inside. The scent of chamomile mixed amid the rushes filled her every breath. The welcoming glow of the wax candles greeting her did little to ease her nerves.

She stepped past two large chairs that graced either side of an elaborate hearth. Ensnared by the beauty, Isabel paused before the chiseled stone. Engraved within the quarried borders stood two falcons, their wings arched high. She turned. Beneath the window sat a small, gilt table that held several unopened bottles of wine. Tapestries decorated the plastered walls, each as elaborate as those sprawled tastefully upon the floor. The bold colors of the decoration exuding a proud elegance, one befitting an earl.

Except there wasn't a bed.

They'd entered Frasyer's sitting room.

Duncan's gaze swept the ornate chamber. "The luxury suits you," he said, a trace of anger sliding through his words.

Turn toward me, she willed, her heart breaking. *Look and tell me what you truly see. Wealth matters not to me. Only you. It has always been only you.*

As much as she wanted to admit the truth, she remained silent. To try and convince him otherwise would further prod his suspicions of her reason for leaving him for Frasyer. God forbid Duncan's anger if he ever discovered the truth.

He walked around the chamber. "You think he has hidden the Bible here? There are no chests, no compartments. Unless he planned to hide it in plain sight."

Heat stroked her face as she tried to think of an explanation for her lack of knowledge about the room. A fool could see the Bible couldn't be concealed here.

Except she hadn't known otherwise. How could she. With her own chamber at the top of the stairs, she'd never been allowed entry into any of Frasyer's private rooms. Her presence on the fourth floor was for appearance only.

"I was unsure." Another lie. God, she was sick of them. "His bedchamber is beyond that door." Isabel gestured toward an adjoining entry on the other wall and prayed she was right.

It should have occurred to her that unlike her own chamber, Frasyer would insist on an elaborate suite of interconnected rooms instead of a single chamber. As with everything else, he thrived on luxury, a show of his wealth.

Duncan crossed to the door and opened it. Fury hardened the sharp angles of his face as he surveyed Frasyer's bedchamber.

She drew in a slow breath, aching at what he was thinking, even though for the last three years she was the one who'd encouraged him and everyone else into believing her actions were self-serving.

Not even her father and Symon knew the complete truth of her private arrangements with Frasyer.

"We need to hurry," she urged.

"Aye," he drawled, his burr rich with sarcasm. "I have no desire to remain in your lover's chamber longer than necessary."

With a heavy heart, she followed him inside. As with the adjoining chamber, wax candles fragmented the blackness of the chamber, framing within their tainted glow the massive bed centered against the back wall.

A bed Duncan believed she warmed.

Isabel tried not to focus on the large bed. Or on how the thick posts arched upward in a magnificent display, each adorned by swaths of crème linen that connected and curtained the massive oak frame.

In horrific fascination, her gaze was reluctantly drawn past the golden ties that secured the yards of the finely woven material and offered a blatant view of Frasyer's intimate domain.

Bile rose in her throat at the notion of sharing such luxury with a man she despised.

Duncan walked past, his face carved with an ominous frown.

She tensed. Please let him credit her nerves to his believing she found embarrassment in his being in Frasyer's bedchamber. She forced herself to browse the room as if not awed by the magnificence of the plastered walls, each adorned with wall hangings of painted wool. Or how she was humbled by the intricate biblical paintings gracing the ceiling.

At the sound of muted voices from the corridor, Duncan glanced toward her. "Where do you think he hid the Bible?"

She shot a glance toward the door. "I do not know," she whispered back. "Upon our return, I was immediately taken to the dungeon."

"Does he have a secret room off his chamber?"

"I . . ."

A muscle worked in his jaw. "Well?"

"I am not sure."

With a curse, he strode to the nearest chest. "For a woman who frequents Frasyer's private chamber, you seem to know little of his habits." Duncan dug through a stack of finely woven silks of magnificent reds, greens, and even the coveted blue of royalty.

Her heart pounded as she moved to kneel before another of several chests within the room. She prayed they would find the Bible soon. The longer they remained, the greater the risk of Duncan learning the truth.

Or of them being caught.

Isabel opened the lid. Wrapped within cloths, the pungent scent of ginger, cinnamon, and several other spices reached her.

"Is it there?" Duncan asked.

She shook her head as she closed the lid. "No."

He moved to another chest. A creak sounded at her side as he opened the top. "I have an idea. Where does Frasyer keep his jewels?"

"His jewels?" She frowned as she turned toward him. "You are not going to rob him are you?"

Duncan gave a rude snort. "I want nothing of his." His emphasis on the word *nothing* struck clear to her heart. "I asked where he kept his jewels, because he would perhaps keep the Bible in a place where he stows his most prized possessions."

"We need to keep looking."

Duncan stared at her in disbelief. At her silence, his face darkened with temper.

"I am trying to help."

"Are you?" he demanded. "After three years as his mistress, you expect me to believe that you do not even know where Frasyer keeps his jewels?"

"There were many things I was not privileged to know."

Duncan shot a cold look at the bed. "For the length of time you have lived here, one would think you would know where Frasyer would keep his every article of clothing, along with those things he coveted. Or perhaps, like me, he has learned you are unworthy of trust." He turned toward her, his gaze assessing. "If so, he is wiser than I believed."

Her cheeks burned at the insult, but she let it go. "I will not speak of my private arrangements with Frasyer to you."

"I assure you, they are not details I wish to know."

Isabel's body trembled as she knelt before one of the three remaining chests they had yet to search. "We will not find the Bible by arguing." Her ignorance of Frasyer's private living quarters already hinted that all was not as it seemed. The longer they remained here, the more Duncan's suspicions of why she'd become Frasyer's mistress would grow.

"Aye, on that point I will agree." He turned to the next chest, then stopped. Duncan braced himself against the wall, and she noticed the sheen of sweat coating his face.

Isabel stepped toward him, but his glare made her stop. She glanced to his left arm; he was favoring it. "How badly are you wounded?"

"Continue searching."

"Please, let me—"

He brushed her aside. "Search, so we can leave this wretched place—and I of you."

Worry tightened in her stomach. By the paleness of his face and how his body was shaking, the wound was serious, but Duncan was stubborn and wouldn't allow her to see the extent of his injury. Not without an argument. She hurried to the next chest. Please, God, let the Bible be inside so they could leave. Once away from here, she could tend to him.

She returned to the chest. Inside lay several bolts of silk, dark reds the color of blood. Frantic, she dug deeper.

No!

She shoved aside layers of the slippery material. The Bible had to be here somewhere. What if Frasyer had taken it with him?

Or what if he had hidden it within a secret chamber? Or had burned it for pure spite?

"It is not in this room," Duncan concluded as he sat back with a frustrated sigh, cradling his arm.

"It is!" Her nails scraped bare wood as she shoved aside the remaining bolt of silk.

Duncan leaned over and caught her arm. "Leave it."

"Do you not understand? With the guards scouring

the keep for me, Frasyer having returned, and your wound, we need to leave." She jerked free of his hold and started unfurling another bolt of silk. "Let me search through these bolts one last time, then we will go." Her voice rose. "Perhaps in my haste, I have overlooked it."

"Isabel—"

A thud, then the murmur of voices in the adjoining room had them both turning toward the door.

"Frasyer!" she gasped.

A sword's wrath! Duncan pushed to his feet and for a second, the room wavered before him. With their bloody luck this night, besides the earl, he wouldn't be surprised to find an entire contingent of knights outside the door. "We must leave."

Fear widened her eyes. She shook her head. "The only way out is how we came in. We must hide."

He cursed low and fierce.

Angry footsteps echoed in the exterior chamber. "Isabel, and whoever helped her, could not have escaped," Frasyer's voice snarled.

Duncan smothered Isabel's gasp with his palm, the action making him dizzy with pain.

"I want the guards to search the entire castle again!"

"Aye, my lord." The clack of boots hurried out. A door opened, then thudded shut.

"Lad," Frasyer said, "have a bath drawn in my chamber."

"Yes, my lord." Quiet steps sounded. The door scraped open and then closed.

"The fools," Frasyer cursed, his voice growing louder.

Isabel pushed Duncan's hand away and stepped back. "He is coming in here!"

"I can hear that for myself." Duncan scoured the chamber for any sign of another exit. "Are you sure there is no other way out?"

"None that I am aware of."

Why had he even bothered to ask? She hadn't known if there was a secret passage or where Frasyer kept his jewels. Exactly what did she do here?

No, with the statuesque bed overpowering the room, her duties were all too obvious.

They must hide. Drops of sweat streaked along his cheek as Duncan bent over and lifted the blanket draping over the bed.

"Hurry," he whispered.

Amber eyes pleaded with him as she knelt beside him. "I am sorry. I never meant for you to become involved."

"Move!"

With one last apologetic look, she scrambled beneath the luxurious bed.

Duncan glanced toward the outer door. She was sorry? That wasn't the half of it. Resigned to his fate, he protected his injured arm as he followed her under.

Chapter 5

With his breathing labored, Duncan peered through the narrowed view beneath the bed covering as Frasyer entered.

The earl threw his gloves in a carved, oak chair. "That bitch. She will regret crossing me. When I am through with Isabel, she will be begging to return to the dungeon." His booted feet pounded out his anger as he stormed to the bed. The mattress sagged from his weight.

Duncan glanced toward Isabel, her face illuminated by the dimmed light. Fear glazed her eyes, and her entire body was trembling. He pressed his finger to his lips. If she made any sound, she would give them away.

The clack of hurried steps echoed from the entry. A thin, nervous lad hurried inside. "If you will allow me to help you, my lord."

Duncan sighed his relief. Frasyer's squire.

Inches away from Duncan's face, one of the earl's well polished leather boots landed with a clunk, quickly followed by the other. The shuffle of fabric. Then a pile of what appeared to be Frasyer's traveling garb began heaping on the floor as well.

Dizziness had Duncan closing his eyes. Blast, his arm burned as if on fire.

"Your robe, my lord." The shuffle of cloth. "I will check on the status of your bath."

Duncan opened his eyes as the squire hurried out.

The mattress shifted above them, then Frasyer's feet appeared. Garbed in a thick blue robe, he walked over to a small, rounded table. The slosh of liquid echoed through the chamber as he poured himself a goblet.

What Duncan wouldn't give for a drink. With his arm aching like a wounded boar, several.

As the earl settled into the chair, Duncan surveyed their surroundings, aware he and Isabel would be here for a while. Cobwebs cluttered the underside of the bed, and dust motes dotted the floor as if mounds of hay. He glanced toward the head of the bed.

And froze.

A big black spider, cradled within its web, hung a whisper above his face.

Duncan started to roll away, then held his position. The slightest sound would alert Frasyer of their presence. Sweat beaded his brow. Blast, he hated spiders. They reminded him of how, at the age of twelve summers, his brothers, Seathan, Alexander, and Patrik had hidden one within his boot as a prank.

Even after all these years, he could still remember the feel of it struggling against his skin after he'd shoved his foot inside the sewn leather. When he'd tore the boot free, he'd spied the largest, ugliest black spider he'd ever seen.

Aye, his brothers had laughed as he'd wrenched off his boot, but he'd obtained his revenge. The buckthorn he'd slipped into his brothers' broth had kept them within a sprint's length of the latrine for the next two days.

A cup clattered onto the table. The spider skittered toward the wall.

Duncan breathed a sigh of relief.

"What is wrong?" Isabel mouthed, the worry on her face framed in the meager spill of candlelight. "Your arm?"

He shook his head.

She frowned but didn't press him.

Bare feet came into view as Frasyer returned to his bed. This time, he lay down. The bed sagged with his full weight, leaving a hand's breadth between Duncan and the mattress.

Isabel looked away.

He wasn't liking this any more than she was, but Duncan couldn't help but wonder if what really bothered Isabel was that she was lying beside him, instead of in her chosen place alongside the earl. After Frasyer had thrown her into his dungeon, Duncan wanted to believe she'd wish otherwise.

With a grimace, he slowly stretched his aching arm. He couldn't believe there wasn't a secret passage. But without knowing where it was located, they didn't have the luxury of time to search.

Once the earl had bathed, he would return to his bed to sleep. Then he and Isabel would be stuck here for the night.

The idea of spending the upcoming hours on

the floor beneath the earl's bed in accompaniment with a spider wasn't a thought that filled his heart with joy. Especially stuck next to Frasyer's mistress.

Lying in the silence, Duncan tried to ignore the persistent throb of his arm and the way the room was beginning to blur. He forced his eyes to focus, willed himself to remain conscious.

The exterior door scraped open and Frasyer's squire entered.

"Be quick about it," a stern voice ordered. "And if I see you spill a drop of hot water on the floor, you will be spending the night in the stable."

Steps clattered on timber. A curse sounded. Several men carried a tub into the outer chamber. Time seemed interminable as steaming buckets were carried in and emptied. Finally, when the last lad carrying water had departed, the squire entered the bedchamber and bowed.

"Your bath, my lord."

Frasyer's bare feet appeared again as he stood and followed his squire into the adjoining room.

Duncan tried to envision himself anywhere else, riding through the fields on his steed, taking a long plunge into the icy waters of the loch, or battling an angry opponent on the field. The latter holding great appeal with his contender amazingly similar in appearance to the earl.

The slosh of water announcing Frasyer had entered the tub sliced through Duncan's thoughts like a ragged blade.

Isabel shifted at his side.

Duncan waved his hand for her to stay still, his effort shooting a blast of pain throughout his arm. He smothered a groan.

She edged near him. "What is it?"

"Quiet!" he whispered. He gritted his teeth, as she leaned closer. With her entire length pressed against him, he could feel her every curve. He tried to ignore the softness of her breasts and smother his inconvenient thoughts in his wound's mind-numbing pain.

Instead, his body hardened.

A cursed nightmare. As if at any moment he'd open his eyes and find himself in his bed at his brother Seathan's home, Lochshire Castle. Then he'd laugh at himself and forget the entire chaotic event.

"Duncan?" she whispered.

Enough! He turned to tell her to remain silent once and for all. And found her lips inches from his own.

"He cannot hear us in the other room," Isabel whispered, "He is taking his bath."

Duncan stared at her mouth, wanting to lean forward and claim its softness.

Isabel touched his brow.

"What are you doing?" He didn't need her touching him. He was a man. Not a saint.

"You have a fever."

He closed his eyes against her tempting mouth, convinced his last wisp of sanity had fled. It must be the pain in his arm making him giddy. His mind was befuddled as if caught in a dense fog. How could he want a woman who had betrayed him? A woman he now hid with beneath her lover's bed?

A drip of sweat rolled down his cheek and plopped on the floor. Another wove along his neck to pool on his chest.

Isabel frowned. "You are trembling. We have to get you out of here."

"How?" he hissed. "Walk past Frasyer and nod a good day? I am sure he will thank me for escorting you from his dungeon."

Her mouth tightened. "I did not ask you to stay."

"No, that was my own foolish decision."

Isabel remained silent.

Frustrated, he turned his head sideways to scan the room through the gap in the bedcover. At the movement, more pain lanced up his left arm.

Duncan leaned his head on the floor, closed his eyes and waited until the dizziness passed.

"What is wrong?"

"Nothing." Everything. "I was looking for another way out."

"Oh."

"As I trained with Frasyer often during my youth," he said slowly, fighting to keep his breathing steady, "if nothing else, I learned that although the previous earl loved his wealth, he enjoyed the complex. I would be surprised if he did not have a secret passage leading from his chamber. Mayhap two."

"He could have them, but like I said—"

"There were many things you were not privileged to know." To find balance in her relationship with Frasyer, Duncan could understand Isabel conceding on some issues, but by all appearances, their relationship had little to do with fairness. Or respect. Both foundations of the woman he'd once known.

Or had he known her at all?

"Duncan—"

"Nay, lass." Why did he mull over an event long past? He rolled away from her and onto his injured arm. Stars exploded in his head. He groaned and sagged back.

"Your arm?"

"Is fine." Throbbed as if skewered by a hot iron. Heat poured over him as if standing next to a smithy's fire. His hand shook as he mopped the sweat from his brow. He opened his eyes and forced himself to focus. They had to escape while he was still strong enough to protect her.

Shifting onto his good shoulder, he scanned the walls. In Seathan's castle, a secret passage lay hidden in each of the family chambers.

"Bring me a cup of wine," Frasyer ordered.

The earl's squire hurried to do his lord's bidding.

Once the lad left his view, Duncan continued scanning the wall for any hint of an opening, a fine line separating the rocks, or through uneven stone.

He followed the lower edge of the tapestry and started to move on, but an uneven shadow had him glancing back. There. Almost flush with the bottom of the woven cloth appeared to be the outline of a door. If he hadn't looked for it, he would have missed the discreet indent altogether. Exactly as the lord of the castle would have wished.

"Look at the tapestry by the far wall," Duncan whispered to Isabel. "It is hiding a door."

She inched up on her forearms, and her breasts pressed against his shoulder; he all but groaned. "I do not see anything."

"Along the lower edge." It again struck Duncan as odd that Frasyer's mistress didn't know the whereabouts of his secret passage. What did they do, tear at each other's clothes as soon as they entered his room? One would have believed they would have at least talked after they'd made love.

A bizarre kind of love if you asked him. What kind of lover threw his mistress into the dungeon? And how did her father, Lord Caelin, fit into all of this?

"I see it now," she whispered with excitement. The warmth of her breath skimmed over his neck. "Perhaps it is where he keeps his jewels. If so, the Bible may be in there as well."

"With the opening against the interior wall, more than likely, it is a secret passageway."

She leaned back. "Oh."

Though he didn't want to return to Moncreiffe Castle, with his body growing fevered, he couldn't risk remaining and, if challenged, being unable to protect her.

"Isabel?" he whispered.

"Aye?"

Duncan took a slow breath, hating his admission. "If the door proves to be an exit, we must leave, Bible or no. I must have my arm tended."

Concern darkened her eyes. She glanced at his wounded arm and resignation settled on her face. "Then we had best pray the passageway leads out."

Her calm acceptance surprised him. In the dungeon, she'd adamantly refused to leave Moncreiffe Castle without her mother's Bible. What guided her decision to go without an argument now?

Isabel's agreeing wasn't out of concern for him. Her broken betrothal to him three years ago to become Frasyer's mistress attested to that. Nay, something was amiss. Aye, she was afraid for her father's life, but Duncan sensed her fears went deeper than that.

When he'd given his word to help Isabel find her mother's Bible, he'd done so not only due to his vow to Symon, but for Lord Caelin's sake. Now, he added another reason for staying—to learn the truth of Isabel's relationship with Frasyer.

"Can you walk?" she asked.

"I have a wound on my arm, not my leg. Of course I can walk."

A disgruntled frown dragged across her brow. "Or crawl if you had to. You are barely holding your own. Not that you would be admitting it," Isabel charged. "You have not changed, Duncan Mac-Gruder. You are still a stubborn, mule-headed fool."

"Do not start flattering me now, lass," he hissed through the pain. "Why, I will think you still favor me."

Her expression faltered. "Duncan, this is serious."

He grunted and then started to shift to a more comfortable position. A shadow on the far wall caught his attention. "Look, behind that tapestry on our left. There is another door."

Isabel leaned forward. "That might be where he keeps his valuables hidden."

"Mayhap. When we return, we will search there."

She turned toward him, uncertainty haunting her face. "I am sorry. I never meant to involve you in any of this."

A solid knock echoed on the outer door.

"Enter," Frasyer said.

The master-at-arms strode in. "My lord, Lady Isabel is not within the keep."

"Continue looking," Frasyer ordered. "She has to be here somewhere. When she's found, secure her in the dungeon, then inform me."

"Aye, my lord." The master-at-arms bowed, then left.

Water sloshed as Frasyer stood. "Incompetent fools. Once I have Isabel back, I will show them how to break a woman's will." His squire rushed to dry him off. After Frasyer had donned his robe, he stormed into his bedchamber and slammed the door.

Isabel jumped, and Duncan squeezed her hand in reassurance. If the bastard hadn't subdued Isabel's spirit after three years, how did he believe he could do so now?

The earl poured himself a drink.

Duncan willed Frasyer to keep drinking. If the earl passed out, that would solve their immediate problem of his noticing when they made their escape.

After downing the single goblet, the second since his arrival, Frasyer walked toward them. The bed shifted above them as he settled in for the night.

Duncan gritted his teeth in frustration. Frasyer had not consumed enough to inebriate a toad. Unless he was exhausted from this day's travel, then all chances of escaping were for naught.

Duncan pantomimed Frasyer sleeping to Isabel. Then he mouthed, "Is he a heavy sleeper?"

In the meager light cast by the taper, she shrugged.

Unbelievable! How did one not know how soundly their lover slept? Duncan closed his eyes and waited.

At this moment, their only option.

Time dragged on. The throbbing of his body a potent reminder of his weakening condition. After what seemed an eternity, Frasyer's breaths became regular. Another long pull of time passed before, finally, he began to snore, a fact Duncan owed to the earl's hard travel this day.

The bells of Matins tolled.

Duncan glanced toward the open window. They'd lain here for two hours.

He shifted, muffling a groan as he tried to relieve the cramping of his joints. He and Isabel couldn't wait until daybreak. Delaying would serve to weaken him further. However slow they traveled, the cover of nightfall would shield their movements as they crossed the open field to reach the woods.

"Let us go," Duncan whispered.

"Can you make it?" she asked in his ear, her soft breath feathering across his skin. The bed creaked above them, and her eyes widened with fear.

He held up his hand for her to remain silent, then he reached for his dagger. If Frasyer discovered them, Duncan might not last long, but he'd give the bastard a solid fight.

With another shifting of the bed, the earl's feet came into view. He lumbered across the chamber. Frasyer was leaving! Then he paused at the table and extinguished the tapers.

Blackness smothered the room.

Steps closed, then the bed sagged.

With a silent curse Duncan closed his eyes and fought to suppress the shudders that continued to rack his frame. So much for making it through one of the hidden doors. It would seem they were doomed to remain here this night. He could only pray that if they weren't discovered before morning, when it came time to leave, he could physically make it.

The scent of freshly extinguished candles singed the air as Duncan continued to tremble beside her. Isabel reached over and touched his brow. Heat greeted her touch. Panic welled inside her. He was consumed with fever. If she'd tried, she couldn't have dreamt of such a disaster.

Why hadn't he told her about his injury and its severity when he'd returned to the chapel? However much she needed to find the Bible, she wouldn't have remained at the risk of his life.

His admission they needed to leave convinced her that his condition was grave.

But with Frasyer asleep above them and his squire standing guard in the antechamber, how could they escape? Even if they managed to slip past the earl, how far could Duncan travel in his injured state?

Tears burned her eyes as she struggled to overcome the sense of impending doom. Nay, she'd lost Symon, but to her last breath, she refused to lose Duncan as well.

Mayhap she should surrender to Frasyer. Then Duncan would be safe. That wasn't an option. In his deteriorating condition, Duncan couldn't escape by himself.

Neither could she allow Frasyer to find Duncan within his bedchamber. The earl wouldn't hesitate to end Duncan's life.

And her father. If she were caught, proof of his innocence would never be found and delivered to Lord Monceaux.

"Isa . . ."

"Duncan?"

His teeth had begun to chatter.

Guilt clung to her. As much he needed to rest, before he began to ramble and expose them, she had to get him out.

"Shhhh," she whispered into Duncan's ear. Isabel glanced toward where moonlight illuminated the tapestry upon the wall. Before she'd hoped one of the doors held her mother's Bible. Now, she prayed one of them held a route from which they could escape.

"Duncan," she whispered in his ear. "Stay here and be quiet. I will be right back."

"Wh-Where are you going?"

"To crawl over to one of the secret doors and see if I can open it."

"It is too risky."

This was so like him. Stubborn to the point of unreasonable. "And you are thinking with your wounded arm and a fever you could be doing better?"

He wiped the sweat from his brow. "I promised to keep you safe."

"And you have." She gentled her voice, aware he was persecuting himself for their situation, when in fact, this was all her fault. Why did he have to be so noble? "This once you will do it my way. After I have the door open, I will wave you over."

He reached over and clasped his hand over hers, his hold a pittance of his strong grip in the dungeon. "I . . ." He hesitated. "Be safe."

"I will." Isabel withdrew her hand from his and immediately missed his touch. Even after three years, he still felt so much a part of her. A part she could never again have. Her body ached with the need to have him hold her, want her as he once did. She longed to tell him the truth. That she still loved him. A fact she never could.

"What is wrong?" Duncan asked, tearing her from her musings.

"Naught." She inched to the edge of the bed. Holding her breath, Isabel rolled from beneath and then lay still.

Above her, a cool breeze sifted into the room, spinning up fragments of dust to shimmer within the moonlight like a faerie's trail. The occasional shout from a guard outside blended with the blustery wind and Frasyer's occasional snore.

After peeking over the edge of the bedding to ensure Frasyer still slept, Isabel crawled across the floor. Each placement of her hand seemed to form another drip of terrified sweat upon her brow. Each second a dark promise that Frasyer would awaken and catch her.

At the bottom of the tapestry, she ran her hands over the cold, rough stone. A finger's width from the floor, her nail slipped into a crevice.

She'd found it!

Taking a deep breath, she ran her finger along the outline. Halfway up the side of the door, her nail dipped into a smooth, half-moon crevice carved into the stone.

Cloth rustled on the bed.

She froze. Expecting to find Frasyer sitting up on the bed glaring at her in outrage, Isabel turned.

Instead, she found Duncan inching his way over. What was he doing? She'd told him to wait until she had the door open! Isabel waved him back, but Duncan continued forward. Was he addled? Aye, his fever was causing him to make poor decisions.

She glanced toward the second secret chamber where her mother's Bible might be within. Once Duncan was a safe distance and she'd tended to him, she would backtrack to search the hidden room.

A sleepy grumble sounded from the bed. In the moonlight, Frasyer's face turned toward her. "Isabel?"

Chapter 6

A saint's curse, Frasyer had seen her! Panic tightened Isabel's throat. She couldn't have answered him if she wanted to.

She motioned Duncan to halt.

He continued inching toward her. No! He had to go back and hide under the bed before Frasyer saw him!

Mumbling, Frasyer shifted.

Isabel froze.

Duncan stiffened.

Grumbling, Frasyer turned his head toward the opposite wall, his limbs tangled in the sheets. After a moment, he lay back and his breathing slowed. Quiet snores began filling the chamber.

Isabel's entire body sagged with relief. Heart still pounding, she glanced at Duncan as he reached her side.

"You lackwit!" she whispered.

He ignored her. "Hurry!"

As much as she wanted to rage at him, they had to go. Her fingers trembled as she wedged them into the carved indent and pulled. Stone scrapped with a soft hiss as the door inched open. Air, musty and damp, poured into the room. She glanced toward Frasyer.

He hadn't moved.

She pulled harder.

Finally, the door swung open enough to allow both her and Duncan entry.

His hand flattened against the door frame. In the moonlight, his determined gaze underscored his intent to leave by his own means, but the paleness of his face as he struggled to stand exposed the cost.

She hurried over and wrapped her arm under his right shoulder. He tried to shrug her off, but the slight tremble in his body made her stay close. His weakness before her wouldn't sit well with him, but right now, he needed her. However much he loathed her, she'd be there for him.

Duncan's grip was heavy on her shoulders as she glanced at Frasyer still snoring in his bed. If he hadn't heard the scrape of stone, he was indeed a heavy sleeper. A grim smile touched her mouth. At least that answered Duncan's earlier question of how soundly Frasyer slept.

Isabel lifted the tapestry, helped Duncan inside and secured the door. Blackness engulfed them. "Stay here," she whispered, as she helped him lean against the wall. She pulled her hand away, shaken at how after three years she could be so aware of him and want him with her every breath. "Do not move. I will check your injury as soon as we are safe."

"It is fine," he gritted out.

She didn't dignify that with a response.

Cold stone ran beneath her hand as her fingers moved over the uneven surface, searching for a candle that should be stowed nearby.

At least with Frasyer never having allowed her into his bedchamber, the earl would believe her ignorant of the tunnels and dismiss them as a choice to make her escape.

Still, that wouldn't stop his search for her.

Or recover the travel time she'd lost to deliver the Bible to Lord Monceaux.

Duncan's boots scraped the dirt as he waited on shaky legs.

She caught his shoulder and steadied him. "I said do not move."

"I am—" He drew in an hard breath. "I am looking for the candle."

"I will find it. You need to rest."

"I will help." It wasn't a request.

Her protest died. If he was strong enough to argue, she'd be thankful for that.

She renewed her search. Their fingers touched, the warmth luring her to lean against Duncan. She pulled away and returned to her task. With him injured and growing weaker with each passing moment, his survival was up to her.

The steady drip of water played cadence with Duncan's raspy breathing as she continued her search. The cool air of the passageway and the musty smell made her wish for a fire to warm by and dispel an unsettling feeling enshrouding her.

"Over . . . Over here," Duncan said, his voice too faint for her liking.

She moved to his side, the heat pouring from his

body reaching her. "Pass it to me and I will light it."
She tried to keep the worry from her voice. How
much longer before he collapsed? Please let them
escape from the castle before he did so.

Clothing rippled.

"Duncan?"

Silence.

Isabel reached out. Her fingers brushed his robe.
"Do you need to sit?"

"I am . . . I am fine."

Far from it, oh dear Lord, help them. She followed the stiffness of his arm to where his hand
clenched upon the stone.

His fingers shifted to brush against hers. Despite
the completely ill-timed response, warmth stormed
her body. Her pulse raced, desperately searching
for a sliver of the bond that had existed between
them. A fragment of trust, however fragile.

Duncan muttered a curse and shoved the candle
and flint into her hands. "Light the blasted candle."

Why was she torturing herself wishing for what
never could be? Isabel busied herself stacking dry
tinder wedged in the crevice, left for such a desperate purpose.

Kneeling, she struck the knife to flint. Sparks
raced through the darkness and then faded to
black. She scraped the flint again. Sparks rained on
the slivers of wood like stars of hope streaking
through the midnight sky. Several fragments flared
within the tinder. A tinge of wood glowed for several moments, then ignited.

Isabel held the wick over the tiny flame; it flared
to life.

The waver of candlelight illuminated the narrow

corridor. Near the edge of darkness, steps carved of stone faded downward. An escape route?

Isabel raised the candle chest high. The pale, yellowed light framed the fever burning in Duncan's eyes. By the strain on his face, he was struggling to stay on his feet.

She moved to his side. "Lean against me." When he stiffened, she lifted his arm over her shoulders. "If not for me, then for my father's sake."

A muscle worked in his jaw as he clung to a wedge of rock. Duncan grunted his assent, then he leaned his full weight against her. She steadied herself and started forward, slower than she would have liked. At this pace, how long would it take them to reach the safety of the forest? An hour? Two? One step at a time. She'd focus on that. They would make it.

She refused to believe otherwise.

With care, they worked their way down the hidden passage. Each step an achievement, each floor a miracle. Several times she tried to stop to allow Duncan time to rest, but when she began to slow, he pressed on.

"Bedamned, move!" he growled.

"I am moving for both of us," she snapped irritably and continued on.

At long last, after both of them were gasping for breath and her muscles straining under Duncan's weight, the passageway leveled out. Her head pounded as she tried to remember what level they were on.

"What is wrong?

At Duncan's ragged voice, her fear of leading

him from the castle escalated. "Nothing." And prayed they hadn't taken a wrong turn.

Hot wax dripped on her left hand. Isabel flinched. The candle flickered and then the flame steadied. She would have to pay closer attention. If the candle burned out before they reached the exit, they might become lost in the catacomb of tunnels.

"We need to move." With Duncan shuffling at her side, she started forward. Instead of solid ground, her foot dipped into a crevice. She yelped as she lost her balance and fell forward, her momentum dragging Duncan with her. She landed hard, and the candle flew from her hands.

Duncan cursed as he landed beside her.

"No!" She lunged for the candle that was rolling away. As she caught the base, the flame flickered. Then died.

Blackness engulfed them.

The ripe scent of candle smoke filled the darkness. Sounds magnified around them. Water dripping in the distance. Their breaths rushing out. Duncan's heart beating inches from her own.

With a groan, Isabel sat up. Pain sliced through her right knee. Holding her leg, she slowly bent it back and forth.

"Are you all right?" Duncan's voice pierced through the darkness.

"I am fine." Thank, Mary, it wasn't broken.

If only they could find the correct tunnel that led outside. As they'd descended, the catacomb of tunnels branching off to various parts of the castle had stunned her. She'd never imagined such an intricate web of secret passages existed within Frasyer's home.

Hot sweat greeted her palm as she touched Duncan's brow.

With a grumble, he swatted her hand away.

"Can you get up?" she asked.

"Aye."

By the weakness of his voice, she wasn't convinced. Without giving him an option, she caught his arm and helped him sit. "We need to relight the candle."

Cloth scraped against stone as Duncan leaned against the wall next to her. "Did you bring the flint?"

"I . . . I did not think we would be needing it."

He sighed. "No use regretting it now. We will have to find the exit in the dark."

Isabel ignored the stabbing pain up her right leg and stood. Bracing herself against the wall, she reached down to help Duncan and then paused.

Like a faerie hill to wish upon, a shaft of light cut through the darkness. "Duncan, look up ahead."

"An exit."

"But to where?" she asked. "The bailey? An entry behind the gatehouse?"

"Wherever it leads," he rasped, "it is better than rotting in the dark."

Mayhap, but at least here, however temporary, they were safe. Isabel half pulled, half dragged Duncan to his feet. She braced herself for his weight as he leaned against her.

"Take it slow." Uneven rocks jabbed into her slippers as they inched forward. Near the exit, he stumbled. "No!" She caught him. Barely.

"I am fine," he panted out.

He wasn't. If he didn't rest soon, he'd pass out

from exhaustion. If fever didn't overwhelm him first. "We will stop here for a short rest."

"There is no time."

Isabel wet her lips. His brother Seathan, Earl of Gray, lived but a day's travel from here. "I have an idea. You stay here, and I will go for help."

"And who would you be seeking aid from?"

"Seathan."

He snorted in disbelief.

His suspicion of her good intent hurt, but why would he be believing her after she'd hurt him three years ago?

"What if you are caught?"

"Unless Frasyer's guards have extended their search beyond the castle, I should be safe."

"It is too far."

She didn't argue. For now it was pointless. As long as Duncan could travel, it was safer than leaving him here.

Duncan staggered forward.

She followed in silence.

The purple-gray streaks of dawn cut through the sky as they exited the tunnel. She scanned the field woven with winter-torn heather and took a deep breath, welcoming the fresh scent after the stale, tunnel air. At any other time, she would have enjoyed the beauty before her. Now, the clearing was another obstacle to overcome.

Across the lush expanse, a thick stand of trees outlined the edge of the forest. A short distance within lay the entrance to a hidden cave. One in which she'd secretly met with Symon many times before.

Symon.

Her chest tightened as she thought of her brother.

"What is wrong?"

Duncan's slurred voice had her glancing toward him, his ashen face causing her further worry. "Naught." She set aside the memories of her brother that threatened to rise. "The field is clear." Far from the clutter of emotions wrapped around her heart that threatened to weaken her in a moment when she needed to be strong.

For them both.

A third of the way across the field, the sun peeked over the mountains. At this rate, 'twould be midday before they reached the forest. She scanned the horizon. With them framed within the field in broad daylight, if someone rode by, they would be easily seen.

"There is no sign of Frasyer's men," Duncan said as if sensing her concern.

"No, but by now Frasyer has widened his men's search to extend beyond the castle's boundaries."

"Aye."

As if beckoned by their words, the cadence of hooves pounded in the distance. Through the blades of grass, a small contingent of Frasyer's knights rode into view.

She caught Duncan's shoulder and tried to turn him back.

He resisted.

"We have to hide in the tunnel!"

"Isabel, I . . ." Instead of starting to turn, he collapsed. The chalky whiteness of his face in contrast to the blood staining through the cloth she'd bound over his wound.

"No!" Her arms shuddered beneath his full weight. He couldn't pass out on her now. They'd be caught! "Duncan?"

On his knees, he tried to push her away. "Go." He drew in a ragged breath. "Hide while you can."

"I will not leave you."

"It is not a debate!"

Tears scraped in her throat as she glanced toward the tunnel. No way could she carry him back.

"Lass—"

"You risked your life to free me. Do not ask me to leave you now. I will not."

His mouth thinned into a stubborn line. "There is nowhere to hide."

She nodded toward where several small boulders jutted from the earth. "We will lay behind them." Half stumbling, she helped him hide behind the rocks. Though only waist high, they provided a degree of cover. As long as the men passed at a distance, they would remain unseen.

The earth trembled as the riders closed.

A man shouted.

Isabel tensed as she lay beside Duncan. "Do you think Frasyer's knights spotted us?"

"They are too far away."

She started to rise.

Duncan caught her arm. "What are you doing?"

"I am going to look."

He hesitated, his breathing harsh. "Be careful, lass."

Kneeling against the stone, Isabel peeked above the boulder. She dropped beside Duncan. "They are headed straight toward us!"

"Bedamned!"

When Frasyer's knights discovered them, how was she going to explain Duncan's presence? Numerous reasons came to mind. She discarded each and every one. However untrue, Frasyer would believe Duncan's releasing her from the dungeon was driven by amorous intent. Frasyer knew of her love for Duncan, of how it'd remained steadfast over time. He'd savored every moment of Duncan's belief that she'd broken their vows for Frasyer's wealth.

After uncovering her clandestine meeting with Symon and her father only days ago, Frasyer would believe she'd been meeting with Duncan all along. Once he'd questioned his guards and learned no priest had taken a lad to penance, Frasyer would deduct how Duncan had slipped through his castle's defenses.

"Here." Duncan pressed a dagger into her hands. "In case you need it."

Fear threatened to freeze her, she squeezed her eyes shut, then opened them. "I am sorry to have drawn you into this."

He shot her a hard stare. "Aye, with me you have made many a mistake." He shifted into a crouch, visibly weak. Yet, his weapon was readied. "Get ready, lass."

The cold rock pressed against her back as the steady thrum of hooves increased. Yes, she had made many mistakes when it came to Duncan, but now she wondered if her biggest one was not turning to him for help when Frasyer had first pressed her father for Isabel to become his mistress.

Too late to worry about choices made in the past. Now, nothing good would come from the revelation.

Still, she couldn't stand here and do nothing. Duncan's face was covered with sweat. His hand trembled around the hilt of his sword. Though he believed himself able, he was too weak to fight.

"Listen to me," she whispered. "I am going to crawl a distance from here, then I will give myself up. They will not know you were involved in my escape. Once they take me away, head toward your brother's home." She dreaded returning to Frasyer, and the harsh treatment he would deliver, but no other option remained.

"And what of the Bible?"

The Bible! In the mayhem of the last few hours, she'd forgotten it. This time Frasyer would lock her in the dungeon, but with a guard. She'd never be able to escape.

And her father would die.

Unable to resist, Isabel softly traced her hand along the strong curve of Duncan's face. Neither could she sacrifice Duncan's life. "I will find a way," she lied.

He caught her hand. "No."

Frantic, she tried to pull free, but he held her tight. "Do you not understand?" Her voice trembled. "I cannot risk losing you as well."

Duncan stared at Isabel, working to filter her words past the constant throbbing of his wound. "Three years ago you broke our betrothal to become Frasyer's mistress. A long way from caring for someone if you ask me."

A bird cried overhead. A cloud smothered the sun. The thrum of hooves grew louder.

"Let me go before the knights come too close," she whispered. "They must not find you."

The sincerity of her request resurrected his suspicions of her past actions. Since he'd freed Isabel from the dungeon, it seemed at every turn something else was awry.

"Nay. Whatever happens, we will face it together." And once they were safe, he would find out exactly what she was about.

"You do not understand!" She jerked her hand free. He grabbed for her, but his injury slowed him. Before he could stop her, she crawled into the thick grass.

"Isabel!" The stubborn lass. Dizziness overwhelmed him as he tried to follow.

She disappeared from sight.

Sweat trickled down his face, and his entire body burned as if set ablaze. He sat and rechecked his injury, which was red and warning of infection if he didn't tend to it soon. Blast it!

A stick snapped a distance away.

He glanced through the yellow-brown blades of withered grass broken by an errant thistle. Ten lengths ahead, Isabel stood. Caught within a gust, her straight whisky-colored hair that'd come unbraided fluttered around her face as if a defiant faerie.

"No!" The pounding of hooves drowned out Duncan's cry as she faced the riders. With a curse, he struggled to his feet.

As if a miracle, the riders swerved toward the hidden exit.

Trembling, she turned toward him. And halted. Horror filled her face. "What are you doing exposing yourself?"

"Saving your blasted hide," he growled, refusing to allow her to see how almost losing her had ripped his heart open all over again. He was a fool to care, but 'twould seem with her, it was his lot.

She waved her hands. "Get down." When he remained standing, however unsteady, Isabel ran over and dragged him with her to the ground. "Do you want to be getting yourself caught?"

He scowled at her. "Nay, that was your intent."

"Damn you. I was trying to save your hide."

"So you say." Through the swaying grass, he watched the knights as they slowed near the tunnel's opening he and Isabel had emerged from moments before.

"John," the lead rider ordered as he waved his men to a halt. "Ensure no one comes out."

"Aye," the knight replied as he dismounted.

Motioning his men forward, the knight kicked his horse into a canter; dry glass flew from their horses' hooves as his men rode in his wake. Minutes later, the riders faded from sight.

Through his blurred vision, Duncan spotted the remaining guard. From his vantage point, how much of the field could the guard see? Or would his focus be only on the exit?

Thunder echoed in the distance. Duncan glanced westward. An ominous bank of snow-filled clouds rumbled toward them.

"The guard is going inside," Isabel said.

"To keep dry." A luxury they could ill afford. He sheathed his sword and then held out his hand. "Give me the dagger."

Isabel handed him the blade.

As he stared at the weapon, his vision clouded

to a giddy blur, his mind whirling with unbidden memories. He remembered the day his father had bestowed it upon him to celebrate his becoming a knight.

As well as the halved sapphire hanging around his neck presented by his grandmother during the ceremony. The other half now lay inside a bowl of her abandoned chamber in his eldest brother's home, Lochshire Castle. A room the brothers believed contained magic.

He frowned. Duncan believed in the fey and of powers drawn from the earth, but he had doubts of the gemstone's abilities. Though the sapphire was known for its powers of prophecy, wisdom, and its ability to help the clarity of mind, until the end, he'd never seen Isabel's treachery coming.

As if summoned, the warmth of the stone pulsed against his chest. Duncan scrubbed his face. 'Twas fever claiming his thoughts. Little time existed to be thinking of his past, the fey, or Isabel's betrayal. He clutched the knife.

"Duncan?"

Isabel's worried voice dragged him from his hazed thoughts.

Somber eyes studied him. "Let me look at your arm."

"We must find shelter first," he said.

"I know of a cave nearby."

He nodded. By the time they made it to safety, he doubted he'd care what Isabel did to him, much less remember anything.

She situated herself to give him her support. "We must keep low."

Leaning against her, Duncan forced his aching body forward. Through the haze of pain, he noticed the softness of her curves, how she pressed against him with worry filling her eyes. Once he'd wanted her tenderness. That was before he'd known her tenderness was for sale.

He clenched his teeth and allowed his fury of her betrayal to fill him. He wanted nothing to do with her. But shamefully, a part of him knew he lied.

Snow slapped his face as they moved, the fat flakes icing his skin and further blurring his vision. Wind battered them with a merciless bite as they reached the shelter of the trees, but with his body burning with fever, he savored the icy drops.

Snow clung to Isabel's hair like a faerie crown as she turned toward him. All he saw was a blur. Fragments of the woman he'd once loved. A woman who, damn her, could hurt him still.

"The entry to the cave is up ahead, behind that dense brush."

He nodded, too tired, his body aching too much to speak. Or try.

Isabel guided Duncan over a moss-covered slope. Halfway down, he slipped.

"Duncan!" She grabbed his cloak to stop him, throwing him further off balance.

Clods of dirt flew as they slammed to the ground. Momentum plunged them down the steep incline. Branches, rocks, and sticks jabbed at him.

"Watch out!" she yelled.

The blur of darkness screamed toward them. Instinct had Duncan rolling to place Isabel behind him, and he took the full impact as they crashed into the brush shielding the opening to the cave.

And his mind gave in to welcome blackness.

Chapter 7

"Wake up, Duncan!"

Caught within the tangle of limbs, Duncan fought to remain conscious. Everything hurt. Why hadn't Isabel left him alone. For a second, he'd felt the empty bliss of nothing.

He pried open his eyes. Isabel's face swam into view. Snow clung from her whisky hair. Worry hazed her amber eyes. And her face, though pale to him, couldn't have looked more beautiful.

'Twas his fever misguiding his thoughts, he assured himself. But a traitorous part of him admitted that since he'd first caught sight of her in the dungeon, all his old feelings for her that he'd sought to destroy had become unveiled.

She caught his shoulders and struggled to lift him. "We have to get you inside the cave."

His lids started to slide down. "Sleep," he murmured, wanting only to rest and for a moment not to feel.

"It is too dangerous for you to remain here with Frasyer's men searching for us. You must help me. I cannot carry you."

Frasyer. Aye, couldn't let the bastard find them. Gritting his teeth, Duncan struggled to stand. Halfway, his legs started to buckle.

"Come on." Isabel positioned her hand under his right shoulder and lifted.

Ignoring his body's protests, he braced his feet apart and pushed. The cave blurred before him. By sheer will, he regained his focus.

"Easy now," Isabel cautioned as she helped him into the dry interior. "Food stores and blankets are hidden inside. Once I have tended to your wounds, I will go for help."

"No. Too dangerous. You must . . ." The room spun around him. Darkness threatened. He shoved his palm against the worn rock and braced himself.

"Duncan?"

"I—" His legs crumpled and he landed on his injured arm. Pain tore through him and he struggled to remain conscious. He felt someone shaking him. A frantic voice in his ear.

"Wake up."

He forced his eyes open, but he couldn't focus. Gray sliding to black. The room began to fade around him.

"Stay awake!"

The fear in her voice had him trying to rally, but darkness beckoned with a welcome hand. "A . . ." He fought to swallow over a throat gone dry with fever. "Alert me if anyone comes."

"You are in no condition to move, much less defend me." Isabel smoothed his face with her hand, her touch tender, her chastisement gentle, as if a caress. "I am going to Seathan for help."

Duncan tried to reply, but pain blurred his mind and her words garbled. Darkness beckoned, an escape from the pain originating at his arm and tearing through his body. Dear God, the pain.

His lids began to droop again. A thought clawed its way to the fore. Forcing his eyes open, Duncan reached up. His hand shook from effort as he jerked the halved sapphire from around his neck. He shoved it into her hand.

"Gi-Give this to Seathan."

To Seathan? At this moment Duncan's oldest brother didn't matter, no one did but getting Duncan home alive. Isabel frowned but took the chain holding the sapphire pendant, remembering the day his grandmother had gifted it to him upon his being knighted.

"Why?" she asked, as the gemstone dangled before her, surprised Duncan would entrust her with a possession he valued above all others.

"It is the only way"—he closed his eyes for a moment, then struggled to open them—"Seathan will believe you are telling him the truth."

Isabel stilled. She'd never considered his brother not believing her, but it made sense. After Duncan's father died, without hesitation, Seathan had taken on the responsibility of raising his younger brothers, Alexander, Duncan, and their adopted brother, Patrik. Throughout the years, Seathan had guided them and guarded them with a fierce loyalty. Then she'd ended her betrothal with Duncan and broken his heart. Seathan, like his brothers, had shunned her ever since.

Regret balled in her throat, hot and hard. Regardless, for Duncan's sake, she would do whatever it took to convince Seathan she was telling the truth.

Duncan's eyes rolled back in his head.

"Duncan?"

Silence.

Her chest squeezed tight as Isabel stared at his pain-filled face, the sweat streaking his brow visible in the muted light. Fear roared inside her, but she shook his shoulder with gentleness.

"Duncan?"

He didn't move.

Sucking in a deep breath, she fisted the sapphire within her palm, the pendant a potent reminder of Duncan's belief in her. As she clutched the gemstone, heat slowly warmed her palm. Surprised, she opened her hand to find the dark blue gem seeming to glow upon her skin. Ridiculous.

Many people believed in the properties of this gem, its presence giving them the ability to purge themselves of unwelcome thoughts, to cleanse the mind and bring inner peace. Many people claimed Duncan's grandmother had the sight and had foreseen Duncan's troubled future. Had she gifted him with the halved sapphire upon his knighting to bring him a semblance of comfort in his future?

As if the sapphire or its meaning mattered now. Isabel pulled the amulet over her head, tucked the sapphire beneath her chemise to lay against Wallace's arms. She ignored how warmth continued to pulse within her palm where the gem had lain. Tiredness and her imagination spurred such thoughts.

She had to get Duncan to safety. Breaking down now would only hinder her journey ahead.

After preparing a makeshift bed, she rolled him onto the blankets and removed his garb to tend to his wound. Her hand trembled as she surveyed the depth of the cut combined with the amount of blood he'd lost. Guilt lanced her. He never should have accompanied her to Frasyer's chambers to search for the Bible, much less spent the last few hours hidden beneath the earl's bed, bleeding all the while.

Please protect him from infection, she prayed, unable to prevent tears from burning in her eyes.

She wiped them away with the back of her hand. "Do not die on me, Duncan MacGruder." Even as she spoke the words, she knew that if he lived, 'twould be more than the herbs she'd give him, but her heart, before leaving to find his brother.

Isabel secured a water pouch to her waist, drew on her cape and crept outside. The slap of cold air had her glancing up. The cloud-sprinkled sky of earlier now gave way to thick, dark clouds. The fresh scent of the air was rich with the promise of more snow.

She worried her lower lip. In the distance, a knight guarded the tunnel she and Duncan had slipped from a short time before. Soon, Frasyer would widen the search. She refused to reflect on the dangers of traveling in the forest alone with a snowstorm approaching. Duncan needed her, and she owed him a greater debt than he knew.

With a prayer on her lips, Isabel hurried off into dense forest.

The following evening, eyes as black as the devil's own pierced Isabel as she forced herself to remain standing at the entry to Lochshire Castle. Her entire body trembled with a mix of fear and fatigue as Duncan's oldest brother, Seathan MacGruder, Earl of Gray, strode toward her. Clad in his mail, he was every ounce the warrior.

Fat flakes of snow spiraled between them, each negating to shield her from the man she must face. A man who detested her with his every breath.

She shivered and glanced longingly toward the keep and the warmth waiting within. However much she wanted to, she couldn't remain. A snow-storm that'd begun shortly after she'd left the cave had slowed her travel. The drifting flakes in combination with the night more so. Too many hours had passed. She'd hoped to have returned to Duncan by now.

Please, God, let Duncan be alive.

As another shiver racked her, Seathan halted before her.

With cold precision, he shoved back his snow-littered coif. Sweat clung to his face from his practice interrupted moments ago by her arrival and request for his immediate attention.

Freed from its bond, his black hair tumbled over his broad, well-muscled shoulders. A body honed for war. A mind quick and lethal in its attack.

"You dare much by showing your face at my home." His deep burr reverberated within the tunnel of the gatehouse, his dislike of her clear. "You are not welcome here."

Sadness threatened to overwhelm Isabel as she stared at Duncan's brother, a man she'd known all her life, a man she'd laughed with and told jokes to as a child. Beneath his intense scrutiny, she felt as if a stranger.

For Duncan's sake, she refused to leave. Isabel shook her head. "I cannot go."

Seathan started forward as if to cast her out himself.

She put her hand out. "Wait! Duncan was gravely wounded helping me escape Moncreiffe Castle two days past. I left him hidden in a cave near Frasyer's castle. I need your help in bringing him home."

He glanced over her shoulder to the harsh, snow-covered land, where drifts were growing by the hour. His face, shadowed with the start of a full beard, iced to distrust as he turned back to her.

"Duncan left several days past on an errand of importance to help the rebels."

"He was helping but one rebel, my brother." Emotions threatened to storm her as they had countless times during her journey. By sheer will, she tamped them down. "On a death pledge to Symon, Duncan traveled to Moncreiffe Castle to rescue me from Frasyer's dungeon."

His eyes narrowed further. "You lie. I have neither received word of Symon's death, nor did Duncan inform me of his pledge to help you escape."

Her heart ached. Of course not. Duncan would never admit he was going to rescue her. For his vow to her brother, he'd set aside his shame.

"Duncan would not want you to know of his helping me," she admitted.

Seathan's mouth tightened.

"I have proof." Her fingers, numb from her journey, trembled as Isabel tugged the chain and amulet from around her neck. Freed, the sapphire twisted amid the flakes of snow. Errant rays of sun flickered upon the gem to cast prisms of blue and aqua over her hand like a shattered rainbow.

"Before I left Duncan in the cave, he gave me this." She held the jeweled necklace toward him.

Seathan's nostrils flared as he seized the pendant. His ebony gaze filled with suspicion.

Isabel's chest tightened with panic. Oh God, he didn't believe her! "I am not lying. If Duncan is not rescued and tended to soon, he will die. Please, help me."

Wood scraped behind them as the door to the guardhouse slammed shut. Hard steps crunched beneath the snow, closing fast. Isabel turned.

Dressed in mail, Duncan's middle brother, Alexander, strode toward her. His lean build was similar to Seathan's and Duncan's. Hair, black as midnight, framed his hard countenance. A scar ran along his left cheek, adding to his daunting presence.

Alexander's gaze pinned her. Suspicion seethed in his deep blue eyes hardened by an edge of violence. "I see she dares to try to enter our home." He scowled at his brother. "Why have you not yet tossed her out on her arse in the cold where she belongs?"

Aware Alexander's passions often guided him, Isabel held her ground. He was only protecting Duncan, a brother he loved against a woman he despised.

"Duncan is seriously wounded and needs your help," Isabel insisted.

"So you claim." Seathan handed his brother the sapphire pendant.

Alexander's brow slammed together as he laid it over his gloved hand. "Duncan's amulet?" He scowled at her. "Why does *she* have it?"

"Isabel said Duncan gave this to her to convince us she is speaking the truth."

"There is only one way Duncan would part with this amulet." Alexander took a menacing step toward her, the sapphire strangled in his grasp. He leaned forward until his nose was but a hand's breadth from her, his mouth curled in a fierce snarl. "What have you and Frasyer done to Duncan?"

"I swear to you, this is not a trick," Isabel replied, her voice unsteady. "Duncan was injured when he helped me escape Frasyer's dungeon two days past. We reached a cave. Before he passed out, he gave me the amulet. You must believe me!"

Alexander snorted. "I would be believing that bastard Frasyer would toss his mistress into the dungeon. A fitting place for the likes of you. Now you want me swallowing that Duncan would be helping you escape Frasyer's lair?" He shook his head. "Nay, lass. After you betrayed Duncan three years ago to wallow in the earl's bed, he would not trust you with a maggot-infested chunk of venison."

Seathan stepped closer. "She also claims Symon is dead and that Duncan gave her brother his vow to help her escape before he died."

"Another bloody lie," Alexander spat. "Think we are foolish enough to believe you?"

With Duncan's brothers towering over her, needing distance from their fury, Isabel stepped back. And bumped against the hewn wall. Cornered by the intimidating males and pinned by the hard glares of the nearby guards, she wanted to sink to the ground and cry. Since she and Duncan had escaped the dungeon, she'd had no food, rest, or water. Her muscles screamed from strain of the arduous travel, her body ached from the cold, and worry for Duncan had weighted her every thought.

Isabel glared from one brother to the next. Damn them both. "Loan me a palfrey. I will retrieve Duncan myself!"

"Aye," Alexander said with sarcasm, "and let you steal the horse as you did Duncan's amulet?"

"I told you, I did not—"

"Is Duncan dead?" Seathan demanded.

Her heart ached as she recalled Duncan's sacrifices to help her—and of his promise to Symon. "No, he is alive."

At least he had been when she'd left him.

No, she refused to think of such dismal thoughts. She'd lost her brother, was unsure if her father still lived, and but a slim chance to find the Bible and save her father existed. A hope that with each passing day was fading away. But she'd not let Duncan down.

She started to say more, but her vision began to blur. Isabel braced herself against the cold, stone wall. Gathering her strength, she squeezed her hands into tight fists and stepped forward to face the formidable warriors in one final stand.

"Do you not understand? If you do not help me bring Duncan home, he is going to die!"

Alexander crossed his arms and Seathan only cocked a speculative brow.

Tears streamed down her cheeks as Isabel tried to shove past the two warriors. "To Hades with the both of you! I will find a palfrey and manage to bring him back myself."

Seathan's calloused hand caught her shoulder. "Duncan would only part with his amulet if the situation was dire, or, as Alexander says," he continued, his voice solemn, "he is in Frasyer's hands and you are part of his devious plot to capture us as well."

She jerked from Seathan's hold. "I would never lie about something as critical as Duncan's life, not even for Frasyer. Despise me, it matters not, but each moment we delay in leaving is time lost in saving your brother."

Alexander snorted. "You think to deceive us with this pathetic tale of—"

Seathan raised his hand cutting off his brother's reply, his hard gaze never leaving hers.

Alexander's face reddened. "You are not telling me you are believing Frasyer's whore?"

The blood rushed from her face. Whore. Yes, he would think that. Everyone did. But their opinion of her at this moment mattered not.

Seathan's eyes bored into her with a look so deep it was as if he could see clear to her soul. At last, the earl nodded. "Order our mounts readied posthaste."

"By my sword," Alexander seethed. "She shows up dressed in naught better than rags with a far-fetched story that reeks of Frasyer's doing, and you are believing her?"

"Go," Seathan said. It wasn't a request.

Alexander's muscled frame stiffened. "Rest assured"—his glare pinned Isabel—"we will be on the lookout for Frasyer's treachery. And may God help you if you are telling us a lie, for I will end your deceitful life with my own hands." He stalked toward the stable, the crunch of snow haunting his steps.

Seathan's gaze on her never wavered. He watched her like a hawk focused on its prey.

"Thank you," she said unsteadily.

Surprise, then understanding flickered in his eyes. An odd tingling crept over her skin. Did the earl suspect she still loved Duncan? No, Seathan believed her loyalty lay with Frasyer. Only the amulet had swayed him to believe her of Duncan's peril.

Still, the intrigue in Seathan's eyes worried her more than Alexander's anger. Rousing the Earl of Gray's curiosity meant regardless of the time or obstacles faced, Seathan would rout out the truth.

A truth she could never unveil.

Seathan rubbed his thumb against the hilt of his sword. "I find it odd that after walking away from Duncan three years ago, you appear on my doorstep begging us to help save his life."

She hugged herself for more reasons than the cold. "As I explained, he was wounded as he helped me escape the dungeon."

"A tale, I assure you, I will become intimately familiar with upon our return." At the whinny of a horse, Seathan straightened. "Had I more time, we would discuss your true reasons for wanting Duncan safe." He nodded to a guard.

A red-haired knight stepped forward. "My lord?"

"See that Lady Adair is given food and a room within the keep." He paused. "And is not allowed to leave Lochshire Castle until my return."

The knight nodded and took Isabel's arm as Seathan started to turn away.

She struggled to break free; the guard held her arm tight. "No, you must take me with you!"

Seathan paused, his look fierce. "There is no need. I know the area well."

He couldn't leave her behind! She had to know if Duncan was alive. "There are several caves in the knolls to the north of Moncreiffe Castle. With the falling snow, even with a familiar eye, they will be difficult to find. And if you do not discover Duncan quickly . . ." She steadied herself. "I have lost too many hours in my journey here. Please, for Duncan's sake, we cannot lose more."

At her mention of evading Frasyer's men, the earl's eyes narrowed. "For Duncan's sake," he agreed. "If this is a trap, I am agreeing with Alexander's frame of mind, it will be your last." He nodded to the guard. "Bring her a dry cape and some warm meat wrapped within bread and some cheese."

"Yes, my lord."

As his guard departed, Seathan waved her forward.

Afraid he'd change his mind, Isabel hurried to catch up with him as he walked toward the stable, ignoring her exhaustion and the coldness numbing her from head to toe.

"Once we have returned, Duncan is cared for, and you have rested," Seathan said as he walked at her side, "I will be knowing the details of why Frasyer would sentence you to the dungeon."

She didn't answer. Somehow, she had to keep Seathan from prying further. And she couldn't do that by remaining at Lochshire Castle.

After Duncan was home and she was confident he would recover, she would slip away and return to Moncreiffe Castle to find her mother's Bible.

Alone.

The steady thrum of the church bell reverberated through Duncan's skull like the pounding of a siege engine. He opened his eyes, wincing at the effort.

A half-burned taper flickered on a corner table. A blurred, luxurious tapestry hung on the far wall. He squinted and tried to focus. His head pounded harder. Frustrated, he struggled to sit and pain shot through his left arm.

His arm.

The confrontation with the knights at Moncreiffe Castle streaked through his mind. The long hours throughout the night that he and Isabel had hidden under Frasyer's bed, and how, with Isabel's help and sheer will, they'd escaped and made it to a cave.

Then nothing.

He must have passed out. What of Isabel? Had Frasyer found them? Or had Isabel deceived him from the start and waited until he'd fallen unconscious to lead Frasyer to him?

Duncan frowned. That didn't make sense. She could have called for help while they'd hidden beneath Frasyer's bed. Or sought aid anytime during their escape for that fact. Still, Duncan couldn't shake the feeling that something about her intent in helping him was amiss. Even if he was safe, she had far from earned his trust.

So where was he? If he was indeed captured, he doubted Frasyer had shown compassion for his injured state and moved him to one of his luxurious chambers. After Duncan had sworn fealty to William Wallace, Frasyer had branded him an outlaw.

He forced his eyes open again and struggled to focus. Slowly, his vision cleared. Between the taper near his bedside and the flames within the fireplace, he recognized the wooden chest at the end of the bed, then the muted design woven within the rug hanging upon the wall. He sagged with relief. 'Twas his chamber in Lochshire Castle.

A vague memory of giving Isabel his amulet tangled in his thoughts. He reached up to his chest. Nothing. Duncan frowned. He had no memories of travel, which had certainly occurred.

The amulet must have convinced his brothers she was telling the truth of his needing help. Even as he'd handed it to Isabel, doubts plagued him that the pendant alone would convince his brother that her request was the truth. What else had she explained to them? Or rather, how much?

"Isabel?" Raw, his throat ached at his effort to speak.

"Duncan! You are awake."

The grogginess of her voice behind him alerted Duncan that he'd awoken her from wherever she'd been resting out of his sight.

She walked into view and knelt beside the bed, her eyes moving over him with worry. "How fare thee?"

Despite the lingering disorientation, the sight of her relieved a pressure in his chest. Had he been able to, he might have heeded the temptation to draw her into his arms and assure himself they were both safe.

"Well enough."

She filled a goblet with water and held it to his lips. "Here."

His fingers trembled as he wrapped them around

her own. Irritated by the warmth contact with her brought, after a sip, he pushed the cup away.

She set the goblet on a nearby table, concern edged in her face.

"How long have we been here?" Duncan asked.

"Three days. Your fever broke early this morning."

That explained his weakness. He moved his wounded arm.

"You need to keep your arm still. I have wrapped it and it is still healing."

"It is a little stiff is all." He'd suffered worse discomfort many times before.

"You are lucky the gash didn't become infected."

"Thanks to you," he replied, realizing her efforts had kept the wound clean.

She cleared her throat. "I did naught but what anyone else would have done."

Not true. Duncan had no delusions of his fate had Frasyer caught them. "Did you tell my brothers about Symon?"

The pain in her eyes bespoke her reply. She nodded.

Bedamned. He'd not meant his brothers to learn of Symon's death this way. Neither had he meant for them to discover his vow to Symon concerning Isabel—the very fact he'd excluded from his missive to Seathan. Had either of his brothers learned of his intent to sneak into Moncreiffe Castle they would have stopped him.

Now they knew. They would be furious, more so now that they'd realized he'd twisted the truth about helping the rebels. But he'd not lied. As a loyal follower of Wallace, Symon counted as such. Except, they wouldn't see his explanation that way.

He sighed. It was too late to worry about their anger now.

Duncan took in her rumpled dress and the tiredness weighing heavy in her eyes. "You have slept little." With her having half carried him to the cave, then having struck out on her own to reach his home, she had to have been exhausted. From her rumpled gown, he assumed she'd stayed within his chamber until now. Her reason derived from guilt, but the motive did little to ease his worry.

She shrugged. "I have caught naps."

"Not enough."

Her expression grew remote, as if she were a stranger. "I am well. Your growing upset will only tire you further."

Refusing to be swayed, he shifted to a more comfortable position on his side. "It would seem the amulet convinced Seathan in believing I needed help, but that does not explain how you convinced my brother to allow you to care for me?"

She looked away, her expression remote. "He is a practical man."

Her guarded words furthered his interest. Practical, aye, but his eldest brother was fierce in his protection as well. When their father had died, without hesitation, Seathan had taken responsibility to raise him, Alexander, and until his death, Patrik. The day he'd learned of Isabel's betrayal, Seathan had sworn she would never again set foot in his home.

Now, for him to have permitted Isabel to remain within Lochshire Castle, much less tend to Duncan, something significant had passed between them.

"What did you say to Seathan to convince him to allow you to tend me instead of our healer?"

Wind whistled through the window in a soft hush. The candle sputtered, then held its own. The rich scent of burning wax filled his every breath as he waited for an answer.

She sighed, a soft and lonely sound. Then, as if a trick of the light, tears shimmered in her eyes. As quickly, they vanished. "That you almost died saving me, and I had a great debt to repay."

"That may be true, but there is more that you are not telling me."

At her silence, his suspicions built. What could she have told Seathan, that she loved him? Quickly, he cursed the foolish thought. Even if Isabel wanted him, he would never accept her back now. Neither could he believe that Seathan would accept such as truth from her.

Disgusted with his musings, he glanced through the window and into the night. Stars filled the sky, tinged with the hint of the oncoming morning. So like many of the nights of his youth. Nights where he'd looked out and crafted his dreams. Except now he was a man grown. And everything had changed.

His dreams of forever with Isabel, like his trust in her, had shattered.

The door eased open and Seathan stepped inside.

At the interruption, relief flashed across Isabel's face.

Duncan caught the expression. He would discover the truth, but from Seathan's hard look, it would be a blistering telling.

"You are awake then," Seathan said.

"Aye."

Isabel stiffened at Duncan's side. "My lord."

Seathan's mouth tightened as he turned to Isabel. "Leave us."

Chapter 8

Isabel tensed at Seathan's command, but Duncan didn't miss the shimmer of distress on her face. Again Duncan wondered what had transpired between the two while he'd slept. From the ire brewing in Seathan's eyes, he'd find out soon enough.

"He awoke but moments ago," Isabel cautioned, "and needs to rest."

Seathan stepped forward, nodded his dismissal. "I will see to his welfare."

"As you wish." With a nervous glance toward Duncan, she left, closing the door in her wake.

Silence echoed between Duncan and Seathan like ice pellets against forged steel.

Seathan's obsidian gaze narrowed on him. "The missive you sent stated you were helping the rebels. You deliberately omitted to both Alexander and me about Symon's death and your vow to him to save Isabel. Now, I will be knowing why."

Duncan lifted his body up and braced himself on his arms, the movement igniting a pounding in his head. Every inch of him ached and the smallest movement cost him. Already the lure of sleep pulled on his senses. But he'd been lucky.

Unlike Symon, he had lived.

Before he could speak, the door was shoved open. His brother Alexander strode inside. "Good, you are awake."

The ire in his voice framed his scowl, assuring Duncan neither of his brothers would yield in their outrage. "It would seem so."

Alexander sent Seathan a questioning look. "What has he said?"

"Naught as yet." His oldest brother kept his gaze skewered on Duncan. "But he will be explaining why he lied to us."

"Aye, he will," Alexander agreed.

"Symon was a rebel," Duncan said.

"And a friend," Seathan stated. Grief dug deep lines in his brow as he stoked his thumb upon the hilt of his dagger. "You should have told us immediately of Symon's death—not left us a missive skewed with a version of the truth before you rode off."

Alexander gave a grunt of disgust. "You have the wits of an ass. Had Frasyer caught you, he would have gladly delivered you to King Edward. Longshanks would revel in displaying the head of yet another Scottish rebel upon a pike."

Alexander's use of the slang name given for the English king, Longshanks, assured Duncan of the depth of his brother's fury.

Humbled, embarrassed he'd not given his brothers a full explanation from the start, Duncan nodded. "I was wrong. For that I am sorry." He held his hand up when Alexander made to speak. "Because it was

Isabel, I felt it was personal. Something I had to do by myself."

"Personal? Nay, you were ashamed because it was her," Alexander challenged. "And for that, you almost bloody got yourself killed."

Seathan stalked toward him and towered over his bed. "You made this task personal—by choice. Your going to Moncreiffe Castle stemmed from your vow to Symon before his death, not a request from Isabel. Since she broke her betrothal to you three years past, you have neither tried to see her nor spoken of her."

Duncan rubbed his brow to try to quell the pounding in his head. And failed. Mayhap Seathan was right, but over the past three years thoughts of her had haunted him like a curse. Still, he wouldn't admit that. A man could only concede to being so much of a fool.

"Right or wrong, I left a missive stating my reasons for going alone." Duncan shot a hard look first at Seathan, then toward Alexander. "Did Isabel tell you that Frasyer has charged Lord Caelin with aiding the rebels and has sent him to Lord Monceaux's to be hung?"

Seathan nodded. "Aye. I have sent several runners to Rothfield Castle in England to explain the situation to Lord Monceaux."

Relief swept through Duncan. Why had he not thought of doing the same? With Alexander's marriage to Lord Monceaux's sister, Nichola, the English lord would surely help them. Not to mention the fact that although Griffin was King Edward's Scottish adviser, the English were unaware he was a spy for Scotland who worked under the code name of Wulfe. The information Lord Monceaux passed to Wallace ensured the Scottish rebels stayed one step ahead of the English king. God help Griffin should King Edward ever learn the truth of his secret identity.

"Griffin will ensure Lord Caelin's life is spared," Duncan said.

"He will try," Alexander said. "But furious at the embarrassment served to his troops by the rebels, King Edward will settle for no less than Wallace's head. Nay, Longshanks spares no one whom he believes knows the whereabouts of Wallace."

"And with his rage of having Wallace slipped past his knights' searches several times now," Duncan agreed, "to vent his anger, the English king would cling to a lie."

"A lie indeed," Seathan agreed. "One that Frasyer will no doubt ensure reaches Griffin."

"Wanting to earn royal praise," Duncan added, understanding the self-serving bastard too well, "Frasyer will send a missive to King Edward as well, which negates Griffin ensuring Lord Caelin is unharmed."

Seathan and Alexander nodded in unison.

Pain throbbed in Duncan's head. "Frasyer would sell his mother if it earned him praise in the king's eyes."

"We will do all that we can to save Lord Caclin," Alexander said solemnly, "but we must take care to preserve Lord Monceaux's identity. If we should lose Griffin's aid to the rebel cause, it is a blow I doubt from which the rebels could recover." He shot Duncan a serious look. "Nor would I wish to deal Nichola such news of her brother."

Like the sputter of a windswept flame, Duncan's

hope for Isabel's father wavered. "Wait!" He sat up straighter and winced as the movement pulled against the stretch of healing skin. "There is proof of Lord Caelin's innocence. Isabel explained to me that before her father was hauled away, he told her to look in her mother's Bible!"

"Her mother's Bible?" Seathan asked.

Alexander frowned. "She nay mentioned a Bible to us. Or the fact that any proof of his innocence exists."

"Which makes no sense." Duncan shook his head. "Why would Isabel not tell you that we delayed our leaving Moncreiffe Castle because we tried to find her mother's Bible to save her father?"

Fresh anger clouded his brothers' faces.

"She said you were hurt while fighting guards, which delayed your escape," Seathan said, "but no more."

A sword's wrath. What else had she omitted? "The only reason I can think of why she wouldn't tell you about the Bible is . . . because it is a lie." Frustration churned within Duncan like a cauldron boiling over. "No, it cannot be. When she told me about the Bible, she pleaded and begged me to leave without her. Isabel was determined to find it on her own. She acted as if she truly cared that I was safe. Though I found her actions confusing, I believed, and still do, that she was sincere."

"God's steed! The two of you need a good shaking," Seathan muttered; Alexander grunted in agreement. "You both have given me enough of the truth to serve each of your purposes."

Duncan bristled. "My original intent was to spare

you from seeing Isabel again. One of us being afflicted with her presence was enough."

Seathan raised his brow. "Afflicted?" He waved a hand when Duncan would have spoken. "Start at the beginning and tell me the truth about what happened between you and Isabel. The entire truth. I will tolerate no more deception."

At thoughts of Isabel, a barrage of unwanted emotions stormed Duncan.

Desire.

Unanswered longing.

The sting of old betrayal.

But to avoid his brother's demand would only cause further chaos where too much lay at stake. "I will tell you, but first, explain why have you allowed Isabel to remain at Lochshire Castle."

Alexander's mouth thinned into a hard line as he slanted Seathan a hard look. "A question I have asked him as well."

"I have my reasons," Seathan stated.

And Seathan believed Duncan was stubborn, Duncan mused. He couldn't keep pace with his oldest brother. "Since she saved my life, I would think they are reasons I would deserve to be knowing."

"Since your thoughts have misguided you as of late," Seathan said, "I will determine when a reply to your question is necessary."

Alexander walked over to stand beside Seathan. He spread his feet shoulder width and crossed his arms. "Out with it, Duncan."

Aware that his brothers wouldn't be budged and thankful that his dizziness had abated, for the next few minutes, Duncan relayed the facts—from Symon riding up to him mortally wounded, his vow, freeing Isabel, and their escape.

Seathan curled his hand around the hilt of his sword until his knuckles grew white as he listened. "Had I known of what you were about—"

"You would have stopped me," Duncan said.

Alexander's nostrils flared with anger. "Which is why you did not wait for Seathan and me to return from Selkirk Forest after our meeting with Wallace."

"I had not anticipated such trouble. Had Isabel but cooperated, she and I would have been long gone before the dungeon guards noticed her absence." His throat parched, Duncan reached over for a goblet of water. His arm began to shake, and sweat beaded his brow.

Alexander stepped forward and handed him the pewter goblet filled with water.

"My thanks." Duncan took a long drink. After a moment, some of the dizziness passed. He wished he could say as much for how his body ached.

"What will you do about the Bible?" Seathan asked.

"I will be going back for it," Duncan said.

"Go back," Alexander scoffed. "With your wounds still healing, you will not be setting one foot inside—"

Seathan raised his hand, silencing his brother. For a long moment he studied Duncan as if he weighed a decision of import. "Do you trust Isabel?"

The question caught Duncan off guard, more so that it was a question he had asked himself many times over. A question that still gave him doubts. From Alexander's grimace, his brother was as surprised by Seathan's change of topic as well.

"I am not sure," Duncan admitted.

Seathan dropped his hand to his side and strode to the window. After a moment, he turned to face Duncan. "If indeed she is telling the truth, we must consider that Frasyer has taken the Bible with him, if not hidden it elsewhere."

"Or destroyed it," Alexander added.

Frustration collapsed atop Duncan's already mounting pile. "I am well aware those possibilities exist."

Seathan's eyes sparked with fury. "Are you? As Alexander stated, you are unfit to travel, much less fight Frasyer or his knights if confronted."

Duncan pushed himself into a sitting position, ignoring his body's protest. "It will take me a day, two at most to be up and about."

Alexander grunted. "You are as weak as a babe. You need rest, not to be pushing yourself."

"I will hand select two of my most trusted men to return with Isabel," Seathan said.

"Nay." Duncan threw off the covers and ignored the black spots dancing before his eyes. Clenching his teeth, he slid his feet over the side of the bed. "I will go. It is my responsibility."

Seathan shook his head. "Your vow to Symon to free Isabel is fulfilled. You owe her nothing more."

Words Duncan had repeated to himself a hundred times over, but shamefully, they didn't ease the anxiety spreading through him at never seeing her again. Which, after she'd abandoned him but days before they were to wed, made absolutely no sense.

"I have also given her my vow to help find the Bible." Duncan looked from one brother to the next.

Anger flared in his brothers' eyes, but in Seathan's gaze, he also noted understanding.

Unsettled, Duncan curled his hand into a fist, then slowly released it. What was there to understand? Or rather, after Iuliana, the woman Seathan loved had betrayed him, why would his older brother hold nothing but contempt for Isabel? Yet, he had allowed Isabel to remain within their home.

"Regardless of what either of us wishes," Duncan added, "with Frasyer's men in search of Isabel and her accomplice, for the next few days it would not be wise for anyone to try and reenter Moncreiffe Castle. If the knights I fought with within Frasyer's castle recognized me, Frasyer will have posted a watch upon Lochshire Castle to intercept me, or any of my kin, upon my return."

"True," Seathan agreed. "But garbed as a priest, I doubt they recognized you. If so, Frasyer would have arrived at my gates with a contingent of men demanding you and Isabel."

"Aye," Alexander grunted. "Still, with Frasyer's ire peaked, it would be foolhardy for any of us to ride upon his lands. Like it or not, we must wait a few days."

Seathan tapped his finger on the hilt of his sword. "I will increase the guard around Lochshire's borders in case Frasyer's men grow bold."

"I do not like the waiting, but it is a wise decision." With a sigh, Alexander began to pace the room. When he reached the far wall, he turned and stopped. For a long moment, he studied Duncan, his face hard. "A question Seathan asked earlier will not let me be. You said you are not sure if you trust Isabel, Duncan, but do you believe she has changed?" He stepped toward him. "Do you believe yourself immune? That your continued involvement with the lass will not lead to another round of hurt?"

Duncan didn't miss Seathan's watching him with interest at Alexander's question. He shoved to his feet. The room spun, but he braced himself. Out of sheer will, he remained standing.

"Do either of you think I could forget that she betrayed me?" Duncan demanded. Neither could he deny that the familiar spark, the warmth that'd always existed between them, thrived. An awareness that until he'd held her in the dungeon, he'd deluded himself into believing had faded. Now, despite her treachery, he wanted her. If he allowed Isabel back into his life, she could hurt him once again.

Except this time, he doubted he could recover.

"Though you would deny it," Alexander said, cutting into his musings, "you still carry feelings for the lass, want them or not. Your actions say what you will not."

"To Hades with you!" Duncan's legs began to tremble beneath the effort of standing. "I owe you no explanation other than the one that I have given."

"Enough," Seathan stated. "Arguing will change nothing."

Redness slashed across Alexander's cheeks, then his face softened with regret. "My words are driven from worry. Damn you, Duncan, you almost died."

The concern in his brother's voice tempered Duncan's anger. Tiredness washed over him, and he rubbed the back of his neck. "I know." Still, he couldn't help but wonder what was going through

Isabel's mind. Though she'd not spoken of her relationship with Frasyer, one would think with her imprisonment in Frasyer's dungeon, her father threatened with his life, and her brother killed, a woman would leave her lover. Except with Isabel, life had taught him not to expect the obvious.

"Rest, brother," Alexander said, "before you collapse and reopen Isabel's careful binding."

As Duncan slid back in bed, Seathan walked over to the table and poured himself a glass of wine. "Has the lass given you a reason why Frasyer imprisoned her?"

Duncan stiffened at his own idiocy. So caught up in emotions for Isabel, he'd neglected what he should have explained from the first. "Frasyer did so because she refused to tell him where Wallace is hidden."

"She knows?" Seathan and Alexander asked in stunned unison.

The shock on his brothers' faces matched Duncan's when he'd learned the fact. "Aye. Symon must have told her. It is the why of it I am unsure of." He shrugged. "With her living with Frasyer, one would believe the last thing her brother would discuss with her was Wallace, especially his location."

Seathan slammed the goblet upon the table. Red wine slopped over in angry puddles. "Or any rebel activity."

"What other rebel information has she been privileged to?" Alexander demanded.

"And why did she not mention this to us when we questioned her before? By God's steed, I will find out!" Seathan strode to the door. "I assure you, when I speak with her this time, she will leave nothing out."

"Stop!" Duncan jumped up again to intercede, but his legs gave way and he collapsed to the floor. Biting back the pain, he accepted his brother's help. With his hands braced on the bed as he sat up, he met Seathan's gaze. "I will talk to her in the morning."

"No," Seathan replied. "The luxury of time or tenderness is long past. With her ties to Frasyer, he may already be aware of other information dangerous to our rebel cause. Whatever she knows, we must learn posthaste and pass on to Wallace."

Alexander stepped forward. "I will go with you."

"Then we will all speak with her," Duncan said, aware the trio would be intimidating to Isabel, but also because he wanted to be there. "I want answers as well, but if Frasyer knows of Wallace's position, why has he not attacked the rebel base before now?"

"Now you protect her?" Seathan challenged.

"No. I but offer thoughts to consider." Duncan paused. "Tending to me, she has slept little since her arrival. Do you think in her exhausted state we will learn more than if she is allowed a bit of rest?"

"Exhaustion will make the finding out easier," Alexander snapped.

"She saved my life, I cannot forget that," Duncan replied. "Besides, do you think a few more hours truly matter?"

Tension built in the air between them. Seathan hesitated a moment longer, then stated, "At first light, but no longer."

On a slow exhale, Alexander relaxed. "As much as I want answers, on this I will respect your decision, but only because the lass reached us in time to save Duncan."

Thankful, Duncan nodded, aware this was far from a reprieve, neither should it be. Isabel's poor decisions in not confiding to him had created this muddle. She would bear the resultant burden. Still, that didn't mean he would allow his brothers to browbeat her unchecked.

If for no other reason than the vow he'd made to Symon, he would see to her safety.

"Rest now," Seathan said. "You woke but a short while ago and are still fevered."

"And your moving about has reopened the wound," Alexander chided.

Duncan looked down. A line of blood stained the wrap. He would be more careful, but he had a greater concern that had haunted him since he had released Isabel from her cell in Moncreiffe Castle.

"Do you think Isabel is a spy?" Duncan asked. "That Frasyer's tossing her into the dungeon was a trap?" Before either brother could reply, he continued. "I want to believe it is my mind concocting such doubts, that she would not betray us. As I explained, since I approached her in Frasyer's dungeon, she has acted and spoken as if her worry for me is sincere. But with her past actions, I am unsure."

"Something is amiss no doubt," Seathan agreed. "Exactly what, is the question."

Alexander nodded. "My thought as well."

A light knock sounded on the door.

Seathan stepped to the side. "Enter."

The door opened and a very pregnant woman,

her ivory face embraced by a cascade of auburn tresses, walked into the chamber. Eyes serious, she nodded toward Seathan, then turned to Alexander in silent question.

Alexander's face softened as his gaze fell upon his wife, Nichola, the love in his eyes making the empty void within Duncan's heart deepen. The depths of his feelings were those he'd once felt for Isabel. Feelings he'd cast aside when she'd abandoned him for Frasyer.

Surprise cascaded across Nichola's face as her gaze rested on Duncan. She shoved her hands on her hips. "You are sitting up when you should be asleep."

"From the look of you," Duncan said with tenderness, always amused by her English accent, "it is you who should be off your feet."

A warm glow shone on her face as she laid a hand atop her stomach, round with her and Alexander's first child. "I will be soon enough. First I wanted to help Isabel get settled in the chamber above. She was so tired, she was asleep before I left." Nichola frowned. "I told Seathan after she'd stayed within your chamber for two days that he should order her rest in another room. Since your arrival, she has refused to leave your side."

From the tiredness he'd noticed on Isabel's face, it was as Duncan had suspected. "My thanks for taking care of her." Then Duncan realized what Nichola had said. His gut churned. "What did you mean you helped Isabel settle in the chamber above? There is naught above us but—"

"The tower room," Nichola finished.

Silence floundered in the room. The brothers eyed each other.

Nichola scanned their faces, her own growing wary. "What is wrong?"

"Naught," Seathan replied.

Stunned, Duncan glared at his brother. After Isabel had broken their wedding vows, her staying in their grandmother's room seemed sacrilegious— at odds with his grandmother who had offered him naught but warmth, love, and a generous heart.

Since her death, neither he nor his brothers had changed or removed anything from her room— including the bowl of halved gems. Within the bowl, their grandmother had kept the other half of the gems she'd had made into pendants for himself and each of his brothers upon their being knighted.

Two halved gems still remained, the other half of Duncan's sapphire, and that of Seathan's moss agate.

And what of their grandmother's spirit? The residents within Lochshire Castle knew of her presence within the tower room, a chamber Duncan and his brothers also believed held magic.

In his mind, too many reasons existed as to why Isabel should never have been allowed entry there. The fact that only one other person had stayed within the room since his grandmother's death scraped at his mind. Imprisoned, he corrected. After Alexander had abducted Nichola, an English maiden, for ransom, he'd locked her in the tower room. Through a twist of fate, Alexander's captive had become his wife.

Not that Duncan was foolish enough to believe

Isabel staying in the room meant anything, Duncan silently scoffed. But a man who believed in magic and was of a suspicious nature, he wasn't taking a risk.

Duncan turned to Seathan. "She will not remain there."

Lines of worry deepened on Nichola's face. "Alexander, what is wrong with Isabel staying within the tower chamber? With her having saved Duncan's life, I thought you would wish to offer her the luxurious comfort found within?"

Her husband took her hand and gave a gentle squeeze. "Naught you should worry about. We will talk later."

Duncan ignored the pair, his hard gaze on his eldest brother. "She will be moved to a lower chamber."

"Nay," Seathan said. "As you so vehemently pointed out moments ago, she is tired. And I agree, Isabel saved your life. Nichola's actions in placing her there were innocent. Or, perhaps Nichola was guided by a higher power?" Though Seathan's voice remained solemn, for a second, humor twinkled on his face. As quickly, it fled. "Regardless, she will remain there."

Put in his place as easy as that. Duncan quashed further argument. True, Isabel had saved his life, but had she left the castle when he'd first released her from her cell, they would have escaped untouched. And she would most likely be reunited with her father by now. Still, they needed the Bible to prove Lord Caelin's innocence.

"Before I would be forgetting." Seathan withdrew Duncan's amulet from a pocket and handed it to him.

"My thanks." Duncan slipped it around his neck, the gem cool against his skin.

"You were right," Seathan said. "Had you not given the amulet to Isabel, I would have turned her out and you would have died. Go to bed, Duncan. It is rest you are needing, not further debate. I will return later." He nodded toward Nichola. "My thanks for seeing to Isabel's needs."

"You are welcome," she replied, looking a bit unsure.

Without another word, Seathan turned and left.

Alexander walked over and took his wife's hand. "Get off your feet, Duncan. If you remain awake and walking about, you will only prove the extent of your foolishness."

A muscle worked in Duncan's jaw.

"Your face is flushed and tiredness weighs heavy on your face," Nichola said before Duncan could speak. "Please, listen to your brothers and rest."

With one last warning look, Alexander guided his wife from the room.

The door closed and left Duncan in the flame-lit silence. Yellow fingers of light flickered over the door like amber claws. His legs trembled from his effort as he stretched out on the feather-stuffed mattress. He mulled over Seathan's words, more so at the oddness of Isabel's actions since he'd helped her escape.

He had no illusions about his doubts on a personal level. After she'd broken his heart, he could never fully trust her with his feelings again. In that, he'd not allow her another chance. Though three years had passed, the familiar ache of the hurt still cut too deep.

And what of Frasyer? Whatever lay between her and the earl was a mystery in itself. The more he learned, the less her relationship with the earl made sense. Not that she'd attempted to clear up that matter. If she tried, did he want to hear about her past with a man he despised?

Duncan's thoughts turned to another lingering worry. The tower chamber. His reaction to Isabel sleeping in their grandmother's room was about trust and loyalty to his grandmother's memory, naught more. As for the magic within the room, he doubted her stay would have any effect on him.

Chapter 9

Faeries stared down at her.

Isabel squinted in an effort to focus from her sleep-clogged haze. Then slowly, she opened her eyes. Moonlight spilled through a single, arched window in an iridescent swath, embracing everything within the chamber. Including the faeries.

A dreamy smile touched her mouth. No, not real faeries, but beautiful, hand-painted images captured in various aspects of flight adorned the ceiling. Her favorite was a raven-haired faerie in a moss green gown, her silver-tipped wings caught in mid-flutter, hiding behind a lush, purple-tipped thistle.

Laughter trickled around her. She blinked at an odd feeling of disconcertment. Or maybe it was real, and the faeries were laughing at her, amused by her confusion?

Awake now, she scanned the chamber, a room she vaguely remembered being led to by Alexander's wife, Nichola. Exhausted at the time, she'd noticed neither the luxuriousness, nor had she asked where she was being taken. Once she'd lain upon the featherbed, sleep had claimed her.

Exactly where was she? In the many times she'd visited Lochshire Castle as a youth, she'd never entered this chamber. It was utterly feminine, not the decor she would picture as Seathan's choice. Was it his mother's room?

Intrigued, Isabel sat up, slipped her legs over the bed and stood.

An elegant, hand-stitched coverlet, the color of moon-kissed daisies, lay rumpled on the bed where she'd slept. Nearby, sat a small table, adorned with myriad personal items: intricately carved jewelry, a bone comb, and an ivory-framed mirror. A tapestry hung on the far wall, images of faeries woven amid the leaves. The fey depicted an exact match to those adorning the ceiling.

A fire burned low in the hearth, assuring her that she'd slept for many hours, a beam of moonlight streaming into the chamber confirmed the fact. When she'd laid down, the first rays of the morning sun had guided her to the bed.

The scent of wood and silvery wisps of light lingered as Isabel strolled to the window. And frowned.

She was on the third floor. There was only one chamber she knew of built on this level—Duncan's grandmother's.

A smile touched her lips as she remembered the amazing woman. Duncan, as had his brothers, loved their grandmother, a trim, elderly woman with a quick smile and a warm laugh. And she'd always smelled of a hint of lavender.

A woman the brothers had adored.

Isabel's smile faltered. So why was she here? After

she had broken her betrothal to Duncan three years ago, the brothers would never have wanted her to step foot within this room, much less sleep here.

Except Nichola had brought her here, which explained everything.

Raised in England and ignorant of Isabel's history with Duncan, Nichola didn't understand how wrong it was for Isabel to be in this chamber. Isabel pressed her hand on the cold sill. When Duncan and his brothers found out, they would be furious.

However much she wished she could stay, savor the memories of a time when she had loved Duncan and he had loved her in return, she must leave.

After the grief she had served Duncan, she agreed, she didn't deserve to remain.

Yet, however odd, a sense of acceptance enveloped her. Though it was wrong for her to be within the chamber of a woman so loved by her grandsons, she felt welcome. It made no sense.

A twinkle of light on the opposite side of the bed caught her attention. In another bowl on a stand farther away, lay two halved, shimmering stones. Intrigued, she walked over and picked up one of the halved rocks. Cradled within the gold-encrusted outer layer, captured by the moonlight, lay what appeared to be spirals of moss.

How unusual. Isabel returned the stone and picked up the other gemstone. Encased by a white exterior flecked with speckles of brown lay a sapphire, the dark blue of a midnight sky. A mirrored twin of the halved sapphire Duncan wore around his neck, the one she had carried to prove to his brothers that she hadn't been lying about Duncan's dire condition.

This had to be its mate. A unique gift their grandmother had bestowed to each of her grandsons upon their being knighted. Why then were there only two gems within the bowl and not three, one for each brother? Or rather, four, she mused, as she remembered their adopted brother, Patrik.

Sadness touched her. Patrik had died a year before. In a scuffle with an Englishman over his sister if gossip proved to be correct. With the source, she couldn't be sure if that was the truth, neither did she know who the woman in question was. Regardless, she found it baffling why an Englishman's sister would be in the heart of Scotland alone.

She curled her fist over the roughened gem. An ache built in her chest as she remembered her own family. Her brother. How she wished he were here to comfort her, to offer guidance.

As if a prayer answered, calm swept over her, a deep sense of peace she'd not experienced since when Duncan had first embraced her in their adolescence.

Her pulse raced as if she could feel that very moment, how he'd held her so tight, the heartfelt words he'd whispered in her ear.

Daonnan agus am feast. Always and forever.

How she'd wanted the same. And still did.

The sapphire warmed in her palm.

Surprised, Isabel opened her hand. A soft, blue glow pulsed within the center of the gem. 'Twas a trick of the moonlight. She was tired and allowing her emotions to conjure what could never be.

Except she stood within the shadows.

Shaken, Isabel placed the sapphire beside the other gem. It continued to pulse a soft, blue light. She stepped back and the sapphire's glow grew brighter, as if beckoning her touch. As she continued to stare at the sapphire, moonlight swirled around the room as if it breathed its own life, wisps of silvery light flitting across the ceiling where the faeries lay.

Madness had surely overtaken her.

Isabel backed to the door, turned, jerked it open, and ran straight into a solid wall of honed muscle. With her heart in her throat, she opened her mouth to scream.

"Whoa, lass," Duncan said as he caught Isabel's shoulders, noting the pallor of her face and her trembling body. "What is wrong?"

"Naught," Isabel replied, her voice breathless as she glanced behind her, wary. "You but scared me."

True, but he saw more than fear in her eyes.

Concern narrowed her brow. "What are you doing out of bed?"

A question he'd asked himself several times over. "I came to check on you."

Hurt streaked her face, but understanding as well. "Once you learned of the chamber Nichola had taken me to, you came to demand I leave."

"In part," he agreed.

"And?"

He placed his left arm against his side where it had begun to throb. "To thank you for saving my life."

"A life you should not have risked by staying within Moncreiffe Castle after I told you to go."

"A fact that is in the past," he replied, annoyed

that even now, with them both having made it safely to his brother's home, she would fight him still.

He scanned the familiar room. Everything remained in place. Untouched. "Why were you leaving in such a hurry in the middle of the night when you should be asleep?"

"I awoke and did not know where I was. Then I realized—"

A telling blush crept up her cheeks, assuring him he was right. "You are in my grandmother's tower chamber." He couldn't help the coolness in his voice. How was he supposed to feel knowing that Isabel had slept in a room he and his brothers considered sacred?

She nodded. "I was so tired earlier, I did not realize it until I woke."

That he could believe. "Nichola does not know of our past. She *assumed* you were a welcome guest."

"Please, do not be upset with her."

"My anger does not flow to those undeserving, something that you should understand." She stiffened, but he didn't apologize.

Silence filtered between them, a quiet hum edged with awareness.

Though he'd not intended to, his gaze traveled the length of her body, taking in the soft swells that invited him to touch, the curves that bid him to linger. Beneath his heated gaze, her nipples tightened against the softness of her gown, offering their own invitation.

"Nichola is English," Isabel finally said, her voice cautious with a throaty edge.

"She is." Duncan damned the rasp to his voice, betraying that he wanted her.

"With Alexander a rebel . . . I never would have believed he would court an Englishwoman, much less marry her."

"If asked before he met her, Alexander would agree."

Isabel arched a brow in silent question.

"He abducted her a year ago to raise coin for the rebels."

"But he married her," Isabel stated, clearly confused. "That makes little sense."

"Aye, it does not. Then, neither does life."

"No," she whispered, "it truly does not." The crackle of flames echoed into the somber silence. A frown creased her brow. "A year ago? Is that not when Patrik died?" Apprehension sheathed her face. "Oh, God." She swallowed hard. "Please, tell me the incidents are not related."

Even after the months past, the reminder of his adopted brother's death weighed heavy on Duncan. "Aye. When Alexander returned from England with Nichola as his captive instead of her brother, Alexander was half in love with the lass." He grimaced, remembering his brother's personal struggle with the fact. "Not that he wanted to be. It seemed fate would dictate otherwise."

"How does Patrik's death relate with Nichola being Alexander's captive?"

"You remember how my father adopted Patrik when he was a lad?" Duncan asked.

Isabel nodded.

"The reason is known only to a few, but Patrik came to live with us after the English butchered his family before his eyes. He escaped, but with the horrific memories of that day. Ever since, Patrik's thirst for English blood had been unquenchable. When he realized Alexander was falling in love with Nichola, he crafted lies to Alexander about her being an English spy. When those untruths failed to dissuade Alexander's growing feelings, Patrik tried to kill her."

Isabel covered her mouth in horror. "God in heaven!"

Duncan nodded, the turmoil and the sadness of losing a brother he loved still tearing at his heart. "Alexander and Patrik fought. The knife Patrik held during the struggle slipped from his hands and wedged between two rocks. In the end, Patrik rolled onto his own blade."

"How tragic," she whispered.

"Aye, his death haunts us still." Duncan rubbed his brow, tired, saddened by the regretful memories, of his heartbreak at watching the guard leave with Patrik's body. It was the last time he'd seen him. When they'd arrived home hours later, the guard had already buried Patrik's body, so they'd gathered for a private ceremony.

"But from the tragedy, happiness arose as well. After the fight, Nichola's brother, Lord Monceaux, whom Alexander was sent to abduct, showed up in search of his sister. When he saw Alexander with her, believing Nichola was in danger, her brother attacked Alexander in an attempt to save her life."

"An Englishman dared venture this far into Scotland alone?"

Duncan hesitated. Though Isabel may be privy to rebel secrets from Symon, she was still Frasyer's mistress. He would not divulge that Nichola's brother, Griffin, the Baron of Monceaux, who was King Edward's

Scottish adviser, was also a spy for Scotland known by most by the code name Wulfe.

"He and his sister are close."

"And the ransom?"

"Was paid." Duncan didn't add the details of the payment, specifics he would have informed her of before her betrayal. "Afterward, and with her brother's blessing, Nichola married Alexander."

"It is hard to believe the English noble would allow such a union, more so with his strong ties to King Edward."

"It is."

"I heard something about an Englishman being here during Patrik's death," she said, "but no more."

Duncan nodded. An easy silence fell between them, a closeness that he'd missed. But to remain alone with her, to invite Isabel back into his life, was a mistake.

He stared at her, wishing this moment could be as simple as standing beside the woman he'd grown up with, the woman he'd once loved, a woman who'd also embodied his every dream.

She moved against him, and the moment shifted. Desire flooded him hot and hard. Her scent wrapped around him making his body ache with it's demand. He could all but taste her on his lips, knew the satiny way her skin would feel against his hands.

Bedamned. He stiffened and shifted away.

At his action, worry marred her face. "I have kept you up when you should be asleep."

"No, I . . ." He could hardly tell her the truth. That his body seemed to have a will of its own when in her presence.

"You are too weak to be up and about. You will reopen your wound."

"It is healing."

"And hurting you now by the way you are favoring it."

He remained silent, refusing to confirm her words. Too aware of her, Duncan glanced around his beloved grandmother's chamber, expecting to feel anger at Isabel's breach within the room. Instead, a sense of how appropriate it was for her to be here washed over him.

Isabel gently caught his hand. "Sit for a moment and rest. Then I will help you to your chamber."

Duncan held his ground. He didn't want to feel the silkiness of her skin, or the intensity of his need to draw her body against his. "Why did you not tell Seathan and Alexander about the Bible or that Symon had told you of the rebel movements?" he asked, grasping on to other reasons that had spurred his midnight visit when most were asleep.

Her expression grew guarded. She released him. "I will be here but a short while. The Bible is mine to find. The conversations of my brother and I are in the past."

At the stubbornness of her reply, anger stewed in his blood. "As for the Bible, I gave my vow to help you find it."

Amber eyes blazed fire. "And was almost killed in the trying. Nay, your part in helping me is done. On the morrow, I will leave."

The seriousness of her tone roused panic inside him. "You cannot."

Isabel folded her arms across her chest. "I would

think you, as your brothers, would be pleased to be rid of me."

An excellent point, one he should have agreed with. So why was he protesting her intent to leave?

"Have you forgotten that Frasyer's men are scouring the forest for you?"

"For us," she corrected.

"Aye," he agreed. "And at the very least, they will be searching every nook and cranny for the next couple of days. This afternoon, Seathan's men reported seeing Frasyer's men scouring his borders. With the continuing snow shielding their movements, we cannot say if their suspicions that you are here have not prompted them to keep a watch on Lochshire Castle."

Despite his warning, Isabel held his gaze, her courage a trait he'd always admired and, begrudgingly, did so now.

"Frasyer would risk much if he infuriated Seathan," she said.

"With you holding key information about the rebels, infuriating Seathan would be of low concern to Frasyer."

She turned away and crossed her arms in a protective measure over her chest. "I would take my life before I would tell Frasyer of the rebel movements."

A belief her brother had obviously shared. Not that it made sense. As if anything did since Isabel had walked away from their betrothal.

Needing to touch her, Duncan walked up behind Isabel and laid his hand upon her shoulder; she stiffened.

"Each day that goes by is one that I cannot lose,"

she whispered. "Already, too much time has passed. For my father's sake, I pray that I am not too late."

Her obvious worry had him wanting to reassure her that he would protect her, to reveal the steps he and his brothers were already taking to ensure Lord Caelin's safety. But could he trust her? He still didn't know.

"Trying to return to Frasyer's home is a foolish idea," he said. "Do you not understand the folly of such an attempt? However much you wish to return to Moncreiffe Castle, to do so now would surely find you captured."

She turned toward him with defiance. "I cannot stay here and do nothing."

"No? How much good will you do your father if you are locked in Frasyer's dungeon?"

She remained silent, but he saw the anger in her eyes, upset at the feeling of one's hands being tied, a sense he understood too well.

"Promise me you will not try to leave until three days have passed."

She shot him a hard look.

At her silence, Duncan stepped toward her. "I will have your word."

Her jaw lifted in defiance. "Or you will have me imprisoned?"

Irritated she'd dare to push him, he caught her hand and clasped it within both of his. "I will do what I must to keep you safe. I promised your brother. It was his dying request."

The bravado on her face crumbled. "Damn you, Duncan." She pulled free and walked over to stare through the window into the star-filled sky. Moonlight streamed around her in a silvery embrace as if she were an abandoned faerie from the Otherworld.

As she had in Frasyer's dungeon, she looked so fragile. Isabel was hurting, alone and feeling the outsider. She'd earned that and more. The anger he'd experienced in the past, and had expected when seeing her again tonight, did not come.

Only desire.

Her frailty appealed to his masculinity, to the warrior wanting to protect a woman he cares for, to a man who needs to defend his mate. Instincts were deeper than the emotions wrought by betrayal and infidelity.

He grimaced, frustrated that after she'd hurt him so deeply, he wanted her. Duncan exhaled a long sigh, walked over and stopped beside Isabel.

"I am surprised that Seathan and Alexander did not storm this room once they learned that I had not told them everything," she said without looking his way.

"They wanted to," Duncan admitted.

She turned to face him, moonbeams framing her face, and to Duncan, she couldn't have looked more beautiful. "And what did they think when they learned of where I slept?"

He shrugged. "It is not where we would have chosen."

"I know."

For a long moment they stood in silence, each watching the other, the whirl of emotions plaguing Duncan falling away one by one. Until it was only him, only her, alone in the chamber.

As if a trick of the light, an aura seemed to surround her and slowly grow brighter.

Drawn, he reached over and touched her.

She gasped and stared down to where their flesh merged.

Warmth tingled up his arm, beyond the sensation a mere touch induced. An energy as if alive arched between them. Stunned, he pulled away.

Eyes widened with surprise met his. "What is it?"

He shook his head. The illusion of an aura had faded. Naught but moonlight grazed her skin. He owed the odd sensation of tingling heat to fatigue.

"What did you feel?"

At the waver in her voice, he studied her face. Lines of concern tugged across her brow.

"You sensed it as well?" she prodded.

"What?"

She looked around as if seeking something, then shook her head. "This chamber is . . ." She stepped to the side, putting much needed distance between them. Except that the lure, the pull to touch her, seemed to intensify. If he was smart, he'd let her go.

"I should move to another chamber," Isabel said.

But he had to know. "What did you sense? What did you feel when I touched you?" As soon as the questions left his mouth, aware of their unearthly potency, Duncan wondered if they were questions best left unasked.

Isabel looked around the chamber as if searching for something. "The room is beautiful. I have never experienced anything quite so warm and welcoming in my life."

"My grandmother would not allow anything else." But she was hedging answering his question.

A blush touched her face. "I remember her. She would tell me stories of faeries. I should have guessed she would have had them painted on her ceiling and embroidered in her tapestries as well."

"The embroidery was a gift from King Alexander III."

Her brows raised in surprise. "She knew him?"

The story of their meeting so long ago filled Duncan's mind with familiar fondness, and was a welcome distraction to whatever had occurred between them moments ago.

"Treated him is more like it," he explained. "A healer, she was in the woods gathering herbs. The king was hunting with several men. His mount stumbled and the king was injured. She witnessed the entire event and offered to care for him."

"And the king rewarded her with the tapestry?"

"Aye."

"Then the faeries on the ceiling were painted to match?"

"Nay, they have always been there."

Amazement shadowed her face. "But they match the tapestry as if copied. Do you not find that odd?"

"Not really. This room is said to be filled with magic. I grew up with my grandmother telling us that she often spoke with the wee folk here."

She again looked around as if seeing the chamber for the first time. "Then it was not a dream." She hugged herself, which didn't suppress the shiver that shook her.

"What?"

"Earlier this night, the sapphire in the bowl seemed to glow. Not the rays of moonbeams, but that of an unearthly glow, almost as if the air was alive, breathing."

The awe in her voice stoked Duncan's irritation.

He glared at the bowl as if a traitor, remembering too well Alexander's story of how Nichola had mentioned a similar reaction when she'd first entered the chamber, or rather, was imprisoned within this room a year ago. He and Seathan had had a fine time teasing Alexander that their grandmother's presence and penchant for matchmaking guided Nichola's reaction.

Neither could he forget noticing the aura that seemed to surround Isabel but moments ago.

Though he believed in the fey and of his grandmother's abilities, *he* would guide the decision of his life, not those of an old woman's fancies. That he found Isabel alluring stemmed from their years together, of the dreams they'd once shared, not from a spell cast by a woman given to magic.

"What you witnessed was the moonlight shining upon the gem," Duncan declared, "nothing more."

Amber eyes sparked with conviction. "I know what I saw. And when I picked the halved sapphire up, it warmed in my hand. The same heat I experienced when you touched me moments ago."

A muscle worked in his jaw.

"It means something, does it not?"

"It means that you are exhausted and in need of rest." As he looked around the chamber, he almost sensed his grandmother's spirit, the magic potency of her presence.

Determined to take Isabel from this chamber, Duncan took her hand. A mistake. Awareness speared him with a dangerous heat. His blood pounded, and his every breath filled with the scent of night and the alluring fragrance of woman.

"What is wrong?" she asked.

"Nothing." Everything. He wanted her. Bedamned if he'd take her. Bedamned if he'd be pushed by magic against his will.

Though his body wanted her, his heart never would. Other than those weak moments when he'd almost died, the trust he'd held for Isabel was that of the past. A trust necessary before anything between him and Isabel could grow. A trust that he would never give her again.

It was ridiculous to stand here with her wanting what never could be. He glared around the confines, sure faeries lurked and laughed—at him.

"You look pale as if you have seen a ghost."

"A faerie more like it," he muttered.

She stepped closer, her scent of woman and desire spilling through his senses.

He hissed out a breath.

"Why are you shaking."

Duncan stepped back, wanting to laugh, to yell, to curse this moment of his embracing heaven and Hades. Unlike Alexander's confusion when he'd placed Nichola in this chamber, and after watching his brother's heart guided by magic, Duncan understood the full effects it could have on a man.

"Isabel." He caught her. A mistake. His body ached with the need to touch her, to run his fingers along her delicate curves, to savor her taste in slow, satisfying regard.

She frowned at him, then her pupils darkened with understanding and filled with desire. "You need to lay down and rest." She didn't move, but stood there like a siren stealing his every breath. "Duncan?"

He cursed as he hauled her to him. With her lips

shadowed against his, the heat from her body enveloping him like a fist, he claimed her mouth. His first taste of Isabel was devastating, pleasing, luring him to linger, to feel more than he should, to want more than he had sworn he would ever take.

A moan of pleasure slipped from her throat, destroying the last fragments of his will.

Lost, Duncan angled his mouth and took the kiss deeper, drowning in her softness, the innocence of her response. He cupped her face as he stole her every moan, savored her every shuddered breath, the softness of her silky skin.

"Duncan," she murmured as he skimmed his mouth over her cheeks, her brow, then along the slender column of her throat, her taste pouring over him, filling him, seducing him with ruthless intent. His jaw grazed the curve of her breast.

Stunned, Duncan drew away, his breathing hard, his body urgent in its demand. It was as if time had stood still and three years had not passed.

Her sigh echoed his own sentiment. "It was always you," she murmured.

Always him.

A vision of Frasyer seared his mind, shattering the image like handblown glass against jagged stone.

Furious with himself, Duncan stepped away. Here, within his grandmother's chamber, he'd almost taken Isabel, stripped her naked and made love with her. Made love? As if she knew the meaning? How could he, even for a moment, have forgotten the reasons why such an act would be more than morally wrong?

Eyes glazed, she stared at him, her face flushed with desire, expectation warm in her gaze.

In this moment, if given one wish, he would sever all thoughts of her betrayal and claim what should have been his three years past.

Except Isabel's virginity was long lost. Her choice to become Frasyer's mistress made for her own gain. He'd allowed his mind to fill with needs he had no right wanting.

Frustrated, he turned to leave.

"Duncan?"

"Stay here," he all but snarled and strode toward the door.

"Where are you going?"

The waver in her voice almost had him turning back. Almost. A mistake he refused to make again. He stepped outside the chamber and shut the door.

With his emotions on edge and his body burning its demand, if he returned to Isabel now, he'd take her.

Chapter 10

The earthy scent of porridge teased Isabel awake. Opening her eyes, she found a tray laden with bread and cheese along with porridge on a small table near her bed. Steam slowly curled up from the wooden bowl. She glanced toward the door. A servant must have delivered it while she slept.

The first hints of sunrise spilled through the arched window glazed with ice, brushing upon her face in a warm caress. She took in the budding dawn, the play of prismed light as it sifted throughout the chamber, its fragile aura capturing all within its path. Like a faerie's magic. She glanced at the faeries painted upon the ceiling. Smiled.

Memories of Duncan's visit last night spilled through her mind, his unexpected tenderness, the barely restrained control she'd felt within his hands as he'd cupped her face. And with regret, the shock of realization at what he'd allowed himself to do as he'd pulled away and left her alone.

She hadn't expected him to touch her, much less kiss her. But he'd wanted her with the ferocity of their tarnished youth. The desire burning in his eyes had mirrored that in her heart.

Even now, with the sun climbing its way into the snow-etched sky, her body yearned for Duncan, to cherish the feel of his mouth, the hewn strength of his body firm against hers. If only for a while.

Thankfully, last night he'd stepped away. Only after his departure had she realized what she'd almost given him. If he'd laid her upon the bed, stripped her of her clothing and made love with her, she would have savored each tender moment.

And Duncan would have discovered she was a virgin.

She pressed her hand against her brow at the sobering reminder. God forbid if he learned that truth. It would raise too many questions. Neither could she forget Frasyer's vow to kill Duncan if she ever told him the truth of their union, nor her belief that the earl would use deceit in achieving his goal.

As much as she wanted Duncan and still loved him with all her heart, she couldn't take the risk. Though Frasyer's men scoured the lands for her and an unknown man, the knights' proximity to Seathan's castle assured her Duncan was a suspect in Frasyer's mind. However much she wished to remain here, she must leave before Frasyer found confirmation of that fact.

Except now her need to leave was more urgent. Though she'd resolved to stay away from Duncan, as proven by his visit last night, when he touched her, her good intentions had fled. At least she hadn't vowed to Duncan that she would not leave Lochshire Castle.

A soft knock sounded on the door. Unsure who

would be on the other side, she turned toward the entry. "Enter."

The door opened, Nichola stepped inside, the warmth on her face of last night replaced by guarded hesitation.

Foreboding flooded Isabel. She shifted to the side of the bed and stood. "Is it Duncan?" Fear made her voice sharp, but she didn't care. If anything happened to him because of her, she couldn't forgive herself.

"Duncan is fine." Nichola cleared her throat, obviously uncomfortable with whatever her task. "Seathan has requested that I escort you downstairs to his council chamber. He and his brothers await your arrival."

Fear consumed her. "Is it my father?"

"Not that we have heard news of."

Isabel sagged with relief. As quick wariness stole through her. "Then what is my presence needed for?"

Nichola's eyes shadowed with worry. "I do not know, neither do I believe it is my place to tell you such if I did. I would never betray Alexander's confidence."

"Of course. Nor would I ask you to." But what was so important that Seathan would summon her at first light? A thousand thoughts flooded her mind, each one more ominous than the next.

"When I first met the brothers together," Nichola said, breaking into Isabel's frantic thoughts, "I admit to being frightened. Then, of course, I was not free."

Isabel remembered the story, grasping on to the bit of sanity. "You were Alexander's captive."

"Yes." A blush warmed her cheeks, and she slid her hand along a chain at her neck and the tip of the halved azurite peeked from her gown. "A circumstance that changed to one where I willfully remained."

"Did Alexander not tell you that I have known them since we were children?" Isabel asked, touched by the Englishwoman's attempt to calm her at the prospect of facing the brothers. "I ask as I am well aware that when united, Seathan, Alexander, and Duncan present a daunting force."

"Alexander explained parts of their past where you were concerned, but not all." Nichola held her gaze. "He did mention that you were betrothed to Duncan. I will not ask why the marriage did not occur, but I will caution you that whatever the reason, Alexander stews about it still."

"Why are you warning me?" Isabel asked. "We only met a few days past. I have done naught to earn such trust."

Nichola's face instantly softened. "I watched you while you tended Duncan. I am unsure of the reasons why you did not handfast with him, but from your tender looks, the way you cared for him these last few days, you love him still."

Isabel gasped.

A smile touched Nichola's mouth, then slowly faded. "Is this such a horrible thing?"

"Please, Duncan must never know."

"Living with secrets is an awful chore. They haunt you, sway you to decisions that you otherwise would never have made."

Isabel touched the pendant of Wallace's emblem on a chain, hidden beneath her gown, the sincerity of Nichola's words assuring Isabel they came from her own personal trials. If only it was so easy to admit the truth.

"Some secrets are not within our control," Isabel whispered.

"Life rarely is." Nichola reached over and laid her hand upon Isabel's shoulder. "I know not what guides your decisions in regards to Duncan, neither do you know me but for a brief meeting of yesterday past. But if ever you need someone to talk to, I offer you my friendship."

Humbled by Nichola's generous offer, Isabel felt more the traitor, bound by promises ill made. "My thanks."

"I will send in a maid to help you."

"No, I can tend to myself." And she needed time to gather her thoughts.

Nichola nodded. "I will await you outside while you dress." She departed.

Alone, Isabel tugged on her gown and finished her toilet. A short while later, she trailed Nichola down the curved turret steps. The rumble of dozens of knights talking as they broke their fast echoed from below. Their warmth, their easy laughter and good-natured calls far contrasted the sterile domain of Moncrciffe Castle.

Frasyer's knights and servants lived beneath his strict rule. He despised incompetence and found joviality a sign of indolence. The residents lived with hushed whispers, lowered eyes, and a solid dose of fear.

As she completed the last few steps, the great room opened before her. Meat-seasoned smoke spewed from the fires reaching up to disappear within a mammoth chimney. Women worked over large pots of porridge along with spits heavy with venison to be served later in the day, and lads hurried over with armloads of wood to restock the fire. Benches sat alongside huge trencher tables filled with knights breaking their fast.

The scene was so potent a reminder of her visits here as a child, Isabel's heart ached. She longed for those days of innocence, of the times before her father's gambling had stolen the life she'd known.

Nichola turned down a secluded hallway. "This way."

Isabel followed, her worry increasing with every step. Whatever had happened, please let her father be safe.

Halfway down the stone-laid corridor, a knight guarded an entry. At their approach, he nodded, then opened the door.

With more confidence than she felt, Isabel stepped inside the chamber. Rugs embroidered with subtle colors lay scattered upon the floor, a fire blazed in the hearth taking off the chill, and a large oak table stood centered in the room near the back. She shivered despite the heat as she gazed around. Minimal adornment in a chamber intended for planning, for interviews designed to intimidate, both with the focus on war.

At her entrance, the three brothers, standing beside the hearth, turned to face her. Their expressions ranged from outright anger to honed interest.

An inquisition.

Steadying herself, she lifted her chin and met Duncan's unwavering gaze with her own. His complexion was healthier than last eve when she'd awoken to find him in her room. Thank God he was healing.

Refusing to show fear, Isabel took another step forward and halted. She nodded toward Seathan at the opposite side of the chamber. "My lord."

"Sit," the earl ordered.

No informalities. She'd expected none. A simple carved chair stood empty to her left. Already outnumbered, if she sat, she would give them the edge of height as well.

She cleared her throat. "I would rather stand."

Seathan nodded. "Frasyer's men have been spotted in the distance."

Heart pounding, Isabel turned to face Alexander. "Frasyer knows I am here?"

"I am unsure," Duncan's middle brother replied. "Unless a guard recognized Duncan while you both were in Moncreiffe Castle, he would have no way of knowing."

"My guess," Seathan supplied, "is Frasyer is taking no chances and scouring all lands within a day's ride."

"No," Isabel agreed, her voice a whisper, aware of Frasyer's obsession when it came to her. "He will not stop searching for me until he has me back."

As if sensing her distress, Duncan's expression grew defensive. "You shall be safe here."

The brothers nodded in unison, but a shiver of fear worked its way though Isabel. Though Seathan's fortress was bound on three sides by water, the defenses strengthened by that of a single road gaining access to Lochshire Castle, they didn't understand the lengths Frasyer would go to keep her. Or rather, to ensure Duncan never had her.

She would dearly pay if she was ever again in his grasp. And once she had cleared her father, Frasyer would know where she was. No doubt existed that he had guards watching Lord Monceaux's castle for her arrival. Another hurdle she would face once she arrived there.

"Last eve," Seathan said, breaking into her thoughts, "after you departed Duncan's chamber, Alexander and I learned that you are aware of rebel activity."

"To a degree," she replied.

Seathan's jaw tightened. "Why did you withhold such an important fact from us?"

"My concern was for Duncan and his health."

Alexander folded his arms across his massive chest. "Do you know where Wallace hides?"

Isabel nodded. "In the bogs west of Selkirk Forest, but he and his men recently moved out."

"Bedamned," Alexander muttered. "It is treachery!"

Seathan raised his hand, his obsidian gaze hard. "Why were you privileged to such critical information?"

"Symon is my brother," she said stiffly. "We are family. What information he passed on to me, he chose to do so because he knew I would never betray him and the rebel cause. Never did I query him for what was not mine to know."

Duncan's expression remained solemn as he watched, but he remained silent. He believed her, didn't he?

"Do you not find it odd that Frasyer's mistress holds information that could cost Wallace his life?" Seathan asked with deadly calm that underscored the graveness of this moment.

"You expect us to believe that you do not share such knowledge with Fraser?" Alexander demanded.

"I would never tell Frasyer of Wallace's hideout or any other rebel news." She tamped down her anger. "The belief of my doing so is absurd. Had I told him, with King Edward's obsession to capture Wallace, would Frasyer not have acted to seize him long past?"

Alexander shook his head with disgust. "None of this makes sense. Your claim is as befuddled as lye mixed with clotted cream. Except now, Frasyer knows that you have information about the rebels."

"Yes." She met Duncan's gaze, refusing to back down. "As I explained to Duncan, my refusing to reveal Wallace's position is the reason I was sentenced to his dungeon."

"That satisfies my question of why he imprisoned you," Seathan stated, "but not why you also neglected to mention your mother's Bible."

Duncan's eyes narrowed as she hesitated. "Out with it, lass."

She tilted her chin up a degree more. "I saw no reason to share the fact. The Bible is mine to find, the proof mine to deliver."

"And if you returned and found the Bible," Seathan asked, "how would you have brought it to Lord Monceaux?"

"I would find a way," she replied.

"In the dead of winter with a snowstorm upon us and Frasyer's men possibly having arrived at Lord Monceaux's castle by now?" Alexander asked with disbelief. "Even if you left this day, do you truly believe you stand a chance to reach Rothfield Castle in time to halt your father's fate?"

Frustration balled in her throat. Damn them. "He is my father. Frasyer gave me a fortnight to tell him of Wallace's position. My father will not be hung before then."

"And you believed him?" Duncan asked quietly.

Until this moment, she'd not considered that Frasyer would have lied. A saint's curse! She fought to staunch the rising fear. "He promised." She wanted to believe he would keep his word, but even as she made the claim, Isabel realized that Frasyer's word, especially to her, was moot.

Coldness crept through her, an icy path that drained any warmth from her body. "You are right. When it comes to finding Wallace and delivering him to King Edward, Frasyer would do whatever it takes to achieve his goal." With her escape, had she sentenced her father to death? She clutched on to the hope that, caught up in searching for her, Frasyer had not changed his mind. "Regardless of the possibilities, I must believe my father is alive. I will do what I must to reach him in time."

"Including returning to Moncreiffe Castle to find the Bible," Seathan said quietly.

She glared at Duncan in accusation. Why had he said anything? She met Seathan's gaze head-on. "Yes."

Seathan nodded to his brothers. "Leave us. I wish to speak with Isabel alone."

Duncan stiffened, his surprise assuring Isabel he hadn't expected Seathan's request.

At his younger brother's hesitation, Seathan motioned toward the door. "Go."

With one last look at Isabel, Duncan strode through the exit, followed by Alexander.

The door thudded closed with an ominous echo inside the large chamber.

Alone, with Seathan staring at her, Isabel held her breath and prepared herself for the worst.

Isabel exited the keep needing a moment alone in the courtyard, all too aware of the covert glances of those within the great hall, the whispers of curiosity churning in her wake. A cold wind, littered with snow, swirled around her as she walked upon the stone steps. Emotionally exhausted from Seathan's inquisition, she tugged her cape closer, ignoring the brittle wind.

Thank God Seathan had asked Duncan to leave. She should have guessed that after watching her tend Duncan, Seathan would have gleaned that she still loved Duncan. Hadn't Nichola witnessed the same? But now she had another problem.

Angry at her refusal to tell him why she had broken her betrothal to Duncan, Seathan had ordered that she remain at Lochshire Castle until he learned the truth.

She rubbed her brow. Seathan claimed he was protecting her, that using Duncan's directions through the escape tunnel and the details provided, he would send men into Frasyer's chamber and let them search for the Bible. After the days past, even if Frasyer had hidden it behind a secret door, he might have moved it by now.

It eased her fear little that Seathan had sent a runner to Lord Monceaux's, asking King Edward's Scottish adviser to stay his hand in deciding her father's fate. Though Earl of Gray, as a Scot and a known rebel at that, did Seathan think that Lord Monceaux would consider his request, even if linked through his brother's marriage? Did he not understand Frasyer was a powerful English earl, a lord who held King Edward's favor? Even if Lord Monceaux considered Seathan's request, didn't he realize that Frasyer wouldn't give up until he'd captured Wallace?

As dire the situation, Frasyer's slight hesitation when he'd cornered her and her family within the hut assured her that he wasn't convinced she knew where Wallace was.

A temporary grace. For once he had her in his grasp, he would use whatever brutal means necessary to learn the truth.

With a weary sigh, Isabel looked around, surprised to find she'd walked across the bailey and was nearing the stable. To her left, a merchant stood at the tail of his flatbed wagon stuffed with goods. Exposed pots and pans hanging from the side clanked as the wind nudged the aged wood.

The merchant glanced over, gave her a smile that did nothing for his crooked teeth and layers of weathered skin wrinkled on his face. "I have some fine cloth with me, my lady."

She shook her head. "My thanks, but I am not interested."

Another man walked around the front of the wagon, several large bolts of cloth balanced on his shoulder, their combined presence all but shielding her from anyone within the courtyard. Wanting to be alone, she turned to go around the man, when the merchant caught her arm.

Isabel whirled. "Unhand—"

Another hand clamped over her mouth, her assailant unseen.

Eyes wide, she tried to scream.

"In the back with her, hurry," the merchant ordered. "Hurry, pack up our belongings. Frasyer will pay us handsomely for Lady Isabel's return."

Frasyer? They were taking her to Moncreiffe Castle! She kicked violently as she fought to break free. Her hands were jerked roughly behind her and bound. Another man caught her feet and secured them as well. In a trice, a gag was wrapped around her mouth, silencing her. Trussed up, two of the men caught her and set her among goods within the center of the wagon.

She had to alert someone!

"Do not fight us," the man holding the bolts of cloth warned as he tossed the pile around her in an effective shield. "I have no qualms about beating a woman."

"Not that Frasyer would be caring with what he has planned for you. He has not been happy these days past," the merchant added with a mean laugh. With a leer, he tossed a last bolt on top of her, then draped a length of cloth over her face that sprawled to the bed of the wagon.

Darkness caved in on her. Sweat beaded her brow as she worked her fingers on the hemp to loosen her bonds.

Confident of their success, she heard the merchant and his assistant talking as they finished packing their remaining wares around her.

She had to break free!

"Isabel?"

At Duncan's distant shout, relief washed over

her. She tried screaming through her gag, but only a muffled sound escaped.

"Climb aboard," the merchant ordered the other man in a hiss. The wagon rocked as the two men settled in.

"Have you seen Isabel?" Duncan asked, this time closer.

Isabel screamed, but again her effort was smothered by the thick cloth.

"Nay," a man nearby replied.

A whip snapped. The wagon jerked forward. Hooves clopped on ice and stone with a steady gait. From a small opening between the fabric, created by the sway of the wagon, Isabel caught sight of Duncan several paces away. Frantic, she twisted in an attempt to expose herself.

The bolts of cloth kept her hidden.

She tried to kneel, but succeeded in shifting the bolt of cloth above her only a hand's width.

The bolt of cloth! With all her strength, she twisted onto her back, braced her feet against the rolled cloth above her and shoved. It bounced up, rocked against a pot that clattered before the bound cloth fell on top of her.

Refusing to give up, Isabel repositioned her feet and shoved. The bolt flew up and again a pot clattered. This time, the tinkle of glass sounded in its wake.

"Quiet back there," the merchant warned.

The shadow of the gatehouse slid over the wagon.

No! Isabel kicked the bolt with all her might. The bolt flipped up, this time angling against the bed of the wagon and not falling upon her. The pan clattered again, then fell silent.

The darkness of the gatehouse consumed the wagon.

She'd failed.

"Halt the wagon!" Duncan yelled.

The boom of Duncan's order swept through her like a rainbow filled with hope.

The whip snapped. The team shot forward; Isabel slammed against the bolts of cloth. As the wagon bumped across the icy terrain, Isabel shifted into a sitting position. She saw Duncan, his eyes wide with shock as he caught sight of her.

"Guards, seize that wagon!" Duncan ordered.

Yells of knights echoed within the stone-built tunnel. Horses screamed. The wagon slammed to a halt.

Isabel plowed against a bolt of cloth, her breaths coming fast. Angry voices surrounded her, grunts and curses of a struggle, then the bolt of cloth above her was ripped away.

The wagon creaked as Duncan, his face masked by pain, climbed onto the back and shoved the cloth half shielding her aside.

"Duncan!" Her bonds smothered her words, but she didn't care. He was here, had saved her from Frasyer's wrath.

"Steady now." Relief spilled over his face as he knelt beside her and pulled her into his arms.

She leaned against his chest, his strength, his murmured words soothing her fears. His heartbeat pounded strong in her ears as if a silent promise that he would never leave her. It was foolish to allow such thoughts into her mind, but 'twould seem when it came to Duncan, however wrong, she could think of no other.

"Thank God you are safe," he whispered into her hair. With a trembling sigh, Duncan began to undo the bonds.

The worry in his expression broke her fragile control. Whether Duncan wanted to or not, he cared for her.

Tears slid down her cheeks and she couldn't stop her body from shaking. "I thought . . ."

"You are safe now." He tugged the last knot free, caught her shoulders, drew her back, and made a slow visual sweep of her. His fingers brushed away the tears slipping down her cheeks. "Are you hurt?"

She rubbed her wrists, the skin red where the bonds had lain. "A touch sore is all. But you . . ." She glanced at the binding; fresh blood stained the cloth. "You have opened your wound."

"A wee bit. Nothing to concern yourself about."

The hard slash of footsteps closed. "Take the men to the dungeon," Seathan's stern voice echoed.

"Aye, my lord," a guard replied.

Seathan walked into view, an ominous frown wedged upon his brow. "How fare thee?"

"I am fine," she replied.

"Far from it," Duncan said.

"Hand her down to me," Seathan said.

"I can make it on my own."

Ignoring her comment, Duncan drew her forward. Seathan caught her by the waist and, with ease, lifted her to the ground. "Careful now."

Duncan jumped down, shaken at how close the merchant had come to abducting Isabel. Thank God he had followed her outside to speak with her. He took Isabel's hand. "You will return to your chamber and rest."

"The men," she said, her face pale, her words carved by fear. "They were taking me to Frasyer. I overheard that he is offering a reward for my capture."

Duncan shot Seathan a look. "Which confirms that Frasyer does not know where she is."

"And bodes well for your safety," Seathan added. "But we will take no further risks. From this day on, until Lord Caelin is freed, you will remain inside the keep, among people I trust. I will not allow anyone else to catch sight of you here, nor stumble upon you in the bailey."

Her first instinct was to protest, but she remained silent. She would not be held here, except she wouldn't tell him that. "What of my mother's Bible? It must be found."

"And will be," Duncan assured her. "Another day, two at most and I will be fit to travel, but you will remain here." Regardless of his doubts about Isabel, his questions of her loyalty to Frasyer, he wanted her safe. He nodded toward the keep. "I will escort you inside before you freeze."

"I will take care of the men. They will regret they dared to enter my castle." Seathan stormed away.

Alexander met his older brother as he was coming from the keep. As Seathan explained the circumstance, Alexander's eyes widened in outrage. He shot a look toward Isabel, then fell into step with Seathan. The brothers strode toward the dungeon tower with clear purpose.

As much as Duncan longed to beat the would-be assailants within an inch of their lives, at the moment, Isabel's well-being came first. He drew her by his side, ignoring the throb of pain from his injury. As they walked to the keep, snowflakes drifted past, wisps of innocence at odds with the turmoil of the past few moments.

The people within the bailey nodded as they walked by. Duncan returned their acknowledgment, his focus on Isabel and the terror she had lived through these past few moments.

Of how he'd almost lost her.

The irony of his thoughts plagued him. Had things truly changed between them since he'd aided her escape from Frasyer's dungeon? She'd told him little of the circumstances surrounding her imprisonment, each bit of information pulled as if it were a throbbing tooth.

But he couldn't deny that he still cared for her despite his efforts not to. She'd been his friend, confidante, his future wife, his soul mate. Or so he'd believed. But still, she was precious enough to rouse those feelings anew.

A knight held the keep door open at their approach. "Sir Duncan."

"My thanks." Overwhelmed by the questions plaguing him, Duncan took Isabel's hand as they passed through the entry. He ignored the curious looks of those within the keep and Isabel's insistence that he release her. After almost losing her, he needed to hold her, to feel her pulse beneath his hand.

On a shudder, she pressed her face into his shoulder.

Moved, he silently vowed that whatever it took, he would keep her safe.

* * *

"Isabel?"

At Duncan's soft whisper, Isabel slowly raised her lids. Duncan sat beside her on the bed, his face strained with worry and his gaze intent. Warmth touched her. As she had tended him, it seemed that he offered her the same. But with his mind caught up in thoughts of her betrayal, he would not be liking the comparison.

"I fell asleep, how?" she asked, surprised after her near abduction by Frasyer's men, she could have. Then she understood. "The tea brought to me after we arrived at the tower chamber?"

"Aye. After your attempted abduction, you needed to rest. I asked the healer to brew the tea with something that would relax you." On a tender smile, he drew her hand into his and laced his fingers through hers. "How do you feel?"

Groggy, too aware of him, and her defenses dangerously weak. "I need to be out of bed." And away from him. Tucked within the comfort of the bed and lulled by herbs designed to soothe her, it would be easy to give in to the desire-filled fantasies pouring through her mind. She set her hands at each side of the featherbed and started to push herself up.

Duncan helped her sit, but he didn't release her or move away.

With their faces but inches apart, she tried not to focus on his closeness, or how he watched her with a longing that made her heart ache. How she'd prayed for him to look at her so. Now, with the moment here, she could accept nothing. With his worry for her, she doubted he realized he'd revealed the depth of his concern for her.

Regret swept Isabel. She withdrew her hand. "My thanks."

Silence fell between them. The stillness seemed to invite truths—truths she could never give. She closed her eyes, inhaled, savored the soft smell of lavender, the hint of smoke from the fire, and his very male presence.

The last thing she wanted to invite was intimacy, but it surrounded her, entangled with too many emotions she dared not identify.

With a sigh, she looked through the crafted glass. Through the window, a wash of purples infused with gold streamed across the darkening sky. "It is sunset. I have missed the day."

"You needed to sleep."

"And I have." Isabel shifted from the bed to stand. Her gown, rumpled from her hours of rest, clung to her. Heat stroked her cheeks as she caught Duncan's eyes lingering upon her shear gown, the swells of her breasts under the delicate fabric. Beneath his heated gaze, warmth slid through her, and her nipples hardened.

He stood.

Nerves danced upon her skin like faerie's wings. "I . . . I need to be alone." Her request fell out in a rough whisper, one filled with the longing she fought to shield. She turned away, the shudders coursing over her body having nothing to do with the icy winds outside.

He stepped closer.

"Duncan?"

"Aye?"

His breath feathered over her neck with forbidden softness. He could not stay. "You should leave."

"Should I?" He touched her shoulder; she stiffened. With aching slowness, he skimmed his hand along the collar of her neck, pausing at her throat to run his thumb up, then slowly down the soft column.

Isabel swallowed, fought the desire storming her, the heat blanketing her until she struggled to remember why this intimacy was wrong.

Duncan turned her to face him. He pressed his index finger over her lips. "This day, you were almost lost to me." He paused, his face taut with pain, with the struggle that assured her that he fought his own battles when it came to her.

"Once you were safe, asleep from the healer's herbs, I left you under the watch of a trusted servant. I assured myself it was best if I stayed away from you."

He looked away, his gaze sliding over the faeries upon the ceiling, then gave a rough laugh. "I tried. I battled with myself for hours in an attempt to put you from my mind. But since the day our lives again crossed, regardless of my attempt to ban all thoughts of you, my mind betrays me. Even as I sent the maid away from your chamber moments ago with assurances that I would keep watch over you this night, I knew coming to you was dangerous. Yet . . . here I am." He swallowed hard. "Tell me that you do not want my touch, to know the depth of what exists between us?"

Aching with need, Isabel opened her mouth to deny him. Silence fell between them. Trembling, she closed her mouth and turned away.

He caught her chin and gently turned her face toward him. "Look at me."

Tears of frustration blurred her eyes as she

complied. How she loved Duncan, wanted him with her every breath. "You know not what you ask of me."

"I do." He brushed his thumb across her cheek. "Too well." With a groan he skimmed his mouth across her brow, along the angle of cheek, then his tongue toyed with the soft curve of her ear. "Bedamned with the reasons this is wrong. Tell me that you do not want me."

Isabel's pulse raced, heat flushed her body until it ravaged her with destroying heat. She tried to reply, to deny him what she ached for with every fiber.

And couldn't.

Chapter 11

Duncan laced Isabel's fingers through his own. "Tell me that you do not want me," he repeated.

The air, drenched with moonlight, laden with unspoken desire, seemed to ignite between them, a heat so raw, so intense that her body pulsed with unspent energy. However wrong, she could not deny him.

Slowly, as if she'd spoken her deepest desires, Duncan freed his fingers from hers and his hands began a sensuous journey up her arms. Her skin tingled along his path, his every touch warming her blood into a dangerous heat. His hands rounded her shoulders and then edged upward to pause at the sensitive curve of her chin.

He angled her head toward his, drew her forward until the curve of his mouth shadowed her own. "Say you want me."

His husky burr rippled through her with a wanton thrill, her senses blurred with her need for him. "Duncan, I . . ."

"Say it."

She fought to remain silent, but his touch, her wanting his love, broke through all her well-placed barriers. "Damn you, I want you."

Satisfaction flashed in his eyes.

"But your injuries—"

"My injuries be damned." His mouth captured hers, hot, hard, demanding everything and more. She succumbed to his touch, to his taste, to the man she'd wanted forever.

Beneath his skilled mouth, her body began to tremble, her mind tangled into a daze of sensual bliss until she was lost to everything but him. To his male taste, a blend of gentle and demanding. When Isabel thought she couldn't feel more, Duncan angled his head and proved her wrong.

Her entire body vibrated beneath his wondrous assault. The reasons why she'd resisted Duncan fell away to euphoria.

This moment was theirs.

Now.

Forever.

Isabel pressed her body flush against his, appreciating his every muscle, the gentle strength with which he held her, the controlled power of his touch. Memories of their youthful passion hadn't prepared her for the desires of the man, but she savored the learning.

Firelight illuminated Duncan's body as his hands caressed her cheek, sliding to tease the curve of her ear, along the silken edge of her jaw, and all the places she'd not known could make her feel so wonderful.

Joy swept through her at his rumble of pleasure, of how his body hardened against hers. This was the moment she'd sought, a moment she'd never dreamed to experience.

Until now.

Lost to her own desire, the brush of cool air upon her sensitized skin had her opening her eyes in surprise to find him watching her, his gaze scalding.

"I need to touch all of you." Duncan leaned back as he spoke, watching her as he untied the next knot.

Her gown fell open, exposing her fully to his view. The shame she should feel at her wanton desire never came. Satisfaction filled her instead.

Green eyes held hers with reverence as the pads of his fingers eased across the swell of her breast to linger. They dipped and teased, making her knees tremble until she believed they'd give way. Still holding her gaze, he leaned down and caught one tip within his mouth, toyed, teased her with his tongue until she moaned from the sheer pleasure of it.

Never had she known it would feel this amazing to be with a man, his touch a dangerous heat that ravaged her soul. No, not any man.

"Duncan."

Isabel's voice, thick with desire, poured through Duncan with a scorching heat. With his body an inferno, he claimed her mouth and savored one more long, drugging kiss, then he drew back and looked his fill. Her lips were slick, swollen with his kisses, her eyes glazed with passion, and her nipples taut beckoning his touch. In the moonlight, she looked like a rumpled faerie who'd lost her way.

A faerie who this night would be his.

His body demanded he take her, and he would,

but he would see to her pleasure first, taste her in all the ways he'd only imagined.

Helpless to touch, to savor what for so long had been denied, he trailed his hands along the soft curve of her breasts until he cupped their full weight, then he gently squeezed her nipples.

Her lips parted, her eyes darkened with passion, inflaming him further.

With his body aching for her, Duncan lowered his head to again taste, caress, inhale her woman's scent that drove him insane. He wanted her like this, exposed before him without doubt, her desire splayed before him without regret.

Need built inside him like a fanned flame as he skimmed his tongue across her silken skin. With each taste, he wanted more. With his every touch, he sought her complete abandonment. One he would have. Isabel, if truth be told, was an addiction he could not refuse.

Slowly, he inched her flimsy gown away, relishing the pale skin exposed beneath the flickers of firelight. Soft curves framed within slender angles designed to lure, a body meant to seduce.

Naked before him, he took in her every detail, his hands mirroring his visual path. With aching slowness, he followed her flat stomach, the curve of her hips, to the tumble of amber curls shielding her most prized possession.

Beneath his touch, she inhaled deeply.

He met her gaze, her tremulous smile he owed to a reaction of nerves. "You are beautiful," he whispered.

Redness stroked her cheeks in an inviting blend of hunger and innocence. "I think . . ."

"Nay think, just feel."

On a soft breath, she nodded.

"Feel me as I touch you. See how I want you so much my body trembles with the need of it." With her watching him, he splayed the folds of her sultry mound to expose her, the warm essence of her pulsing against his fingers. Drawn by an elemental force, a need to claim her, he knelt and leaned forward to taste.

"Duncan?"

The quiver in her voice struck him as somehow odd, but a hand's length from his goal, his mind was glazed with imagining the beauty their union would bring.

Until he looked up and saw worry fragmented her brow.

"Shhh," he soothed. "Only pleasure will come."

"It . . . It is not that. I . . ."

Coldness swept him. Did she think of Frasyer? Wish she were with him? Bedamned! He'd not be a stand-in for the man she wanted.

Duncan jerked his hand away and stood. His entire body vibrated with anger.

Her face blanched.

The guilt carved within her face incensed him further. "Get dressed."

"What is wrong?" she asked, seemingly bewildered.

He gave a harsh laugh. "As if you know not?"

"I—"

"Why do you hesitate when I touch you?" he asked, hating the question, the anger pouring through his voice, aware jealousy incited his words. But he had to ask, to know. "Why act the virgin with me when for the past three years, you have given yourself freely to Frasyer?"

Amber eyes widened with horror. "I would never think of Frasyer when I am with you."

"That is something at least." But doubts engulfed him, damning what should have been beautiful between them now a catastrophe. Duncan glared at her, stunned by what he'd almost done. So caught up in wanting to make love to her, for a moment he'd forgotten her betrayal. And for what, a meaningless romp? No, for him it had mattered. "Would you have slept with me?"

She looked down. "Yes."

At her shame-laden reply, hurting, he was disgusted with himself that after everything, he could still want her. A fleeting hope came to mind. "After we have proven your father's innocence, do not return to Frasyer."

Isabel blanched and turned away. "I cannot promise."

"Cannot or choose not to?"

"You do not understand."

"An answer that seems to suit you often since I rescued you from Frasyer's dungeon."

At his charge, she faced him then, her eyes wrought with pain, but determination as well. "Once you freed me from the dungeon, I did not ask you to stay."

"Nay," he said, drawing himself to his full height. "You did not. And when this is all past, if you choose to return to Frasyer's bed, a mistake I will not be making again." Before he could make himself more the fool, he snatched her gown and shoved it toward her. "Dress yourself."

Isabel drew it against her nakedness like a shield, as if to hide what moments before she'd freely offered. She didn't look at Duncan, and he found himself wanting her to. To lift her head and swear that Frasyer meant nothing to her. That it was always Duncan she'd wanted, that circumstances unknown to him guided her to walk away from her vow.

She remained silent.

A yell from outside caught their attention.

Breaking away from the spell she wove, Duncan strode to the window and frowned. The distant groan of the drawbridge sounded as it was raised, followed by the clatter of chains on the portcullis. "A runner arrives. I pray it is with good news."

Her heart pounded as Isabel hurried to stand by his side as the single rider cantered across the narrow road leading to the castle, the bordering water on either side of the pathway frozen and dusted with snow.

"Do you think he carries news of my father?"

"Nay. With the past storm, our man will not return for at least another day. It is most likely a messenger whom we are expecting." He gave her a sober look. "I must leave. Put on your gown and return to bed." He paused as if debating his words. "I will be away from Lochshire Castle on the morrow, as well as my brothers. We will be gone but a day, two at most. You will be safe here."

Worry flickered on her face. "You have not fully healed. You need at least another day to rest."

"I will determine my needs," he said sharply.

With her body still throbbing with the desires he'd ignited, the fury in Duncan's gaze was a chilling reminder of the cruel reality that stood between them. She wanted to urge him not to travel, to explain that her innocence this night hadn't been an act, that it was always him she'd ever wanted.

Then what?

Warmth swirled around her like a cradle of hope. *Trust him,* a soft voice murmured in her mind.

She wanted to, desperately. His every step away from her was tearing her apart.

As he stormed from the chamber, Isabel could only watch as the last of her heart crumbled. The slap of the door echoed in his wake. Angry steps faded as he hurried down the stairs.

Isabel closed her eyes, aching. Over the past three years, she'd convinced herself she could live the role she'd played of Frasyer's mistress. Now, with Duncan's touch still lingering upon her skin, his unspoken promises unfulfilled, she realized she was wrong.

But how could she exit the role she'd chosen to play? To keep her father out of debtor's prison, after she'd delivered the Bible, she must return to Frasyer. In that she had no choice. Now when she returned to Moncreiffe Castle, she would be even more aware of the cell he'd crafted within her chamber. A cruel imprisonment, one without bars, without love, a chamber offering only an empty life and promises of a cold future.

Isabel tugged on her gown and stumbled to her bed. She crawled beneath the covers and curled into a ball. But she didn't cry. She hurt too much, wanted Duncan too deeply to succumb to such a petty show of emotion.

Pillowing her hands beneath her cheek, she stared at the faeries painted on the ceiling. Before they had seemed so close, as if she might reach up and touch them. Now they seemed distant, an elusive dream.

Like her time with Duncan.

Her attraction to him would always be strong. How could it not be? She loved him. She'd been a fool to believe she could remain with Duncan, even for a while, and resist.

Though Seathan had forbade her to leave Lochshire Castle, with him as well as Nichola having already guessed she still loved Duncan, their knowledge of her feelings would lead to further trial. She must depart before she weakened and, *God* forbid, before she told Duncan the truth. Thankfully, Duncan was healing quickly if he planned to travel in the morning with his brothers. The way he'd stormed from her chamber moments ago attested to the fact.

But then, how she could ignore Duncan's request for her not to return to Frasyer? Tears built in her throat. How she'd wanted to say yes. Another dream lost.

Resigned to her fate, Isabel slipped from the bed and walked to the window.

The runner's horse had cantered from beneath the gatehouse and had reined to a halt. The portcullis, as the drawbridge, remained up, which meant they expected the runner to depart in a short while.

Her heart lurched. She could leave now. With the cover of darkness and the brothers preoccupied, the many hours before her absence was noticed would increase her odds of escape. And with them leaving the castle early on the morrow, it gave her another day before a search for her would begin.

Oh, but Duncan would be angry. Still, he'd fulfilled his vow to Symon and she couldn't endanger his life further. Otherwise the last three years of suffering at Frasyer's side would have been for naught.

She would find the Bible alone. She had no choice.

A soft warmth brushed over her.

Isabel whirled, expecting to find that a servant had entered while she was lost in her distress.

The chamber stood empty.

She scanned the room. Only the painted faeries above watched her. A shimmer to her right caught her attention. Within the bowl, the halved sapphire seemed to twinkle.

Isabel frowned, remembering how the gem had appeared to glow when she'd first seen it.

Drawn by a force she could not explain, she padded across the chamber. As she drew closer to the bowl, impossibly, the light from within the sapphire strengthened.

A shiver skittered across her skin. She was imagining such. 'Twas moonlight reflecting off the gem. Yet, outside the window, night clung to the sky thick with clouds. Neither did the flames within the hearth reach this corner of the room.

Her fingers trembled as she picked up the gem and held it within her palm. Warmth, then a soothing balm infused her, a gentleness she could not explain. Tears burned her eyes. She cradled the halved sapphire. If she could not have Duncan, with this gem, she would at least have a part of him.

Wiping her eyes dry, she packed her belongings in a small sack, then carefully stowed the sapphire inside.

A soft knock sounded on the door.

Stuffing the few articles of clothing she had beneath

the bed, she straightened the bed coverings, walked to the door and opened it.

An older woman holding a tray of food bowed before her. "As you missed the evening meal, Sir Duncan asked me to bring you food."

"Please, set it on the table."

The woman frowned at her with motherly concern. "You are not feeling well?"

"No." 'Twas not a lie. Her sadness was not tied to her health, but the empty prospects of her life ahead, and her fear of failing to save her father's life.

"No doubt after your trauma this day." The woman tsked. "The merchant should be hung. After spending time in the dungeon, he will be regretting his attempt to abduct you."

Numb, Isabel nodded, not wanting to think of today's near capture. "If you please, do not wake me to break my fast. I have decided to sleep in."

The servant nodded. "The extra rest is needed with all the time you spent awake tending to Duncan." The woman patted Isabel's arm. "Nay trouble yourself further. You will be safe here."

Isabel remained silent. The option for safety on any level was long lost.

Warm gray eyes sparkled as the servant patted Isabel on the arm. "Once you have eaten, you will sleep like a babe. And I will ensure you are not bothered in the morning."

"My thanks."

With a nod, the woman turned and left.

Isabel waited several moments until she was sure the servant had left, then she hurried over and withdrew her sack stuffed with her garb from beneath the bed. She wrapped the food upon the tray and placed it inside as well. After adding another layer of clothing to help fortify her from the cold, she gathered her cloak. Thankful that with the hood pulled over her head it would shield her as would with the shadows, she left her chamber.

With the castle bedded down for the night, Isabel slipped through the great hall with ease. Outside, she was thankful the blanket of clouds remained, casting the bailey of Lochshire Castle in myriad shadows.

Still, she waited along the side of the steps to ensure no one had seen her leave. A gust of wind sent snow spiraling before her, slipping flakes beneath her cape and chilling her exposed skin. She tugged her wrap tighter.

Able to again see, Isabel kept close to the bailey wall, her steps on the newly fallen snow cautious. At least the gusty wind would erase her tracks.

The shuffle of horses and smothered voices raised in terse tones echoed from the stable. The door to the keep opened and Duncan, Seathan, and Alexander strode from the entry and headed to where the runner waited.

She flattened herself against the curtain wall. *Please don't see me.*

Caught up in meeting with the messenger and in deep discussion, the brothers strode past her.

Isabel sagged against the cold stone. Thank God.

At the entrance to the stable, Duncan paused and glanced toward the tower where he believed her asleep.

Her heart squeezed. What were his thoughts? Of anger and frustration, or did he regret their intimacy?

With his frown captured in the flicker of torchlight, Duncan turned and joined his brothers already speaking in harsh tones with the runner.

Steadying herself, Isabel focused on her escape. Satisfied that everyone was occupied with the runner's arrival, she hurried toward the gatehouse. With one last look around the bailey, she stole into the darkened tunnel.

At the drawbridge, she squinted against the darkness and the blowing snow. Across the ice bordering either side of the road, she barely made out the snow-covered field that disappeared into the bordering forest. She saw no sign of either Seathan's or Frasyer's men.

As if, between the night and the blowing snow covering the moon, she could discern any threat. If her absence had been discovered, with visibility poor, odds were anyone searching for her this late would miss her as well.

After a quick prayer, Isabel scurried down the side of the bank, keeping to the shadows along the side of the road.

Wind tugged at her clothes, bit at her exposed skin as she trekked along the narrow path. On shore, after one look around, she sprinted across the meadow. At the edge of the tall pines, she looked one last time at Lochshire Castle. Sadness embraced her. With a hard swallow, Isabel turned and disappeared into the forest.

Chapter 12

The howl of wind roared above the treetops as Duncan guided his mount down a steep embankment. Though shielded from the bitter wind and the lash of snow, once he broke free of the forest, the hard flakes would assault him.

He tucked his gloved hands holding the reins deeper into the folds of his cloak. Thankfully, after he crossed the stretch of field and the road straddling a portion of the loch ahead, his journey would be over.

As he rode beneath a leafless oak, sunlight splintered through the branches, tossed about with an unforgiving force. At least daylight was with him. After sunset, any semblance of warmth would be smothered by the night. He shivered as he navigated around a large fir, careful to keep his mount near the bare ground carved by wind swirling around the base of the trees.

Already his body ached from riding hard this day. Against his brothers' cautions, he'd ridden with them at the break of dawn to meet with Wallace. Afterward, he had left while Seathan and Alexander remained to work out details of an upcoming rebel siege.

The hard ride had taken its toll on him and irritated his freshly healed injuries. Not that he would admit it. However, neither the arduous travel, nor the dangers of having slipped passed Frasyer's men upon his return had kept thoughts of Isabel from his mind.

An image of her standing naked before him in the tower chamber, regret darkening her amber eyes while her body was still taut from his touch, haunted him.

Even now, with almost a day past since they'd almost made love, her intent to return to Frasyer left him baffled. Isabel's uninhibited response to his touch and the intensity of how she'd returned his kisses assured him that she desired him. Yet, she was determined to return to a man who had cast her into his dungeon. A sword's wrath. What other atrocities had she suffered beneath the bastard's hands that she so obviously lived in fear of Frasyer's displeasure?

His each breath spiraled before him, then vanished within the bluster of wind. Had another man told Duncan such a story of a lass's decision to return to such a cruel lover, he would have dismissed it as a tale long told. But it was true, and the idea of her returning to Frasyer tore him apart.

One would think when it came to Isabel, he would have learned that power and wealth drew her, power that Frasyer held, not the meager earnings of a knight. Yet, after their heated kiss, he couldn't stop the resounding belief that something was deeply amiss.

And why had Symon shared rebel movements with Frasyer's lover? Aye, she was Symon's sister, but he'd witnessed his friend's shame when Isabel's name was mentioned after she'd become Frasyer's mistress. Neither could he forget Lord Caelin's subsequent withdrawal from the community upon his daughter's disgraceful choice.

Though her family obviously disagreed with her actions, not only had they met with her in secret, but they had also revealed rebel secrets that none close to an enemy's camp should ever have knowledge of.

Yet she had, in chilling detail.

Regardless of how Duncan tried to find logic in the facts, his musings crafted a tangled puzzle. If only he could speak with Symon, ask him what the devil was going on. He curled the reins within his hand and glared at the snow-covered road stretching out before him. Until they freed Lord Caelin, he would have no answers, especially because Isabel, for whatever her reason, refused to speak on the subject.

He rode in the break between the thick firs, and a field blanketed by snow opened up before him. Framed within the frozen grasp of the lake, Lochshire Castle, Duncan's home since his youth, rose up before him, a majestic stronghold that none had ever breeched. But stone and mortar held little defense against the thoughts in his mind.

Or his heart.

Bedamned! Duncan nudged his mount into a canter, embracing winter's raw scent, the harsh bite of cold as he rode against the wind. His mulling was a waste of time. Her actions and words assured him she would not change her mind when it came to remaining with him.

Upon his arrival, he would check on Isabel, then be done with her. He could not go on this way with her, trapped within a state of perpetual confusion as to his own wants and wishes.

At first light on the morrow, he and another knight were riding for Moncreiffe Castle to retrieve the Bible. He now knew the layout of Frasyer's home, and where the Bible wasn't, which was to their advantage. Isabel would be furious when they returned with the Bible without her knowledge of his going, but at this point, he cared not of her outrage. His goal now was to save her father's life. Once Lord Caelin was safe, maybe then she would realize that life wasn't meant to be squandered on the unworthy, and that her path was of her own choosing.

A path he found himself wishing led to him.

With a heavy heart, Duncan cantered beneath the gatehouse, then drew up before the stable.

A lad ran up and took the reins.

"My thanks," Duncan said as he dismounted, favoring his left side where it was still tender to move his arm.

"Sir Duncan," an older woman greeted as he entered the keep.

He nodded, recognizing the servant he'd asked to bring up a meal to Isabel last night. The worry on her brow had him halting. "What is wrong?"

"It is Lady Isabel."

Well aware of Isabel's stubbornness, Duncan glanced up the steps. "I will tend to her."

"That is not the problem." The woman's hesitation

before she continued sent a chill of foreboding down Duncan's spine. "I cannot find her."

"What?"

"Last night," the woman rushed on, "when I brought Lady Isabel a tray of food as you requested, she stated she felt unwell and would sleep in. She asked not to be awoken in the morn. Thinking she needed rest, I agreed." She worried her fingers in her gown. "But when the bells of Terse rang and she had not come down, I went to check on her." She shook her head. "She is gone."

A swirl of emotions balled in his gut. He wasn't sure how to feel, upset, worried, or furious. "You have searched the entire keep?"

"Aye, including the stables and everywhere else I could think of. Frantic I have been. Thank the heavens you returned when you did."

He nodded. "I will look for her."

"I am sorry, Sir Duncan."

"Nay, it is not your fault." He knew exactly where that blame lay—with his own assumption that Isabel would cause no more trouble. He was over-reacting. She wouldn't leave without a single word. After their confrontation last night, most likely, she'd found someplace quiet within Lochshire Castle to be alone.

Several hours later, streaks of orange raced across the sky tangled with hues of blue and purple as Duncan hurried toward the keep, giving in to his one last hope. The search for Isabel had turned up naught. Even with several of his guards and servants joining in, no one had found or seen her this day. He would check the tower chamber one last time.

And pray she had returned.

The slap of his boots upon stone echoed around him as he ran up the spiral steps, his tension building with each level. At the top, the door stood open. Waiting. Inviting. Beckoning him to enter.

Please be there.

Duncan ran inside.

Empty.

Silence hummed around him, potent with erotic memories of Isabel in his arms, of her standing naked before him, of her shudders of desire against his every touch.

He shook away the visions, furious they would come, that her taste haunted his senses. The faeries above him seemed to glow. He scowled at them, and the sapphire amulet at his neck began to warm.

Heart pounding, he stilled, remembering when Nichola had taken Alexander's halved gem from the bowl before she'd run away. Then later, of how he and Scathan had teased Alexander that her taking it was a token that sealed their destiny.

But now, with the faeries above him seeming as if alive, and the room vibrating with life, he found himself believing such a spell could exist.

No, he was being foolish. *Look at the bowl, lad, and you'll see 'twas a jest that he and Seathan had made up to set Alexander on edge. It held no merit.* Duncan drew in a slow breath, released it. And turned.

The half of Seathan's moss agate lay in the bowl. Alone.

Panic weighed on him, as fast as his denial. It meant nothing except that Isabel must have taken the other half of his sapphire.

And proof that she'd left.

He focused on that, the notion of it being a

token sealing their destiny was too ridiculous to entertain.

When had she gone? Last night? This morning? No horse was missing, which meant she was foolish enough, or desperate enough, to leave on foot. With the snow to wade through, she wouldn't make it far.

Through the window, he surveyed the blast of white broken by forest. What did she hope to prove?

He stormed down the turret steps and strode outside. The bitter wind battered his face, stole through slim openings in his garb to slice into his body, shooting his anger up another notch. And she was out in this? Why was it, when he was ready to wash his hands of her, did Isabel do something beyond foolhardy and rouse his protective instincts to the forefront?

Ready to throttle the stubborn chit, Duncan raced toward the stable.

Crouched within the thick shrubs, Isabel observed Frasyer's knights, whom she'd stumbled across. Her legs ached from hours of travel, her each breath chilling her throat, and her limbs trembled from fatigue.

With the sun whispering myriad gold and purple streamers across the sky, common sense urged her to carefully back away and make a wide circle around where the knights had camped for the night. Except the sight of their horses tied a good distance away and shielded within a bank of fir trees, lured her to remain.

With a mount, she could travel through the night.

And by daybreak, she would arrive at the secret passage she and Duncan had used to escape Moncreiffe Castle. On foot, it would take at least another two days of pushing herself, unless she was caught.

A horse whinnied.

A knight glanced toward the mount, murmured something to the other men, then rejoined them in their discussion.

Relief filtered through her. Since they were on Frasyer's land, their arrogant belief that they were alone would aid her in her plan. After the sun had set, when darkness embraced them and the men slept, she would untie one of the horses and ride away.

Hours later, shivering almost uncontrollably, Isabel crept toward the horses using the path of trodden snow to shield her presence. A full moon hung in the star-filled sky threatening to betray her presence. After checking once again to ensure the guards hadn't noticed her, she hurried the last few paces and hid between the horses.

A larger gelding shifted, another snorted and stamped his front hoof.

She froze, awaiting the sound of running men.

The rustle of wind-blown branches clattered above her. A distant owl hooted into the pristine night. As before, with only a cursory check by a man closest to the horses, Frasyer's knights remained circled around their fire.

She released a slow breath. With care she untied the steed farthest away from the men. Keeping her hand over his muzzle, Isabel led him away. The crunch of snow beneath their every step echoed as if a battering ram. The silence of the night built around her with damning weight.

Not until she'd reached the opposite side of the knoll, did she guide the horse to a nearby fallen tree and mount. The moonlight, which she'd earlier cursed, now illuminated the forest around her with a silvery light.

With a silent prayer that fate's hand would guide her in finding the Bible and reaching her father in time, she kicked the steed toward Moncreiffe Castle.

At a large outcrop of rocks, Duncan halted his mount, his entire body aching from riding hard all night. Through the thick white flakes, he scanned the snow-covered field he and Isabel had crossed after they'd left Frasyer's secret tunnel.

A lone set of hoof prints leaving the forest caught his attention. The tracks faded as they entered the field beneath the new fallen snow, but he knew where they led. In the distance, almost hidden within a thicket of trees near the tunnel's entrance, he caught the flash of a bay.

A guard's horse? Nay, that he refused to believe. Last eve, when he'd picked up Isabel's tracks in the snow, he'd followed them, surprised to discover they led to where Frasyer's men had made camp for the night.

At first, terrified she'd been captured, he'd started around the perimeter in search of where they'd held her. Halfway around, he'd picked up her footprints accompanied by those of a steed moving away from camp.

She'd stolen one of the guard's horses? With them seated casually at the fire, 'twould seem straight from beneath their unknowing noses.

He shook his head in disbelief. The knights would rue their overconfidence when Frasyer learned of their neglect. Aye, Frasyer would be furious, more so as the cause was one slip of a woman.

Duncan grimaced as he stared at the partially hidden bay, unsure if he should laud her move as brave or foolhardy. A fat flake of snow landed on his cheek, quickly followed by another. To linger would invite trouble, the last thing he, or Isabel, would be needing.

He kicked his horse into a gallop. Outside the tunnel and within the shield of trees, he tied him near her stolen one, thankful for the snow that had started falling before first light. With the increasing intensity of the storm, before long, snow would fill any remainder of their trail.

Dismounting, he knelt beside Isabel's footprints. Beneath his touch, the half-filled rim of snow crowning the tracks crumbled. They were fresh. He stared at the beckoning darkness of the tunnel, then stood.

"I will find you lass. And you will regret your leaving." With a quick scan over the landscape to ensure no one was following him, he slipped into the blackness.

Isabel navigated the darkness of the winding tunnel, testing each step upward with the toe of her slipper as she ran her hand against the cold, damp wall. So caught up in her thoughts of Duncan, she'd left his home without taking a candle. An oversight too late to repair.

By now, Frasyer's knights would have noticed a steed missing and would have begun searching for whoever risked such a dare. Praying the snow that had begun falling at the break of dawn had covered her tracks, she slid her slipper along the stone steps as she climbed them one by one.

The musty scent of stale air and blackness continued to greet her. How much farther? How much longer to Frasyer's bedchamber? Or, in the blackness, had she somehow taken a wrong turn?

A faint scrape echoed from a distance behind her.

Heart pounding, Isabel halted. Listened. Long seconds passed, each one filled with vivid images of guards storming her, being thrown in the dungeon, and of Frasyer's laughter as her father was hung.

Stop it! The noise was nothing but a rat or other vermin scuttling in the dank tunnel.

She started to climb.

Another soft scrape sounded, this time closer.

Isabel flattened against the stone wall. Someone was behind her!

The distinct echo of the soft pad of leather upon stone reached her.

Fear clogged her throat. Mary help her, was it one guard or more? No matter, whoever was following her, was closing in on her fast! Did they know she was here? What a foolish thought. Of course they did. The knights she'd stolen the horse from must have tracked her down and discovered the horse she'd hidden in the trees.

Why hadn't she slapped the steed away upon her arrival? Or better, before she'd crossed the open field? Because with the days to reach her father dwindling, once she found the Bible, she would need the horse if she hoped to reach Lord Monceaux in England before her father was hung.

No, she hadn't come this far to be caught. Or to give up. There must be somewhere to hide, something she could use to defend herself. Damn them, they would not catch her without a fight.

Isabel hurried up the steps, cold stone scraping her palms as she used the walls as a guide.

A flicker of light fractured the blackness in her wake. Shadows built around her into huge, ominous shapes.

Her heart slammed against her chest.

She pushed herself faster.

"Isabel!" a deep male voice called.

She whirled, lost her footing, stumbled back and caught herself. Barely. "Duncan?"

"Aye." The tiredness in his voice weighed heavy on her heart. "Nay move."

"Why have you followed me?" she demanded in the growing light; Duncan's shape slowly conjured into form as he rounded the corner, a candle in hand, the anger carved on his face cast within the flicker of flames. Unforgiving, his eyes bore into hers.

"Why did you leave the safety of Lochshire Castle?" he demanded. "I gave you my oath to help."

Isabel backed up to the next higher step, refusing to allow him to intimidate her. "Nay, that you gave to Symon. And kept. I told you before, you owe me nothing. Leave me, I do not want you here."

Duncan reached her, his anger a living thing. "We are in this together."

"Are we?" she charged, hating that even now a

part of her was thrilled to see him. A part of her wanted to throw herself into his arms and thank him for having cared enough to come, even knowing the risk of his decision—that if he was caught by Frasyer, he'd not walk out alive.

He caught her hand; warmth pulsed through her. Tired, afraid, and with her defenses down, if he drew her to him now, she would cave.

Instead, she went on the attack with a suspicion that had been lurking in her mind. "After you left with your brothers, you never planned on coming back for me. You had planned to ride on your own to find the Bible, did you not?"

Surprise flickered in his gaze.

She jerked her hand free. "You were not coming back for me," she repeated, the hurt she'd tried to shield coating her words.

"You were safe at my home," he stated.

"Safe?" She fisted her hands at her sides. "As if that gives you the right to make decisions about my life without my consent!"

"Nay," he replied, his words ice. "I learned the cost of trusting you too well."

"Just like I should not have trusted you," she snapped. "You were only too willing to be rid of me when it suited your purposes. How long, I wonder, would we have been handfasted before you changed your mind about our pledge?"

He looked as shocked as her at her accusation. Her regret was instant. "I am sorry. I—"

With his jaw set, he moved past her and began to ascend the steps. "Do not flatter yourself. I am here for the Bible to save Lord Caelin's life. No more."

Isabel stared at Duncan's retreating figure as he pushed himself up the steps. "I did not mean it."

He kept on walking.

She hurried after him. The candle cast sporadic light within the narrowed cavern, revealing trickles of moisture weaving down the wall, bits of moss wedged within some of the steps and an abandoned spider web half hidden on a beam near the ceiling.

"Duncan?"

"I will not hear you speak of Frasyer."

"I do not love him," she burst out, unable to withhold the words.

His shoulders stiffened, but he remained silent.

She stared at his back, stricken. She was a fool to admit her true feelings, not that he was likely to believe anything she said. But Duncan's kiss, his touch still burned in her mind. How easy it would have been to have made love with Duncan when he'd drawn her to him in the tower chamber. What she wouldn't give to have had that memory.

"The door is up ahead," Duncan said roughly.

Numb, she looked past him to where the golden light wavered upon the near invisible slit. A thought struck her. "Do you think Frasyer is in his chamber?"

Duncan arched a speculative brow. "Does your lover normally sleep in late?"

And with that simple question, tragically, they were back to where they'd begun. She wanted to scream her frustration, but for what? Duncan still believed she'd chosen Frasyer for his wealth, a presumption she'd allowed.

"He will likely be out this late in the morn," she said quietly.

"Likely?" Isabel's ignorance of her lover's routine

amazed Duncan. "But you do not know for sure?" At her silence, he shook his head with disgust. "Never mind. We will find out together." But a part of him had wanted her to tell him whatever weighed heavy on her mind.

"Ready?" he asked.

"Aye."

He said a quick prayer that Frasyer's chamber would indeed be empty. With his dagger drawn, Duncan pressed his hand against the carved stone and slid open the secret door.

Chapter 13

When the secret door to Frasyer's chamber slid open, sunlight sliced through the tunnel's blackness. Squinting against the painfully bright glare, Duncan scanned the room, one hand clasped on his sword.

Empty.

He lowered his hand. They were safe—for the moment.

When Isabel started forward, he caught her forearm and shook his head. He placed his finger over his mouth for her to remain silent. At her questioning look, he pointed to the outer door.

Understanding shone in her eyes. She nodded.

Duncan crept to the door and listened. Several long seconds passed, but he heard not a sound indicating anyone was in the outer chamber.

"This way." He led her to the other secret entrance. As he passed the massive bed centered against the back wall, Duncan kept his gaze averted. He tried to ignore that Isabel and Frasyer had often slept within the tangle of the sheets. The last thing he wanted to think about was her sharing her body

with the bastard, more so since her taste haunted
Duncan still.

Behind him, Isabel's soft footsteps scraped to
a stop.

Needing to know what thoughts this chamber invoked for her, Duncan turned. Isabel's gaze was
trained on the bed, a flush stealing up her cheeks.
She faced him, her amber eyes wide with guilt, then
oddly, hurt echoed within her fragile features.

Hurt? That made not a bit of sense. He waited
for her to speak, explain, to say anything.

She dropped her gaze.

"What?" he demanded in a harsh whisper.

A shudder flickered over her body. After a long
moment, she shook her head.

That was the way of it then? Fine. If she wanted
Frasyer, she was welcome to him. He'd nay save her
again. No, she'd not asked him to; Symon's plea
had brought him here—to this insanity of a mess.

A cloud shielded the sun, pitching the chamber
into gloom. Scowling, Duncan glanced around,
finding the dismal shadows appropriate.

Disgusted with the entire situation, he strode
across the room, anxious to find the Bible and be
far away from here. He ran his fingers up the wall
in search of the near invisible indent they'd spotted
only days ago when they'd hidden beneath the bed.

Isabel moved to his side, her fingers mimicking his
technique. All too aware of her, of her poor decisions that'd tossed them both into this mayhem, he
focused on his task. As his finger slid near the corner
of the wall, the tip of his thumb found purchase.

"The outline for the door is over here," he said.
"Help me find the opening."

Isabel crouched below him, the top of her straight whisky hair at knee level. She looked up at him.

Beyond her regret, he saw awareness in her eyes. He damned himself over and again for his inability to withdraw from her. "What?" he asked through gritted teeth.

A long second passed. "We need to hurry."

Aye, they did, but with her looking like his every fantasy helped naught. In a foul mood, he began to follow the thin line of the hidden door with his fingertips.

"Here," Isabel exclaimed.

He glanced down as sun spilled into the room. A hand's length from the floor, a small indent lay within the wall. "Good." He knelt beside her. With their fingers near each others, they pulled.

Stone scraped as the door swung open.

Isabel jumped to her feet.

"Hurry."

She slipped into the secret chamber ahead of him. Stilled. "No, it cannot be!"

At the disappointment in her voice, Duncan pulled the door wider. A sizeable stone pallet led to a set of stairs. "Another secret passage?"

"So it appears." Frustration strained her voice. "I was sure this door led to a secret chamber."

"It would seem we were both wrong."

"Now what? I have but days left to free my father and we have yet to find the Bible." She crossed her arms over chest and turned away.

Though she was trying to hide her emotions from him, her shoulders were visibly shaking. However much he wanted to keep his distance from her, he'd not allow her to suffer alone. Lord Caelin was a fine man, one he would risk anything to save.

"We will find the Bible," he said as he drew her to him.

She turned into his arms, and her body trembled against his. "But we cannot be sure."

The echo of her heartbeat pounded unsteady against his; the angst in her voice clawed at his heart. "Nay, we cannot be, neither will we quit."

"No." A quiet strength filled her voice as she looked up. Determination shown in her amber eyes, framed by the fatigue haunting them both. "We will find it." She stepped back, composed once again and nodded. "Let us go."

Candlelight spilled around them in jagged shadows as he pulled the door closed behind them. Duncan held up the taper that fractured the darkness with its yellowed light. The widened flat stone led to a set of stairs that disappeared into blackness.

"Where do you think they lead?" Isabel asked.

He shrugged. "We will soon find out." They started down, every curve, each angle drawing them deeper beneath mortar and stone. Several levels down, a sinking grew in Duncan's gut as to their destination.

The darkness seemed alive, like a thousand tiny eyes following their progress from some secret world. Despite himself, chills prickled up his spine.

"Duncan?"

He shrugged off the foolish sensation that they weren't alone. "Aye?"

"Should we have not found at least one door by now?"

"One would think."

Chilled air tainted with a faint stench increased Duncan's suspicion of their destination.

And he prayed he was wrong.

But with the putrid smell strengthening with each step down, when the stairway flattened out and a door lay before them, he had little doubt to where the passage led.

"Bedamned," he muttered.

"What is wrong?"

"Shhh." He laid his ear against the stone. Muted groans melded with the drip of distant water beyond. Thankfully, there was no echo of guards' voices as they made their rounds. It seemed Frasyer hadn't added a permanent guard after their escape. He grimaced. Why should he? Only a fool would return.

With care, Duncan inched the door open. Though he'd expected the scene before him, confirmation soured the fledgling of hope he was somehow wrong.

"Duncan, where are we?"

The nerves in her voice had him wishing he could offer her another truth. With a sigh, he pushed the door. "Look."

She peered through the opening. Even in the dim light, he saw her face pale. "God, no."

He jerked the door closed, the candle's flame between them jumping wildly.

"Why would this entry lead to the dungeon?" Isabel asked. "It does not make sense."

Duncan nodded, as perplexed as she. "No, it does not."

"If only we had known before."

"What difference would that have made?"

"After you rescued me, had we known, we could

have taken this route to Frasyer's chamber to search for the Bible."

"We could have," he agreed, "but your belief that the Bible was in Frasyer's chamber was a suspicion proved false."

Guilt fueled Isabel and she turned away.

"What is wrong?"

"I should have known," she whispered, damning her ignorance. "I have lived here for the past three years, yet I know little of this castle's workings or routes of escape besides the common entry doors."

Hardness encased Duncan's face and he remained silent, but she knew his thoughts, had witnessed the same damnable look several times as they'd searched for the Bible. He believed that as Frasyer's mistress, her attention had been too focused on the earl's bed to think of such mundane thoughts of strategy for the rebels or otherwise. If he only knew the truth.

Regardless of her reasons, her ignorance of the castle's layout far from alleviated her guilt. Because of her lack of knowledge, Duncan had almost died. As a covert supporter of the Scottish rebels, why had she not explored every inch of Moncreiffe Castle and shared her findings with her brother?

Emotion tightened Isabel's throat. "We have done naught but go in a circle and are no closer to finding the Bible."

"You are wrong. We know where the Bible is not."

Her heart aching, she gave a bitter laugh. "And that knowledge gains us what? Your injury? Days lost. In addition, Frasyer still has the upper hand over my father's life."

"Isabel—"

"Only a handful of days remain to bring the Bible to Lord Monceaux. Yet, I have naught the faintest idea of where it is hidden. For all we know, Frasyer might have taken it with him. And, if he finds you here, damn you, Duncan, he will gladly end your life."

Duncan's gaze softened. "He will not find us."

"Empty words," she breathed, tired of those she loved wounded or dying around her. "Even now his knights could be entering the secret passage, our mounts seized."

"I doubt such. It was snowing when I followed you. Even a few hours behind you, with the storm intensifying, I barely was able to trace your path. By the time Frasyer's knights awoke, even if they began trailing you, before long, any tracks either of us made would be filled."

"You are right," Isabel said, reassured. "I have allowed my frustration to guide my thoughts."

"It is a difficult time for you."

"It is, but for us all. Symon touched so many people's lives. I still cannot believe he is dead." But thinking of him would only nurture the hurt, when time for that must come later. "And what of the Bible? Where could it be?"

Duncan leaned against the wall and rubbed the worried indent of his brow. "We have searched several rooms, which narrows down where the Bible could be. I think we need to start at the dungeon and work our way up."

"How? We will need garb to cover us to get past the guards as before."

He sighed. "We will have to retrace our steps." He pushed away from the wall. "If we do not find any clothes in Frasyer's chamber, another room on his floor might provide us well."

She nodded.

Duncan lifted the candle and turned toward the stairs. "There is one thing I cannot figure out."

"What is that?"

"Why would Frasyer need a private passageway from his chamber to the dungeon?" He started up the steps.

A frown wedged between her brow as Isabel fell into place behind him. "It makes no sense to me as well. It is not as if he has a covert chamber within the dungeon where he hides his secrets." She stilled. "But what if he did?"

Duncan halted, turned. The flicker of possibility in his gaze matched her own thoughts.

"What if Frasyer has a discreet chamber down here where he hides what he wishes others to never find?" she asked. "If so, the Bible may be in there as well."

"Isabel," Duncan cautioned, "there may be another reason for this secret passage." Like Frasyer being so twisted he would covertly watch from a hidden chamber, enjoying as the prisoners within were punished.

"Nothing else makes sense."

"There are other reasons, but on this I agree."

"It is here. I can feel it." He looked far from convinced, but she knew in her heart it was so. "Wait. Why have I not remembered this before? At times, when Frasyer spoke with me, an odd, sour smell clung to him. I had dismissed it as that from hard travel, but I should have placed the smell before, that inherent of the dungeon!"

"We will search the dungeon first," Duncan said. "Though no guards are posted there, they will return on rounds soon enough."

"Then let us hurry."

They retraced their steps. Duncan pushed open the secret door, scoured the dank surroundings, then moved forward. "Stay close behind me."

Torches, spaced at regular intervals within the dungeon, cast splotches of yellowed light, leaving the musty stone walls a jumble of macabre shadows.

Isabel scanned the dimly lit corridor. "Where should we begin?"

"A fine question indeed," Duncan replied. "I doubt that Frasyer would keep anything of value in one of the cells."

"True, but what if one of the doors does not lead to a cell, but a private room?"

"Nay," Duncan said. "When I was searching for you, I scanned most every chamber."

"But not all."

He grimaced. "Nay, not all. Fine then. We will search those cells I did not view first." He pointed to several cells at the end of the corridor. "Those four are the only ones that I did not check."

She glanced past the door where she'd been imprisoned. Sickened by the stench, standing so close to where she'd once been incarcerated, made her want to wretch.

"Isabel?"

"I am fine." She lied, but she couldn't fail now, not when she was so close. "I will take the two doors on the right."

He nodded.

With her stomach threatening to purge, Isabel

hurried along the dank hallway, the groans of men suffering in the distance too clear a reminder of what awaited her and Duncan if they were caught. That was, if after, Frasyer allowed them to live.

At the first door, she peered within the slats, half afraid of witnessing one of Frasyer's unfortunate captives firsthand. Daylight filtered through the narrowed hole carved midway up the wall. Inside, she saw naught but abandoned straw.

"Anything?" Duncan whispered.

"No."

"Nothing here either."

Isabel hurried to the final room and peered inside the narrowed slit. Nothing. Her heart sunk. "Do you see anything?" she asked, praying he had.

"Only another cell."

She touched the chain with Wallace's pendant around her neck. "Damn Frasyer and his game. Where else could a chamber be hidden?

Duncan shook his head and motioned toward the secret passage. "We need to return to Frasyer's chamber and find garb to masquerade ourselves in while we search."

Isabel fell into step beside him.

"Besides the cells," he said, "there is only the stairs leading to the great room."

"What if a secret panel is hidden in the wall up the steps?"

He shook his head. "If indeed another secret chamber exists, it could be anywhere."

The odds against them finding the entry to yet another secret chamber somewhere in the castle was enormous. Each moment lost deprived them of time needed to travel. She scanned the flame-lit corridor, the yellowed light dancing across the indents leaving macabre shadows.

"We should check the stairs before we leave."

Duncan frowned. "Aye, a necessary risk. If we hear anyone coming from above, hurry to the passage." With the groans of the prisoners around them, they hurried to the stairs leading to the great room.

Vivid memories of Duncan's initial appearance overwhelmed her. How he'd appeared within her cell when she'd believed all was lost. How he'd brought garb to help her escape. How he'd stood by her when he'd learned she could not leave without the Bible. And of how he'd been wounded in creating a diversion so they could safely continue their search.

They started past the dark inlet behind the stairs, and another memory jolted her. The shelter she had used to change into the squire's garb.

As they passed the indent, a cool breeze had their candle sputtering. Light from the sporadic wick flickered along the dungeon walls and illuminated the black void behind the steps.

"Wait." Duncan lifted the candle. Yellow light illuminated the shielded door behind the steps, to yet another cell. Or was it. "Look there, where you changed into the garb when I came before."

"Another cell?"

"When I first saw it, due to the lack of grates, I dismissed it as a room Frasyer used to flog his prisoners or worse."

"Mayhap it is a private chamber," Isabel said, trying not to get her hopes up.

"Mayhap." He stepped toward the narrowed inlet shielding the entry.

The creak of a door sounded above. Male voices echoed down the stairway.

Duncan hurried over, jerked open the door. It slid soundlessly open. "Hurry."

She didn't have to be told twice. Nerves slammed her body as she rushed into the chamber, Duncan in her wake.

Candlelight illuminated a room complete with a massive desk, hand-drawn maps of Scotland, claymores, and myriad other war-honed items.

The pounding of the guard's steps on the stairs increased. Duncan pushed her inside, shut the door behind them, and caught her hand.

The guards voices echoed from outside.

Duncan hauled her behind the desk. "Get down."

Heart pounding, she ducked, and he knelt by her side.

He blew out the candle. The room fell to blackness, the taint of smoke from the wick strong.

"Do you think they saw our candle?" Isabel whispered. "Or can smell the smoke?"

"Shhhh."

Silence swarmed them, punctured by the sound of their breaths and the murmurs of the guards.

Seconds passed.

Nearby, a cell door scraped open. The voices grew distant.

Isabel sagged back. "They did not see us."

"Aye, but now we must wait until they have left."

She relaxed, the darkness heightening her senses. Duncan's warm breath slid over her neck with a soft, familiar warmth. He was so close she could feel the heat of his body, the honed muscles a fortifying strength to her frayed nerves. Though she fought to be strong, she wanted him to assure her that they would find the Bible and reach her father in time to save his life. And more, to forgive her. A foolish thought indeed. With all that she'd put him through, she deserved naught of his forgiveness, only contempt.

The scrape of doors and muted voices from the corridor seemed to last forever, the wait made bearable only by Duncan's presence at her side.

Her mind drifted to thoughts of the tower chamber when she and Duncan had almost made love. Her skin prickled with awareness as she remembered the feel of his hands upon her skin, the male taste of him upon her tongue, the erotic sensations his touch invoked.

No, they'd not made love, but for a while, he'd looked at her with the passion she'd believed she would never see in his eyes again.

"They are leaving," Duncan said, drawing her from her musings.

Isabel angled her head and listened, thankful to hear the guards' fading voices as they headed up the stairs.

Leather slid against the stone floor as he shifted beside her. "Wait here."

She caught his arm. "Where are you going?"

"To one of the torches outside so I can light the candle. Stay here until I return." Quiet steps echoed in the silence. A soft shush sounded as he opened the door. Torchlight cut through the gloom a second before she was again plunged into darkness.

Each scrape, each indefinable sound beyond the stone wall had her tensing.

After a long moment, the door reopened. Duncan

stepped inside. Candlelight breeched the blackness like a beacon, illuminating a surprisingly complex chamber.

She gave a shaky exhale.

Unaware of her worry, Duncan gestured toward the chests lined up against the far wall. "I will look through those, you search the desk. If the Bible is not in either place, we will comb through the other chests within the chamber."

Isabel nodded. With the guards surely to return on their rounds in a short while, she prayed the search wouldn't take long. She quickly scanned the top of the desk while Duncan began rummaging through the first of the chests.

Rolled maps, ledgers, and scrawled notes by Frasyer addressing issues of the keep lay neatly upon the hewn wood, but there was no sign of her mother's Bible. Not as if she'd expected it to be lying out for her to find.

"Anything?" Duncan called.

"Not yet." Isabel opened several bindings wrapped in oiled leather, frustrated when only more ledgers for Moncreiffe Castle filled her hand. She glanced over at Duncan. He was searching through the third chest.

She studied the chests along the opposite wall. What if the Bible wasn't there, either? There were so many places within the castle where the Bible might be, but they didn't have the luxury of time to search them all. And if the guards had discovered their hidden mounts, they could be caught before they found it.

Isabel started to step away from the desk when her foot caught on a small wooden chest on the floor.

"Duncan!" Excitement rattled her voice, but she didn't care, if indeed what she suspected lay within.

He shoved the lid of the trunk he was searching shut and stood. "Did you find it?"

"I found something. This may be the Bible!" As Duncan hurried over, Isabel hauled the small chest up, then lifted it onto the table. A part of her feared the Bible wouldn't be inside. She met Duncan's gaze.

"Open it, lass."

With her fingers trembling, she caught the sides of the cover. After a silent prayer, she raised the sturdy top and peered inside.

Isabel's covered her face with her hands. "Oh, God!"

Chapter 14

Isabel's face paled, then she began to sway. Duncan caught her as she crumpled against the desk. "Isabel?" He drew her against his chest. She turned into his arms, tears flowing freely down her cheeks.

"Oh, Duncan," she said, her voice strangled with emotion.

A worn leather bag was crammed into the small chest. Not the Bible. Damn Frasyer for putting her through this, her torment as each search had come up empty, and her every new hope of having found it destroyed. After they'd freed Lord Caelin, he'd find Frasyer. With his bare hands, the bastard would pay.

He stroked the soft tangle of her hair, her trembling body feeling so fragile against his. "Nay worry, lass, we will find the Bible. On that I give you my vow."

"No." Still clutching the leather sack against her chest, she pushed herself away. "This is the Bible." A tremulous smile curved her lips as she tugged open the sack and withdrew a leather-bound book. A tear rolled down her cheek. "We can leave."

Relief poured through Duncan, but another part of him acknowledged a hard truth. This was the beginning of their end. Aye, they could go. Once they reached Lord Monceaux, turned over the Bible and her father was freed, Duncan would ride away to never see Isabel again.

A decision she had chosen.

A decision he should be overjoyed to accept.

Except, standing here, with her but a hand's width away, he realized he'd never stopped wanting her. With the sweet lavender scent of her hair filling his nostrils, and her soft body in his arms, he was hard pressed not to give in to temptation.

At the tower chamber, why had he asked that once they'd delivered the Bible, she not return to Frasyer? What was he thinking? He grimaced. Nay, 'twas more like what was fueling his thoughts.

With the sweet taste of her kisses lingering on his tongue and his body demanding he claim what it believed was his, lust had guided his request. Not that he didn't care for her more than was good. 'Twould seem with her, some things would never change.

"We will use the sack to carry the Bible," Duncan said.

Isabel met his gaze, then she looked away, but not before he caught a hint of regret on her face.

Unease twisted in his gut. "What is wrong?"

"We need to be leaving."

"Aye, but I have known you too long to deny another thought churns in your mind. Tell me."

She scraped her teeth across her bottom lip,

then she shot him a nervous glance. "Now that I have the Bible and a mount, you can return home."

A muscle worked in his jaw. "Had I wanted to slink away after first freeing you from the dungeon, I would have been long gone. I thought you knew me." He gave a bitter laugh. "I thought I knew you. Seems we were both wrong."

"Duncan."

"If you think that I am going to—"

"No," Isabel interrupted, aware that the time had come to push Duncan away for good. As much as she wished it otherwise, the false words she must say to convince him to go without her would hurt him. But there was still time for his escape, for him to be safe. That's all that mattered.

"You are wounded and should still be abed recovering from your injuries. Instead, you take yourself off to travel with your brothers to meet with Wallace, to prove what?" she demanded, allowing her worry for him to fill her words, her anger at his recklessness to drive her forward. "Then, when you returned home and found me gone, when you should have dismissed me and taken care of yourself, you tracked me down, risking your life yet again. For what? You claim for Symon." She shook her head when he made to speak. "Your vow to Symon to help me escape the dungeon has ended." She couldn't keep her voice from quivering at the last. "As is the life we once planned."

His jaw stiffened.

"I belong to Frasyer now, not you," she rushed on. "Do not delude yourself that the kiss we shared in the tower was anything more than a release of frustration, a wanting inspired by our fatigue, of that

any man or any woman would have experienced
under our circumstances." She despised the words
that would hurt the most, a glaring lie to Duncan, a
man she would always love. "I was lonely. You were
there. Had Seathan stood in the chamber instead of
you, had he drawn me to him, I would have kissed
him the same. And had he asked"—she swallowed
hard—"welcomed him into my bed."

Anger darkened Duncan's face to such a dangerous hue that she took a step back. But if she didn't
finish, his pride would force him to remain. "I wish
to be with Frasyer. I cannot say it any simpler. Hear
me, Duncan. I do not want you anymore. I do not
need you to help me carry the Bible to safety. Be
gone."

His green eyes darkened to black, the fury bank-
ing within them making her take another step
back. She'd pushed him, mercilessly, but it would
take his anger to ensure he left.

"And you will ride to Lord Monceaux on your
own?" he said, his voice so dangerously quiet an
other chill rippled through her. "Having not a care
for Frasyer's men who search for you?"

She angled her chin. "I am aware of the challenges I face in my journey ahead."

"And you claim what is between us is over?"

"Yes."

The pain of her words lanced through him with
fiery precision. Yet, something didn't feel right.

Duncan watched her every breath, the nuances
of every shift of her eyes. And then he saw it—the
slightest quiver of her mouth. Understanding ripped
through him. She lied. He drew her toward him
with male satisfaction.

"Do not," she whispered, the slight yearning in her voice giving further credence to his belief.

Fury that she dared deny her true feelings for him pounded in his veins. Did she think him a fool? He raised her up on her tiptoes until their faces were a hand's width apart. The flare of her nostrils and the widening of her pupils told him she was as moved as he.

"It is not I who has lied," he growled.

He claimed her mouth, hot and hard, demanding her response. For a moment her body remained stiff. Then her lips quivered, softened, and accepted. At her moan, he angled his head and took the kiss deeper. Leather slapped upon the desk as she dropped the Bible. Her hands clung to him, dragging him closer, her mouth aggressive, making its own demands.

This was no lie.

The deeper they delved, the more it seemed as if the moment was bigger than them both, as if they were swept up in an otherworldly tide of passion that would consume them both.

Her mouth parted and he plunged his tongue deep inside, savoring her taste, wanting her even more. As her body willingly pressed against him, his hands roamed her every curve, touching, lingering against her silken skin, peeling away garb that denied him the feel of her flesh.

With his blood flowing hot, he scraped his teeth gently against the length of her neck, tasting, teasing until her body trembled helplessly against him.

She gasped, then tried to push away.

He held her tight.

"Duncan, we cannot."

"No?" He slid his hand down to cup her breast, watched as her eyes glazed with passion as he skimmed his mouth along the soft curve. With their eyes locked, he leaned over and swept his tongue across the hardening tip.

She groaned.

"Tell me," he demanded, his breath spilling over her sensitized flesh glistening from his taste. "Tell me that if I chose, we would not be making love here, upon this desk in a trice."

A blush rushed up her cheeks. She looked away, her chest heaving, her body taut. "I cannot."

He released her, a part of him satisfied, another ashamed of the lengths he'd used to force her to admit such. But a man had his pride.

"Get dressed."

She began to, with her fingers fumbling as she sought to fix her underclothes he had mussed.

Watching, struggling to harness his own body's desires, he found himself needing to know. "And if it was Seathan who had come to you that night in the Tower room, would you have invited him into your bed?"

She started to turn her head away, but he stood and caught her chin.

Her lower lip trembled. "No."

"Then why claim such?"

"Damn you, Duncan." She fisted her hands; they fell open, limp at her side. "I want you safe."

"You lie to protect me?"

Anger flared in her eyes. "Yes. To save your thick-skulled life, I will do whatever I must."

"And what else have you lied about?" The yell of a guard outside the entry caught his attention.

Isabel shot a terrified glance toward the door. "We must leave!"

"Aye." Duncan dragged her gown up, then tugged the cape around her body. He blew out the candle, throwing them into total blackness.

Hurried steps echoed from outside. Fading voices.

"What do you think is happening?" Isabel whispered.

"I am unsure, but let us pray they have not found the horses."

Silence. She trembled. "Wait, the Bible!"

"I have it. Come." Their soft steps echoed in the darkness. He inched the door open. The passage within the dungeon lay empty. "It is clear. Hurry."

They bolted down the moist, dank corridor. Halfway to their destination, a shout from outside a nearby opening caught their attention.

She turned toward him, fear framing her face. "Frasyer has returned."

"Go!" He hauled her with him. After they'd entered the secret tunnel, Duncan tugged the door shut. Darkness encased them.

"Did you bring the candle?" she asked.

"Aye, but I need to light it. Wait here." Before she could speak, he returned to the dungeon. He held the candle to the torch. The flame caught, sputtered to life.

Voices drifted from above. He recognized the anger of Frasyer's voice. At the weight of the Bible in his arms, a satisfied smile curved his mouth. Once Frasyer found the Bible missing, the earl would be furious. Duncan's smile fell as he remembered Isabel's wishes when it came to the earl. Even after they'd proven Lord Caelin's innocence and he was freed, Isabel had said she would return to Frasyer.

No, he vowed, not without an explanation! After that kiss, she owed him more than lies.

Duncan hurried toward the secret door, the Bible wedged beneath his arm, his hand cupped to protect the flame.

Shielded inside the hidden entrance, he tugged the door shut. Golden light spilled into the darkness, framing Isabel's eyes wide with worry.

Worry for him? Was that truly why she wanted him to leave without her?

He started up the steps. "Follow me." Tension filled the silence as they began their climb, broken only by the pad of their footsteps.

"What could have brought Frasyer's return?" Isabel asked.

"There could be many reasons."

"What will we do if they have found our horses?"

The odds of their making it safely to the horses, much less to Lord Monceaux's were overwhelming. But Duncan refused to give up hope.

"I do not know," he replied in all honesty.

The steps above them leveled out. He caught sight of the near hidden door. "We are back at the bedchamber," he whispered. Duncan placed his ear against the door.

Silence.

Inching open the door, he scanned the chamber. As always, his gut clenched as he viewed Frasyer's bed. "It is empty." He stepped into the massive chamber, Isabel on his heels as they made their

way around the massive bed toward the other
secret exit.

Footsteps echoed from outside. A door slammed.

Isabel started. "He is coming!"

"Hurry." Duncan pulled the door open, followed
her inside and secured the door.

A split second later, a door banged shut. "Bedamned!" Frasyer's voice boomed from within his
chamber. "Incompetence at every turn!"

"I am sorry, my lord," a shaky voice replied. "The
guards from the campsite are sure the tracks they
found nearby were those of a lad."

At Isabel's gasp, Duncan put his hand over her
mouth and shook his head.

She nodded.

"Or a lone woman," Frasyer snapped.

"My lord, as I said before, we cannot be sure who
left the tracks. With the heavy snow quickly covering the trail, they were unable to follow them and
discover who stole the mount."

"Beneath the noses of four knights!"

"The knights have been punished, my lord."

"Not enough. Six more lashes for each man. I
will not tolerate incompetence." A long pause.
"From anyone!"

"Yes, my lord."

"Be gone!"

Hurried footsteps sounded from inside. A outer
door thudded shut.

At Isabel's pallor, Duncan drew her to him. "Be
patient," he whispered. "We will make it out safely."

A solid knock sounded in the distance.

"Enter," Frasyer ordered.

The slight scrape of a door closing, footsteps. "My

lord. A runner has returned with news that Lord Caelin has been delivered to Lord Monceaux."

Isabel stiffened in his arms.

"And his reply?" Frasyer asked from the other chamber.

"None, my lord. Lord Monceaux was away. The runner was assured that a missive will be sent to you posthaste upon his return."

"As soon as word arrives from Lord Monceaux, deliver it to me immediately."

"Yes, my lord."

"You are dismissed."

"With Lord Monceaux's absence," Duncan whispered once the outer door echoed shut, "we have been offered a few days before Lord Caelin's fate is determined."

"No. When my father was taken, Frasyer stated that my father would be hung in a fortnight," she whispered, her voice laced with anxiety. "The only way the command will not be followed is if when the day arrives for the sentence to be carried out, Lord Monceaux has still not returned to his home."

Duncan opened his mouth to tell her the truth about Lord Monceaux—Griffin—but closed it again.

Though serving as a trusted adviser to King Edward in dealing with the Scots, Lord Monceaux, or Griffin, the name used by their family, was a spy for Scotland. A fact known only by a trusted few.

Duncan, along with his brothers and Griffin, had met secretly with Wallace two days past. In addition to plotting their next strategy against the English troops, they'd discussed Lord Caelin's charge. Though Griffin had vowed to do whatever he could to ensure Lord Caelin lived, Duncan suspected

Griffin's absence from Rothfield Castle was a planned move. Regardless of Isabel's belief, his absence would indeed buy them much needed time.

As much as Duncan wished to ease Isabel's worries, with her continued vow to return to Frasyer, he couldn't take the risk. Besides, she would find out soon enough that her father remained alive and well.

At Frasyer's steps within the bedchamber beyond, Duncan held up the candle. "Let us go."

In silence, they worked their way down the curved stone steps, the stale air tainted with a relentless chill. Guided with candlelight, their progress remained slow.

A long while later, Isabel turned to him. Illuminated by the flicker of the flames, her face softened with relief. "Look up ahead."

He rounded the corner to stand at her side. In the distance, framed within the hewn entry, a wash of golden afternoon light pierced the blackness before fading into the gloom.

They'd made it.

Duncan extinguished the candle and started forward, Isabel's steps echoing in his wake. Near the entry, the snort of the horses had him halting.

"Stay here." With careful steps, he edged forward. Shielding his eyes from the glare of the afternoon sun, he slowly swept the entire area.

"Who is out there?" Isabel whispered.

"No one, but that does not mean Frasyer's knights have not discovered our mounts." He handed her the candle and then waved her toward a darkened corner. "I am going to check for tracks or any other sign that we are not alone. Until I return, hide in the shadows. If you hear me shout, run. Hide. When possible, travel to Lochshire Castle."

Her lower lip trembled. "Duncan, I—"

"Nay worry for me." He handed her the Bible. "In case I do not return."

Isabel caught his hand. "You will come back."

Expectant silence hummed between them. As much as he wished to assure her he would be fine, until they reached Griffin, neither of them was safe.

As if understanding, she swallowed hard. "God's speed."

No time remained to linger, but God help him, if when he walked outside he found his fate death, first he would taste her this one last time.

With care, Duncan drew her to him, slow, to watch, to anticipate how her mouth would feel against his, the way her taste would overtake him in a blissful invasion. At her sigh, he covered her mouth with his, slow, savoring the way she melted against him, the tremors of her body as he deepened the kiss. He wanted more.

He wanted everything.

A fact that fate had woven into a tangled mess.

With regret, Duncan broke the kiss, taking in the way her lips were swollen, how desire entwined with fear in her eyes. He set her away. "Go."

For a moment she held, opened her mouth as if to say something more.

"What?"

She shook her head. "Naught." Isabel slipped into the darkness.

Duncan turned toward the entrance and inched forward, listening for the crunch of snow beneath boots, the snap of a twig, anything to alert him that

Frasyer's men laid in wait. With many of the trees stripped of their leaves, the fir trees they'd hidden their horses among provided only a degree of shelter. Hours had passed. The wind could easily have shifted snow to fill telling tracks of any riders.

At the entrance, he pressed against the cold stone and kept to the shadows. He scoured the nearest bushes first, a wooden tangle against the sprawl of white. Confident they held no threat, he swept the snow-glazed field.

And stilled.

In the distance, tracks disturbed the drifts where Frasyer's knights had ridden. He visibly retraced the tracks, then scanned near the escape tunnel. Nothing indicated a closer search. Duncan owed their blunder to their overconfidence that Isabel wouldn't dare return to Moncreiffe Castle.

Relieved, he stepped into the tunnel and waved her forward. "Come."

Isabel appeared in the light, strain haunting her face, but the eternal hope she carried strong in her every step. Her strength drew him, battled his misgivings, resurrected the doubts of her involvement with Frasyer. But time, not more questions were needed at the moment.

Once they reached the horses, he helped her mount. He secured the Bible to the back of his saddle, then swung up on his own steed.

"We will ride within the edge of trees until a safe distance away," Duncan said. "If we cut across the field, we risk not only being seen if someone is positioned nearby to keep watch, but leaving a trail."

Isabel shielded her brow, her gaze following the

broken trail left by Frasyer's men. "How long ago do you think they passed?"

"As clear as their tracks are, a short while at best. With the wind causing drifts, we cannot be sure how often his men are making rounds."

She nodded.

He took in her layered garb, the cape she wore, pushed away thoughts of her nakedness beneath. "We will travel faster with two horses, but if you become cold, tell me. For warmth's sake, we can ride together."

"I have endured colder weather than we now face." She shot him a surprisingly teasing look. "Including when I traveled to your brother's castle on your behalf."

He smiled, then sobered. "We face two days of hard travel. When we stop, it will be to rest our horses, break our fast, then we push on. The only things to greet us are the cold and the many miles ahead. And your withholding that you are freezing will not speed our travel. If you succumb to the cold, we will be forced to make camp, possibly ride to the nearest home to ensure you do not freeze. Your vow, Isabel, if you grow chilled, you'll tell me."

He didn't realize the significance of his words—the suggestion that he trusted her promise—until her eyes widened, then seemed to blur, as if she were fighting back emotion.

"Aye," she replied. "I swear it."

Nodding, not trusting the moment, Duncan spurred his mount onward toward the forest.

Keeping within the treeline for cover slowed their travel, but he refused to invite further danger. Isabel guided her mount around a broken stump embraced by the sheet of snow. "Will we reach Rothfield Castle before dark on the morrow?"

"If we do not run into any of Frasyer's men, and if the weather holds."

The hours passed with infinite slowness. The snow padded their horses' hooves, the leafless trees offering vague cover. Whenever possible, Duncan kept them behind banks of fir trees and mounds of rocks. Soon, they would have to risk exposing themselves and cross the field.

As darkness smothered the day, angry clouds rolled in and the temperature began to drop. The wind, blowing steady throughout the afternoon, increased with a vicious bite.

Turning his head against the hard flakes of blowing snow, Duncan took in Isabel. She'd tugged her woolen cape tighter and leaned slightly forward against the wind. Tendrils of ice clung to the tips of her exposed hair.

He surveyed the darkening sky. "A storm is moving in." As if to support his claim, a light snow began to fall. Worry crowded her brow. In that he didn't blame her. As much as he wanted to travel straight through, between the storm, terrain, and their exhaustion, they may be forced to seek shelter.

An ignorant lad, he'd foolishly set out during a heavy snow. The large, blinding flakes combined with the spread of white coating the land, soon made recognition of any familiar landmarks impossible. Nay, he refused to risk becoming caught in a whiteout condition again.

As they crested the next knoll, Duncan drew up his steed. He scanned the breaks in the aged oaks, their empty limbs like scrawny fingers arching toward the sky.

Isabel halted at his side. "Do you see something?"

"No. Which worries me as much as it does not. As furious as Frasyer was back in his chamber, one would think he would add more men in the search for you. Or increase their rounds."

"Where do you think they are?"

"A question I have pondered these last few hours. Perhaps he has set up an ambush. If so, I would think it would be nearer to Lord Monceaux's castle, more so if Frasyer discovers the Bible gone."

"But the runner from delivering my father to Lord Monceaux had only arrived while we listened." The breath from her words swirled between them in a white mist in the air.

"True, which makes the absence of his men more confusing. Regardless of his reasons or plans, we will not know if his knights are hidden and keeping watch until we leave the cover of the forest."

"When will we cross?"

"After nightfall. If indeed anyone is keeping watch, with the incoming storm, the clouds will obscure the moonlight. The field narrows up ahead, we will go there."

"Would not Frasyer keep this area under guard for exactly those reasons?"

"Normally I would agree, but in this search, few decisions Frasyer has made make sense. If we see any sign of his men, we will backtrack." He pointed toward a stand of fir trees. "Secure your horse behind the fir. We will break our fast and rest until it is dark. Then we will push hard through the night. The newly falling snow will cover our tracks."

"By morning, there will be no sign of our crossing."

He nodded. And prayed that Frasyer hadn't yet discovered the Bible's absence. When he did, there would be no stopping his fury.

Anger that he wondered if even Griffin's protection of Lord Caelin could stop.

Chapter 15

Weary from the hours of travel, Duncan tugged his cape tighter and scanned the vague outline of trees before them.

The screech of an owl tore through the inky forest, the sound lost quickly by the reckless whip of wind. Shards of moonlight slipped through the clouds, casting the forest in ominous shadows.

Shifting in his saddle, he ignored the tug of pain from his healing wound. Though Isabel worried, he'd endured worse in many a battle. He guided his mount through the next drift, then wove between a thick stand of firs where spiraling wind had scraped free hints of barren ground.

"Duncan?"

At the worry in Isabel's voice, he pulled his steed to a halt and waited until she drew alongside. In the slivers of moonlight, he caught how her body trembled and that she'd shoved her gloved hands deep within her cape.

"You are cold." It wasn't a question.

She shook her head. "It is my ho-horse. He is favoring his left rear le-leg."

Blast. With the forest crawling with Frasyer's men and their travel slowed by the treacherous weather and the night, they needed no further delays. And though she'd deny it, her voice betrayed the fact she was cold.

Duncan dismounted, drew off his gloves and tucked them beneath his arm. With his back to the wind, he gingerly ran his hands along her mount's hindquarter, then toward the hoof. As his palm feathered over the lower leg, the steed jerked.

"Steady, lad." Careful not to startle the horse, he soothed him with words as he ran his fingers over the lower tendon. Horseflesh trembled against his touch. Heat radiated from the muscle beneath.

He gently placed the hoof upon the ground. "He has sprained his leg. Most likely when he slipped on the rocks as we came down that last steep incline. We will have to ride together." Which would have been his decision regardless, considering the shivers icing her voice. Not that she needed to know.

"Wh-What will we do with th-the horse?"

Aware of her pride, he kept the worry from his voice. "Bring him with us. We cannot risk him being found. Even with the heavy snow, we have traveled a good distance." He surveyed the surrounding trees, the rise of the next knoll looming before them.

She nodded.

"This night we will stay at a crofter's hut to warm ourselves and to rest our mounts. We should arrive at Lord Monceaux's before night falls tomorrow."

Her fingers tightened on her reins. "What of Frasyer's men?"

"Few know of the hut's existence. Between the night and the snow, unless someone stumbles upon us, we should remain unseen. The steady wind will erase our tracks."

She shook her head. "No. We ne-need to keep traveling through the ni-night. My father—"

"Will be fine." And prayed he spoke the truth. He walked toward her side. In the first light of dawn, clad with fragments of blowing snow, Duncan saw her tense. He reached up and placed his hands around Isabel's waist, then helped her to the ground. Wrapped within the night she stood before him, their faces inches apart, her breath warm upon his face. As always with her, regardless that they stood in the forest with the air bitter cold, his blood heated, needing her, wanting her.

After Duncan secured her mount's reins to his saddle, he lifted her onto his horse, then swung up behind her. Cold stung her face as he urged his steed forward.

His gloved hand curled around her stomach, drawing her against the hard, muscled length of him. "Relax against me."

A wry smile touched her lips. As if relaxing in his presence was possible. Duncan embodied everything she wanted in a husband. Honor, integrity, a man who gave all for those he loved, and, if necessary, as proved with his vow to Symon, even if it meant risking his life.

The cold had turned her body numb. Concern for her father spurred her on. She'd believed her condition had gone unnoticed. Yet, Duncan had sensed her weakening. She closed her eyes at the evidence of how well he knew her. Of how hard it was to hide from him, except in one regard.

Grief welled up in her gut. As if she had a choice.

Exhaustion weighed heavy on her soul. She was so tired of lies. Of living in a veiled prison unable to help those she loved. She hated feeling torn, aware that the truth would shatter what little feelings Duncan held toward her.

How else could he react when he learned she'd turned away from him in the face of a personal tragedy. A man as proud as Duncan would not see her actions as saving his life, but an issue of trust.

A fragile trust she'd chosen to break.

Wind ripped through the treetops, shaking branches with an angry howl. Snow lashed around them, hard flakes stinging her skin, driving into the smallest opening to stab her flesh. But the elements compared not to her inner ache as Duncan's arm tightened around her.

How had she ever believed she could walk away from him when she wanted him with her every breath?

Secluded within Frasyer's castle over the past three years, she'd savored numerous fantasies of being with Duncan. None compared to this seemingly simple moment.

The rhythmic plod of the horses' hooves offered a soothing cadence. Duncan's arms held her tight, warming her, inciting her need to touch his body, feel the tautness of his flesh beneath her fingers, to know the splendor of their joining at least once in her life. It would be beautiful. How could it be anything but?

Sunlight filtered through the blackened sky, outlining the fading cloud cover they desperately needed to help shield them from view. With each passing hour, they would become more exposed, and with a lame horse slowing them, more vulnerable.

On the morrow, they would arrive at Rothfield Castle and hand Lord Monceaux the Bible. Her father would be freed, and she despised the very thought that she would return to a cold, harsh, and empty life beneath Frasyer's hand.

But tonight . . . Tonight would be the last night she would spend with Duncan. Alone.

Without bonds of propriety or prying eyes.

Regardless of her deepest wishes, once they'd delivered the Bible, her life would not change. With her father's gambling debt to Frasyer unpaid, the threat of her father losing their ancestral home and hauled to debtor's prison remained.

Lost in her tangled thoughts, the steady rocking of his mount, the comfort of Duncan's body and exhaustion dragged her into brief, troubled snatches of sleep. In between, she worried for Duncan's welfare. She'd witnessed him favoring his injured side on occasion when he believed she wouldn't notice.

Twice during the day, caught within the swirl of the wind, they'd heard the distant shouts of men. As the sun moved through the sky, the wind continued to blow, cutting through clothes to skin with a brutal bite.

Heavy snow fell as Duncan guided his horse across an ice-covered stream. Stones frozen in the streambed below merged with other patches dark with the hints of turbulent waters running below.

She took in the roll of white hills, the barren forest dotted with brave firs. "How much farther until we arrive?"

He drew her back in a comforting hug. "Soon."

As they crested the next knoll, Duncan drew to a halt, scanned their surroundings with infinite care as he'd done the entire day.

Fatigued, she found little beauty in the orange-red rays of the sunset that glistened off the firs laden with snow. Or the hare, its coat white of the winter, darting past.

He pointed toward the next rise. "See that thick stand of fir on the top of the knoll? The abandoned crofter's hut is hidden within the trees. We will stay there."

She squinted but could not discern any sign of the building. "I see nothing."

"As the hut is designed."

He didn't say more, she didn't ask. A strong rebel activist, he would know the layout of this land to the smallest detail, information he would use to attack English troops and after, to escape.

As had Symon.

With her mind steeped in emotions, she remained silent. Though an arduous day of travel, now that they had arrived, the exhaustion weighing heavy upon her cleared beneath her fear of the questions she must face.

Duncan kicked his mount forward. As they reached the top of the knoll, he navigated his mount through the thick firs, the breath of the snow-heavy trees easily blanketing their horses from view to any outsiders. As they rode between the next set of firs, the abandoned crofter's hut came into view.

Weathered timber vied with aged thatching woven on the roof, now coated by a deep layer of snow, but both stood solid against nature's force. More comforting, unbroken drifts of white swirled around the hut, evidence no one else had ridden through here as of late.

At the entrance to the hovel, Duncan drew his horse to a halt and swung to the ground. He put his hands around her waist.

She leaned into his hold, too tired to fight the dangerous mix of seduction and comfort his closeness brought as he lifted her down.

Duncan handed her the reins. "Wait here. Though no signs of anyone else having visited recently exist, I need to be sure." After a quick inspection of the hut, he returned. "Go inside. Wait there while I bed the horses. I have lit a taper so you can see."

She scanned the wall of trees.

As if sensing her unease, he shook his head. "We will be safe."

"How long will we stay here?"

"Until first light. We should reach Lord Monceaux's before the sun sets on the morrow."

With a nod, she left him and stepped inside the hut. Erratic flickers from the near-gutted taper illuminated the tiny home. The musty scent owed to the building's infrequent use, further supported by the sparse interior.

To her right lay a decaying fireplace that, with luck, would hold a fire and not set the entire hovel ablaze. In the far corner sat a roughly hewn, straw-stuffed bed, covered with old blankets. A sturdy table stood against the opposite wall, on top, several bowls laid haphazard.

The shambles around her would have sent many a lady running in fear.

And yet, a hominess existed within this crude interior, a sincere warmth that drew her. Isabel touched the laced bed covering, evidence of a woman's hand.

Weariness settled over her. It had been an incredibly trying day. A day of exhaustion and fear and she was barely clinging to sanity. But standing here, surrounded by remnants of a past life, contentment settled in her chest.

A woman had lived here.

A woman with a man to call her own. Given the secluded location and arduous life she must have endured, she'd still taken the effort to leave her mark in this otherwise barren room.

She touched the embroidery she'd made for Symon in her pocket. Though the lace cover was but a simple thing, she had not even that chance to show Duncan she loved him.

In but hours they would reach Rothfield Castle. Then she and Duncan would go their separate ways.

This time forever.

But daylight was a long way off. The choices over the next few hours would be hers. Isabel hugged herself. Did she dare give him the ultimate gift, that of her innocence?

She wanted Duncan with her every breath, had for many years. But if she gave herself to him this night, he would learn she was a virgin, the very fact that had kept her from making love with him in the tower chamber days before.

But now, with the uncertainty of the morrow

looming before them and given the depth of her love for Duncan, the magnitude of losing him again overwhelmed her.

Like the rose unfurling to catch the golden glow of the sun's rays, she knew her decision. Peace infused her, a warmth so sweet it assured her that she had made the right decision. She wanted Duncan. However selfish, however wrong, for this one night, if he accepted her into his bed, she would give herself to him.

If making love with him made her damned, then so be it. For he already held her heart, she would gladly give him her soul.

The soft creak of the door announced his return. Steadying herself, she turned in time to watch him enter and close the door in his wake.

Their gazes met.

Tension snapped between them, edged with awareness and heat. Her body trembled, her reaction far from incited by cold.

"The horses are taken care of," he said, his voice a dark calm, that of a man who was weighing the situation with a seasoned hand.

She nodded. A shiver swept through her body. The room seemed to crowd in on her, steal the air from her next breath. "You are tired. We are both—"

"I will begin a fire." He strode to the hearth and knelt. The shuffle of twigs, clunk of larger wood atop the small pile echoed in the silence as her mind spun.

He scraped his knife against a piece of flint. Sparks showered the dry moss. He blew on the glowing embers until a flame punctured the blackness. As he continued to coax the fire, it grew, spreading beneath the carefully built pile. Within moments, flames licked higher, greedily consuming the dry wood.

Satisfied, Duncan stood and turned. Unaware of her thoughts, he braced his feet shoulder width apart, hands on his hips. A warrior's stance.

At the intensity of his gaze, nerves trickled down her spine. She inhaled deeply, then slowly released, her heart pounding.

"I need to know what is on your mind." For a moment she doubted he would answer.

Duncan tilted his head and appraised her with eyes that held a combination of ice and heat. "I was thinking you are the most beautiful lass I have ever seen." As she caught her breath, he added, harsher, "and the most deceitful." He stepped toward her. "I have waited for the truth, Isabel, a truth I will have this night."

She held his gaze. "Any lie I have made had a purpose."

"Purpose?" His face darkened with anger, his body cast in the outlines of flames at his back adding to the ominous image. He strode to her and caught her face between his hands. "Hear me, Isabel," he said between gritted teeth. "You will tell me everything."

"It is not so simple," she whispered. Frasyer's threats to kill Duncan if she broke her vow of silence of their arrangement clattered in her mind, more so of the twisted ways he would seek vengeance.

"Nothing of importance is."

She could not allow harm to come to Duncan, but neither could she lie to him further. Already, too many mistruths had passed her lips, but she'd given them to save Duncan. Except he would not see it as that.

And he would hate her.

When she loved him with her every breath.

Wanted him as no other man.

"Isabel!"

His harsh voice unnerved her further, but she held her ground. "I will tell you what you want to know, but first"—her voice trembled, but she reached her hand over to cover his—"can we not share this one night?"

Chapter 16

Awareness heated in Duncan's gaze and he stilled. His mouth tightened. At the flash of denial in his eyes, her heart slammed against her chest.

"What difference will a few hours make?" Isabel asked.

He watched her for a long moment. "And after, you will tell me everything."

"Yes." Isabel exhaled slowly. "I promise."

At her vow, Duncan arched a brow, his disbelief easy to read. As nerves threatened to overwhelm her, she damned them and held her ground.

"I want you, Duncan," she breathed, allowing her dreams, her desire for him to seep into every corner of her words. "I want you as I have no other man."

Fire crackled in the thick silence. Tension thrummed in the endless void. Oh, God, what was he thinking? What was he feeling?

It took all of her courage to hold his gaze, but she refused to look away. She wanted him more than any man, more than life itself.

As he continued to watch her, his eyes hot, hard

to read, panic overwhelmed her. He was going to deny her. She knew it with every beat of her heart, with every breath she took.

Then he stepped away, putting more space between them.

"Duncan." Panic had her stepping forward. "Make love to me this night. I see the questions in your eyes. I feel them in your gaze. I swear to you that afterward, I will tell you what you want to know."

With her heartfelt plea wrapping around his thoughts, threatening to overcome his good sense, Duncan took in the desperation lining her face, the pale outline of her skin in stark contrast to the worry troubling her eyes. He should leave her untouched, walk away. God knew if he had but an ounce of common sense he would. Had the past not taught him the depths of Isabel's treachery?

His body burned with need, his blood pounding hard with the thought of finally, finally taking her.

Making her his.

Promises or no promises.

He caught the haunted look in her amber gaze. Secrets. Aye, she had them. And even knowing that, it took sheer will not to succumb to a long-denied passion, where logic and hurt and betrayal came second to seduction.

Her throat worked as she struggled to speak. "Duncan?"

She looked to where her fingers lay atop his, then dropped her hand, where it formed a trembling fist.

Something in Duncan snapped.

On a hiss, he lifted her chin with his hand. His

first mistake. He wanted answers, but touching her, the silk of her skin soft against his fingers, he realized he wanted her more.

He claimed her mouth, hard, hot, demanding. At her taste, an inferno surged through him with mind-numbing need. Heat arched, sizzled between them. His body trembled with the need to touch her, to expose her every inch, to bury himself deep inside her.

The press of her lips against his drove him wild, so he angled his head and took the kiss deeper. A disbelieving part of him expected her refusal, for her to push him away as before, her words no more than another ploy.

Instead of trying to break free at his hungry demands, Isabel leaned her body full against his, curled her hands around his neck and dragged him closer.

With his blood pounding hot, her every moan, her every sigh ignited a new wave of need. Desire, fueled by a lifetime of wanting, destroyed his logic. So he took, demanded, masterfully teased with tongue and teeth until her eyes grew blind with desire. It wasn't enough, he wanted more, he wanted her complete surrender, to take her up until she screamed his name in release.

The coolness of the past few hours fled as she moved her body against his.

With his mouth firmly possessing hers, he walked her backward until he trapped her against the wall near the fireplace. The growing warmth within the small space was but a trice of the heat pouring through his veins.

Duncan wedged his body firm against hers, leaving

her no doubt about his intent, of what they would share this night. He set a hand on each side of her head, effectively trapping her, then he broke the kiss.

The pure need swirling in her eyes matched that storming his body. "You will not leave me. Tonight, or ever."

The words spilled out before he could stop them. She gasped.

He blinked, and even before he registered the shock in her features, he realized he meant them.

Gazing into the soft curves of her face, the soul-searching amber eyes, the soft, full curve of her mouth was like creating a new man in him. Someone with hopes and wishes that lived on despite what life had thrown at him.

A shaky breath spilled from her parted lips. "Duncan—"

"Ever!" He claimed her mouth to seal his words. Merciless to her struggles, he seduced her, using every sensual tactic to drive her wild, until her body relaxed against his and she was once again kissing him back.

Inside him, fear that she would refuse him ebbed.

Whispering her name, while her unsteady breaths trembled from her lips, Duncan slowly skimmed his mouth along the soft curve of her jaw, loving her taste of woman and silk, how she arched with genuine pleasure at his every touch.

"Watch me," he whispered, wanting her like this, wild with need, her mind blazed with passion. And more.

Savoring this moment, their very first time together, he held her gaze as he slowly untied her garb.

He inched the loosened garb from her shoulders, relieved her of the layers, each one landing with a soft, satisfying plop on the dirt floor, until his fingertips grazed bare flesh.

She shivered, but with the way her eyes watched his, desire, not the cold embracing the falling night, ignited the response.

His gentle shove had the final, flimsy chemise joining the heap on the floor. The pendant around her neck, a lion in silver complemented by a background of deep red, hung between her breasts. Wallace's arms.

Before he could think to question the revelation, she stepped toward him and his thoughts shattered.

The muted glow cast by the firelight caressed her nakedness in a soft gold, in direct contrast as he stood before her fully clothed.

As if a parched lad offered the first glimpse of life-saving water, he drank in the sight of the soft curves of her body, the fullness of her breasts with taut, dusky peaks. Then his gaze swept lower, slowly. He lingered on the flatness of her stomach, then edged slowly downward to the amber curls lying in soft folds to shield her most precious gift.

He dragged in a raw breath. She was everything a man could ever dream of and more.

Beneath his steady gaze, her body began to tremble.

Painfully aroused, he looked up, met heated eyes filled with desire that matched his own. Duncan stayed the urge to release himself and drive into her in search of relief. This time, their first time, he wanted her blind with passion. When she cried her release, it would be his name on her lips, he who claimed her.

Except this time, she would not walk away.

Emotion welled up inside him to a painful ache. A need that went beyond physical attraction. She was Isabel.

She was his.

He splayed his hands on her shoulders, then slowly wove his fingers over her satiny skin, his own body trembling in anticipation. He cupped her breasts, savored the play of firelight upon her skin, the contrast of calloused hands to satin. He looked up.

Her mouth parted as if in surprise. Expectant, she watched him.

"Say you want me," he whispered, needing to hear the words, hear the desire in her voice.

"I want you, Duncan."

Slowly, he tasted her skin, the unique blend of woman and lavender infusing his every breath, savoring the soft roundness of her breasts. He drew her tip into his mouth, took until she arched against him.

While he worked her with his mouth, he skimmed his hands over the soft angles of her body, the flatness of her stomach, the sensitive flesh framing where he wanted to touch the most.

Her breath caught and she trembled as would an innocent.

But he only skimmed his mouth lightly against her skin, wanting to build the tension and the inevitable pleasure the waiting would bring. He continued to stroke her until her body trembled beneath, then he lowered his head and followed the wake of his hands.

She arched against his lips. "Duncan."

He knelt before her, catching her hips to frame her before him.

Redness crept up her face, a flush ignited by the fire of desire.

"You are amazing," he whispered, in awe of her precious response when the past three years had surely left her anything but innocent. He inhaled her scent, and his body burned straight to his groin.

His breaths shook as he skimmed his fingers over her most sensitive flesh, needing to see, to feel the slick softness within his hands. A soft moan tumbled from her throat as he caressed her slowly, soft, lazy circles feeling the texture, softness of her amber curls to the silky smoothness of her velvet skin.

Needing to see her, he placed his thumbs against her and slowly opened her to his view. Beautiful. Simply amazing. His nostrils flared at her scent, as one would with their mate. A powerful urge consumed him, to taste her, claim her to be his.

When he lowered his head toward her most intimate place, Isabel stiffened.

Eyes wide with shock, she grabbed his hair with her hands, halting his progress. "What are you doing?"

How could she not know? Surely Frasyer—no, he refused to taint the moment. "Relax."

"You cannot."

Her frantic words had him drawing back. Had she not learned the touch of a gentle lover?

Duncan took in her lips swollen with his kisses, the glazed look of pleasure in her eyes, how her pulse at the base of her neck raced.

A satisfied smile edged his mouth.

That he was not her first left a harsh taste in his

mouth, but he would not think of that. This night he would sear her mind with images of their intimacy.

"Aye, I can and will." He touched her softness, pleased to find her warm and wet. At her sharp intake of breath, Duncan glanced up.

Fear flickered in her eyes.

"I will not hurt you," he promised. "You can trust me."

"I-I know."

"Then what is wrong?"

She swallowed hard. "Naught."

There was, but he understood her shyness. "You are nervous."

Relief eased the lines on her face. "Very much so."

Which made sense. Untutored in the proper way of making love, to her, his actions would seem odd. Duncan skimmed his finger around his silken destination in a slow sweep. Her skin tightened beneath his touch. Trembled.

As if her body understood what her mind did not, Isabel leaned into his touch.

His body hot with need, he opened her to his view, took in her beautiful treasures, sleek with the evidence of her desire for him. He held her gaze as he leaned forward to taste.

More shock, then pleasure radiated in her eyes as he drew her into his mouth, teasing her with his tongue. She leaned her head back on a gasp.

The soft crackle of flames sounded as he plundered, using teeth and tongue until her body bowed beneath his every caress and her breaths grew shallow. Wanting more, for her to give him everything, he used his hands to tease her, exploiting the soft curves as he feasted.

She shuddered, the movements of her hips becoming uncontrollable.

He slid his finger within her slick heat, matching her rhythm.

"Duncan!"

"Let yourself go," he urged, wanting her like this, her body lost to sensation, finding her release for him, knowing that he had brought her this intensity.

Another shudder tore through her. Her muscles tightened around his fingers. He caught her sensitive bud within his teeth, and she cried out her release.

With her entire body shaking, Isabel sagged against the wall. Her face glowed with a combination of daze and awe. Soft moans fell from her lips.

His body on fire, Duncan stood, drew her to him, enjoying her every shiver, the catch in her breath as she rode the remainder of her release. He ignored the hard demands of his body to take and kissed her slowly, softly across the sheen of dampness on her brow.

"I ne-never suspected," she whispered brokenly, "that one person could touch another so."

How could she possibly not know? Ruthlessly, Duncan focused on the moment. On Isabel.

"Pleasure does not come merely in the joining," he said hoarsely, "but in the touch, the building, the anticipation of the journey shared." He skimmed his hand along her cheek, then ever so slowly, slid the pad of his thumb along her bottom lip to curve around until he lifted her face to meet his. "Feel your senses. Experience the rush of heat. Revel at how your passion builds, how every part of you comes alive in the building of pleasure."

He leaned down to catch her nipple with his mouth, swirl his tongue around the taut skin in a slow circle, again savor her silken taste until she groaned with pleasure. Then, and only then, did he look up and meet her eyes glazed with passion.

"This night," he whispered, "I will show you the many ways a man can make love to a woman."

Her blush deepened at his words.

Duncan savored her shyness as he roamed over the soft curve of her shoulder, then sliding down, teasing with his tongue, nipping gently, enjoying the hitch of her breath, how her heartbeat pounded in her chest.

"Duncan?"

Her rough, passion-filled voice curved a smile on his mouth. He left a trail of kisses across her neck, marveling at her silky softness.

"Duncan." The soft tremble in her words sent his own pulse racing.

"Aye."

"You . . . You are still dressed," she said, her voice shaky.

"I am at that," he murmured as he knelt on one knee and framed her waist with his hands, pressing a kiss against the flat of her stomach.

She reached over as if to stop him, but he caught her hand. "I am not done with you yet." Before she could speak, he lifted her and carried her to the bed.

Lying naked before him, Isabel made to cover herself.

"No, let me see all of you."

Had he not already seen all there was to see? Touched everything there was to touch?

Isabel hesitated, lulled by the heat in his eyes. She'd anticipated making love to Duncan, but in her mind it had been hurried, frenzied, a mating rather than a deep joining of the bodies.

Never had she anticipated it being so much more.

Had he truly done those intimately wicked things to her? Had she truly let him? Her body quaked with the aftereffects she wasn't sure she would recover from.

Was this normal? Did all women find such enjoyment?

Emotion welled up in her at Duncan's thoughtfulness, at how he caressed her, watched her as if something to be cherished—his reverence something she'd believed she'd lost.

With her nerves receding, the warmth of moments ago flooded her body, tingles of pleasure rippling through her to tease her most sensitive places. She embraced each sensual shiver, the warmth pooling in her most private place, the rush of anticipation coursing through her body.

Never had she known being with a man would be so exquisite. Heat infused her as she remembered the intimacy of how he'd touched her. How he'd used his tongue with such indecency. And his fingers. He'd caressed her everywhere, stroked her until he left her blind with need. Even now, tremors from her release rumbled through her in silent ecstasy.

Wanting him to see her, Isabel uncovered her breasts. His gaze riveted on her, the intensity of his desire leaving her aching with anticipation. He scanned her body with mind-spinning slowness.

Wherever his gaze roamed, her skin fluttered with excitement. She recognized the sweep of anxiousness, how her body tightened in readiness for Duncan's touch. Was her response what he would expect from a seasoned woman as he believed her to be?

Nerves wove through her bravado. Duncan had known many women. Had he discovered her innocence? Unsure, Isabel started to look away.

Duncan caught her face in hands. Frowned. "What is wrong?"

Ashamed, she shook her head. "I know so little about the joining," she whispered. "You are a man who has known the pleasures to be found in making love. And I . . ."

"Have been treated poorly."

She looked at him then, the flicker of anger, of remembrance on his face in opposition to the softness of his words.

"No," he said when she made to speak. "I do not want to know any details. At least for this night."

Isabel swallowed hard, then nodded.

Tomorrow would come soon enough, and with the daylight, the reality that kept them apart.

He lay by her side, brushed a swath of hair from her brow. "This night is for us." He kissed her gently, with urgency until doubts left her mind and her body filled with a languid heat. On a soft groan, he placed gentle kisses across her cheek.

"Your clothes," she murmured through sensation.

"A fair request," he replied through the next kiss. He stood. With infinite slowness, he removed his garb piece by excruciating piece. Muscles bunched, rippled up his arms and chest as he withdrew his shirt, exposing his hewn frame. A body made for war. A body that knew how to make love to a woman.

Piece by piece, he exposed himself to her. With his eyes locked on hers, he slowly untied the final garment shielding him from her view. Loosened, he slid his thumbs beneath the woven cloth, paused, then released. The tangle of cloth dropped to the floor atop the last of his garb.

He stood before her naked, totally exposed. Taut muscle honed to sheer perfection crafted a warrior's chest, angled down to where blond hair narrowed to a tangle of twists leading to where he stood readied for her.

Heat stroked her cheeks as she looked her fill. His masculinity jutted proudly from a profusion of unruly curls that added to the power he exuded. She swallowed, trembling, unable to look away.

Duncan shifted and she jerked her head up to find him watching her, his gaze, dark, intense, and sensual.

"You are beautiful," she breathed.

Desire kindled in his eyes as he knelt before her, his gaze never leaving hers. He traced his finger in a slow trail from the pad of her bottom lip across her chin, along her throat to pause where her pulse raced wildly.

"As are you." His hand skimmed along her shoulders, curved to flow beneath her breast. "Touch me, Isabel."

Curious, she reached out. His muscled body quivered beneath her fingers.

He caught her hand within his, set it over his heart; it pounded beneath her palm. "My tremors are from the wanting of you."

He sealed his words with a kiss, one meant to seduce, to excite, to wash away all thoughts of everything but him. She savored the thrill of her naked body against his, the roughness of his maleness pressing against her soft, sensitive flesh.

Her hands slid over the hard planes of his body, the taut muscles exciting her more.

"Isabel," he whispered as he positioned himself intimately against her. Propped on his elbows, he watched her a moment before he dipped to nuzzle her neck. "You taste like seasoned honey made only for me."

With Isabel's moans of passion firing his blood, Duncan pressed her onto the bed, enjoying her every shiver, her every twist of delight as he teased her with his tongue. Her taste exploded in his mind, a combination of innocence and woman, an intoxicating mix that he wanted forever.

Though there was a mix of questions and contradictions, these past few days with her had taught him that he still cared for Isabel. Now, with her in his arms, her taste potent in his mouth, he realized his feelings for her went deeper than he'd ever believed possible.

A shiver stole through him, but it had naught to do with how the slide of her body against his drove him wild, or that for the first time since she left he felt whole. The emotions storming him were more than he'd expected. More than he'd ever anticipated feeling for Isabel ever again.

A sword's wrath, he loved her.

Except this time, there was no turning back. He'd not seen the moment coming, or if he had, he'd deluded himself with thoughts of caring, of his feelings of those growing up with her, of having wanted to marry her. How could he be such a fool to think he could ever have stopped loving Isabel?

The demands of his body moments before, the urge to take her, claim her, deepened to a fierce level. Aye, he wanted her, would make her his, but this time, he was offering her the greatest gift.

That of his heart.

If he was a fool to love her, so be it. He loved her too much to give her up now.

With his mind steeped in emotions he'd never again believed he'd experience, he poured them into his every touch, his every kiss. His fingers teased, lingered across her sensitive skin, wanting her to know what she made him feel. How he felt, for her.

With incredible care, he wove his hands over her skin, sliding along the flat of her stomach to the gift she'd given him this night. This time, when he reached his destination, the shock in her eyes of before darkened to needy expectation.

He inhaled her woman's scent as he opened her fullness for his view. "You are so ready for me." Unable to hold back, he tasted her, the warmth of her body's invitation, his own body pounding its need.

"Duncan," she gasped as he slowly suckled her most private place, his tongue teasing, then swirling to outline where she pulsed for him.

He pressed his thumb against the moist walls of her sheath, and her hips raised in response.

With her body writhing beneath his, silently begging for release, Duncan aligned his body over hers, his hardness pressing intimately against the warmth of her dewy entrance.

Glazed with passion, Isabel watched him, her breaths short and coming fast. She caught his hips, pulled him closer. "I need you so much."

The pulse of her warmth throbbed against his sensitive shaft, testing his will. He held on to his control, barely. Covering her mouth with his own, he drew her into a long, drugging kiss.

Need built within him like a river gorged. As he inched deeper, Isabel cried out. She jerked and her body began contracting around him. Swept away by emotion, he pulled back and drove deep.

The slight resistance was his only warning as he tore through Isabel's innocence. He didn't miss the flicker of pain tangled within the passion.

Her slick walls tightened around him. Desire tore through his thoughts, suffocating all but the elemental need to take her. So he moved, withdrew to submerge himself in her heat, until his strokes grew fast and his mind blurred with the taking. Somewhere in the blinding haze of need, Isabel's release broke his fragile hold.

Duncan poured into her, his body racked with blissful spasms that left him drained. Exhausted. He crumpled to her side. Out of sheer reaction he drew her to him, cradled against his nakedness.

Next to him, her breathing calmed. The rapid pace of her heartbeat slowed to a steady, normal pace when this moment was anything but.

Tears shimmered in Isabel's eyes, but her emotion couldn't navigate through the dark fury building within Duncan's soul.

He wished they were simply lovers, not caught up in a web of deceit so he could relish lying in the arms of the woman he loved.

Loved.

Bitterness tainted the beauty thoughts of the word should bring. Pain twisted inside him. "How," Duncan asked with lethal calm, "could you still be a virgin?"

Chapter 17

"No more lies," Duncan said between clenched teeth. "You will explain everything now!"

At the anger churning on his face, Isabel's guilt at hiding her innocence and about Frasyer doubled. "Yes, I did lie to you," she whispered, aching inside, "but I had a reason." She reached out to touch him.

As if scalded with hot water, Duncan released her. He sat on the edge of the bed, his face cast in harsh lines. "A reason for lying to me these past three years? A reason for convincing me that you were Frasyer's whore? What possible reason could you have for denying our love a chance to grow? Nay, no need to explain," he seethed, "the reason is clear. You wanted Frasyer's wealth more than you wanted me."

"No!"

With her body still throbbing from their joining, she wanted to weep. She had envisioned the beauty of making love with Duncan, of the memories she would take with her and cherish. Now, because of her deceit, the consummation of their love, a sacred moment to revere, was destroyed.

She drew a steadying breath and sat beside him, not touching him, the smoothness of his gleaming skin marred by the cruel scar of his recent injury, another to add to those faded from previous battles.

"I have never loved Frasyer or was lured by his wealth," she quietly said.

He glared at her in clear disbelief. "Prove it," he said flatly. "I offer you one final chance to be honest. To tell me why you have lied to me in a way that has never left my mind. By God, Isabel, had you tried to hurt me, you could not have chosen a straighter mark than through your betrayal!"

His gaze strafed her still naked body. "Now I understand the innocence I sensed. How is it that he has never savored what I have tasted, never touched you with a lover's hand? Isabel"—his voice seemed to catch—"if you ever loved me—nay, if there was anything true about our prior relationship, you will be, for once, completely honest about what has transpired between you and Frasyer!"

Looking at him, hearing the torment in his voice, the sadness in his eyes tore her apart. Oh, God, how could she have done this to Duncan, to the man she loved with every inch of her life? She folded her hands before her. Of course, she'd had no choice, but her soul wept for her role in all that they had lost.

But what if she told him the truth? What would happen then? Duncan, too, was not a man to give up what was his lightly. And she now saw that, however much he fought it, he knew they still belonged to each other. Would he confront Frasyer and force him into a fight if he learned of the tragic events?

For so long she had tried to protect Duncan. Look at what her efforts had brought. More confusion. More pain. Her mouth dry, she ran her tongue across her lips. Maybe it was time to put more faith in Duncan as a man.

She drew in a nervous breath and exhaled. "Three years past, I was so excited as it neared our time to wed. I loved you so much and looked forward to our life together. But as you know, since my mother's death, my father has struggled to go on with his life. Raising two children on his own compounded his strife."

"He loved you both," Duncan agreed.

"Aye, but we were a reminder of the woman he loved. I have my mother's smile, and Symon has—had our mother's eyes." She closed her eyes as the memories of Symon's protectiveness swarmed her, his outrage when she'd left to become Frasyer's mistress.

She reached up and worried the pendant around her neck bearing Wallace's arms as she continued. "As the years passed, my father's broken heart never healed."

"And he turned to drink," Duncan said, his expression softening a fraction.

She nodded. "He tried to be a good father." Her heart ached as the memories of the past tumbled through her, her father's struggles, his tears when he believed no one was around. "But hazed by drink, often his choices were poor."

Isabel caught Duncan's gaze, needing him to understand how much she regretted hurting him.

"Then I met you. You will never know how much during those troubled years your friendship meant to me. When we fell in love, indeed, it was a miracle. I believed . . . I foolishly believed with you I would find happily ever after."

She dropped her hands to her sides, then looked at the fire where yellow-orange flames flickered upward. "Late one evening, a week before you and I were to wed, my father came home drunk." She shook her head. "Distraught, his eyes empty, his body slumped in defeat. I had never seen him so broken, except when my mother died."

She paused to steady herself. "Before he spoke a word, I knew something horrible had happened. Sobbing, he begged me for forgiveness, even before he began to explain. When I eventually pulled the reason for his distress from him, I wished to God I had not." Even now the memories of that night tore her apart. The anger had come as the life she'd planned shattered around her like a cold rain.

Tears filled her eyes and her body began to tremble.

"Isabel."

The gentleness of Duncan's voice had the tears flowing faster. She shook her head.

"Look at me, please."

On a shaky breath she turned toward him, the softening of his gaze tearing her apart.

"Tell me."

She wet her lips. "Th-that night my father had gambled with several men, one of them being Frasyer—a man who detests you."

He nodded, slowly, thoughtfully. The beginnings of awareness flickered in his eyes. "A hatred he has made clear since I beat him after a practice spar in our youth."

"That night my father lost heavily to Frasyer, gold my father did not have. He begged the earl not to take his home, promising to do anything in payment." Her voice wavered, but afraid she'd fall apart, Isabel didn't stop. "Frasyer's request was so unthinkable that at first my father refused. But Frasyer gave my father until morning to agree to his offer, or he would be arrested and cast into debtor's prison for life. A proud man, I believe my father would have ended his life before he allowed himself to be locked away."

"What was Frasyer's request to Lord Caelin?" His voice had become a rough whisper, as if Duncan suspected the truth, but couldn't bring himself to voice it.

Tears burned in her eyes as if time had spun back to that terrible night. "There was something Frasyer wanted more than money. That only I could save our home and my father from spending the rest of his life imprisoned."

Her words echoed into the somber silence, fractured by the crackle of the fire burning cheerfully within the hearth.

Duncan's face paled. "Frasyer asked that you become his mistress?"

"Yes, except he made me swear to secrecy the reason why. He wanted you to believe I'd left you for coin, for a man of more wealth. He swore that if I ever revealed the truth to you, you would be killed. Besides my father, Symon was the only other person who knew the truth."

The transformation on Duncan's face was chilling

to watch. Heedless of his nakedness, he launched to his feet. "The bastard. I will kill him!"

Fear piled atop the emotions swirling within her. "Do not say that. I have been trying to protect you."

He rounded on her. "I do not need your protection now any more than I did then. I needed your love." His eyes blazed hot, agitated, as if he itched to strike something. "You should have trusted me with the truth."

"And what would you have done? A knight against a powerful lord. A man whose passions guided him, a man who acted before he mulled things through." Duncan started to speak, but she continued, needing him to understand, regardless of his fury. "I wanted to tell you, desperately. But I knew if I did, you would confront Frasyer."

"And die?"

His sarcasm fed her anger. "Do you not think I believed you could best him in a fair fight? Aye, of that I had no doubt. But in this Frasyer had proven that he would not fight fair. Though he swore if I told you, he would kill you, I also believed his methods would not be those of an honorable man. Do you not understand, I loved you too much to endanger your life? I loved my family too much to allow them to lose their home and leave them in disgrace."

Duncan struggled to accept everything. "So you became Frasyer's mistress," Duncan stated, her story severing the tangle of emotions in his mind. "How could your father ask that of you?"

"He did not," she corrected. "I made the decision on my own, knowing it was the only choice we had."

Everything made sense now, her shocking decision to become Frasyer's mistress, her father's desperate grief when he'd explained Isabel's whereabouts to an enraged Duncan.

And Symon. Oh, God. Over the past three years he'd witnessed Symon's silent struggles since Isabel had become Frasyer's mistress, had tried to convince him to open up to him, but Symon never would. Each day Isabel spent in Frasyer's control would have destroyed her brother more.

Duncan began to pace, hurting, aching, but mostly furious at himself for not suspecting there was a deeper motivation than money behind Isabel's actions.

He stopped. Turned to face her. "You are a virgin. Or were. I—" He blew out a rough breath. "We all believed you were Frasyer's mistress."

Heat slid up her cheeks, but she didn't turn away and his love for her grew. "Initially, I as well. But he never touched me in that way or any other. At first I was convinced that all he wanted was to have me so you could not. Over the past year, I overheard a couple of the knights talking when they thought they were alone. It would seem that in a battle years before, Frasyer was injured. They expected him to die. Somehow he lived, but the wound left him scarred and unable to father a child. I owed his embarrassment to his paternal inability as to the reason he has left me untouched."

The news should have relieved him. Instead, guilt weighed on his mind. "I have blamed you wrongly."

"No more than I have blamed myself." She slid her hands up and down her arms. "Perhaps one day we can move past this."

A muscle worked in Duncan's jaw. "You are too forgiving. These past three years I have satisfied myself with believing the worst about you."

She shook her head. "I let you. No, I wanted you to. Duncan"—she said his name softly—"you have no idea how many times I wished, I prayed, things could have been different between us."

"They will," he vowed, emotion vibrating through him.

"No, however much I desire it, nothing has changed. After this is over, I must return to Frasyer."

"No! You are mine." The thought of losing her again turned his thoughts dark, vicious. "I am my own man. I have my own resources. I would rather fight Frasyer to my death than have you go back to him, thinking to protect me."

She rose, a naked nymph that sent a surge of desire racing through him. "But I must also protect my father, and he depends on me to deliver the Bible and save him from certain death. He will depend on me again to keep him from going to debtor's prison. And Bible or no, if I refuse to return to Frasyer as his mistress, my father will hang."

He shook his had. "There must be another way. There are people we can petition—"

"I would give anything if there were, but my father assured me that he'd pleaded with everyone he knew when he fell into debt." She held out her hands in a gesture of frustration, dropped them to her sides. "There is no one. All the men I love have been torn from me."

The sadness in her voice battered his heart. Muscles bunched beneath his skin. He clenched his fists, wanting to scream his frustration, his mind sorting through options. His brothers would help, as would Griffin. With Griffin's political link to King Edward, anything was possible.

Could he impose on his brother-in-law's position with the English king to intercede?

The rebels needed the information Griffin covertly fed them under the cloak of his secret identity, Wulfe. How could he put his own needs and wants against those of a whole kingdom?

He could not.

Agonized, he pulled free and strode to stand before the hearth where flames greedily consumed the dry tinders. The odor of wood filled the space, a warm welcome to an empty heart.

What did he do now—give up, walk away from Isabel after realizing he still loved her?

He hadn't even told her how he felt. What good would revealing that he loved her do? It would change nothing if and when they parted, making both of their pain worse for the brevity of its acknowledged existence.

However much he was disappointed that she had not turned to him, he found himself almost humiliated by the truth they faced.

Even now, three years after Frasyer had bartered for Isabel, with his sole intent for gaining her to hurt Duncan, he could do nothing. Bedamned, she was naught but an innocent pawn in a brutal game. Anger mounted atop his frustration until it was if he'd burst.

A sigh sounded behind him.

He did not turn.

Long moments passed.

The shuffle of sheets announced that Isabel had

withdrawn to the bed. A bed where he'd lain with her. A bed where they'd made love. A bed where he'd taken her innocence. Duncan leaned his forearm against the stone hearth and bowed his head.

A virgin.

A ludicrous notion claimed his mind. What if she now carried his child? An ache built in his chest. He envisioned Isabel round with his child. A girl—one with her mother's smile, a father's pride.

A child Frasyer would claim as his.

He curled his fist against the stone. Nay, if indeed Isabel was pregnant, Frasyer would not claim his child. Whatever it took, Duncan would have Isabel back.

But how?

He stared at the yellow flames reaching toward the darkness of the cold night. For the first time in his life, Duncan was unsure of what next to do.

The howl of the wind woke him. Duncan surveyed the blackened space with a warrior's eye. Shadows fell with meager relief, broken by the low, blue flames of the burning coals. Otherwise, he saw nothing to alert him of imminent danger.

The soft warmth of skin pressed against him. Isabel. Long after she'd fallen asleep, without any answers as to how he could free her from Frasyer, he'd climbed into bed beside her. While she'd slept, he'd held her close and wished for a miracle.

A hopeless wish if ever there was one.

What had started as a simple rescue mission had tumbled into a fine quagmire—one without answers. With the amount she'd stated that Lord Caelin had lost in his gaming to Frasyer, it was even beyond his brother Seathan's reach. Then there was the added expense of recovering Lord Caelin's home.

Duncan drew Isabel against him, the steady beat of her heart beckoning him to make love with her and never let her go. The desperation of losing her had him kissing the silky skin of her jaw and slowly working his way up to tease her lips.

Soft sighs tumbled to moans of need as she slowly awakened. "Duncan?"

Her soft, sleep-roughened voice thrummed through him. He covered her mouth and kissed her with infinite slowness. With each caress he showed her what he could never tell her. With their bodies entwined, they each found their release.

Isabel snuggled up against him, his heart still racing from their joining. "I love you, Duncan."

Deeply moved, wanting to reply the same, instead he drew her closer. Moments passed. A sleepy smile grazed her lips, then she closed her eyes. Her soft even breaths assured him that she'd fallen back asleep.

Restless, he slipped from the bed. Coals glowed dimly in the fireplace so he applied himself to the simple task of building the fire, blowing on the coals until they ignited the dry timber. Flames built, snapping cheerily. He sat and watched as the fire continued to grow and warm the room, but inside coldness clung to his soul.

He rubbed his temple where a pounding was gaining ground. From the corner of his eye, he caught sight of the tip of the Bible peeking from the leather sack.

If only it held the answers he needed. He sighed.

The Bible held the information to save Lord Caelin. That would have to be enough for now.

Another blast of wind buffeted the side of the crofter's hut, promising their travel this day would be arduous at best. He walked to the slit used as a window, lifted the heavy tarp and looked out. Darkness clung to the sky, casting the surrounding trees and landscape into vague outlines that muted into sheer blackness. Hours remained until the first rays of sun would sever the night.

He looked toward Isabel. She slept soundly, what he needed to do as well, but with his mind spinning, he doubted if he'd find any more sleep this night.

The tip of the Bible again caught his attention. What exactly was the proof Lord Caelin spoke of? A chilling idea crept through his mind. What if whatever the drink-addled Lord Caelin claimed as proof of his innocence was naught more than a worthless writ? Or in his skewed mind, had he re-called evidence that didn't exist?

He glanced at Isabel, thankful to find her lost in sleep. Please, God, let proof of Lord Caelin's inno-cence exist. With his hands trembling in fear, Duncan withdrew the Bible.

On a prayer, he opened the aged leather, worn smooth by overuse. A hint of frankincense greeting him. Hundreds of pages of yellowed parchment, filled with handwritten inscriptions lay before him. Notations penned on some pages caught Duncan's eye as did the folded edges on others. With each marked page he reviewed, he found naught but writings of a believer, a man struggling to under-stand why God had taken a loving wife from him.

His fingers flew through the rest of the pages, but

found not a torn scrap or any other document that represented anything bearing proof of Lord Caelin's innocence. Duncan flipped through the last few pages of parchment, each one driving his sense of doom deeper. As he turned over the last page, his worst fear was recognized.

Nothing.

No proof existed.

He closed his eyes. Their entire journey, the dangers he and Isabel had faced, was all for naught. A lump built in his throat as he turned toward Isabel. He rubbed the thick leather of the back cover. How was he going to tell her? The news would break her heart. Bedamned, why had her father told her such a lie?

Was Lord Caelin drunk at the time of the telling? A hysterical laugh festered Duncan's throat. He'd never thought to ask. No, if her father had been inebriated when cornered by Frasyer and hauled away, she would have told him.

So why did Lord Caelin want her to fetch the Bible? After Frasyer had taken it, one would think he would have scoured it to ensure it held nothing of worth.

It didn't make sense.

Nerves had him tracing his thumb across the hand-sewn stitching securing the leather to the hard cover of the back. Frustrated, he followed the intricate stitching.

Odd. Instead of a steady seam sewn around the back cover to bind it, the threads made an odd, intricate pattern. No, the strange sewing was only along the inner side near the bindings. Unless a person was looking for it, they would miss the finely sewn detail.

He stilled. A hidden compartment? Was the proof they sought inside? Relief swamped Duncan. Thank God.

Upon closer inspection, he found the hidden indent within the fabric that allowed him entrance to the secret compartment. He reached inside. His fingers grazed several pages of parchment.

His heart pounded as he withdrew the aged documents. He unfolded the fragile sheets, noted the dates starting the various entries, recognizing Lord Caelin's writing. He frowned. A diary?

With a sinking feeling in his gut, he began to read the penned notes. Upon the first entry, he stilled. Stopped. Reread it.

Sweat beaded on his brow as he glanced over to where Isabel slept in peace, ignorant to the magnitude of the documents he held.

'Twas no wonder Lord Caelin desired to have the Bible delivered into safe hands.

The reason had nothing to do with Lord Caelin's needing proof of his innocence. It had everything to do with Isabel.

Hands shaking, Duncan continued to read each dated entry, the decisions made, the risks taken by Lord Caelin throughout the time he'd raised Isabel humbling Duncan more.

He finished the last sheet, closed his eyes and hung his head. Oh, God, Lord Caelin wasn't Isabel's father.

No, that honor belonged to Sir William Wallace.

Chapter 18

Stunned, Duncan stared at the worn pieces of parchment, then turned toward the woman who lay in the bed.

A bed they'd shared.

Was Isabel truly William Wallace's daughter?

He again scanned the pages documenting in detail how Wallace, desperate to protect his only child from threats, had been forced to give up Isabel while he fought for Scotland's freedom.

But how could a father give up his daughter?

With each line Duncan read, he felt the enormity of Wallace's sacrifice in leaving his infant daughter with Lord Caelin, how he'd asked his friend to play the role of Isabel's father until their country's safety was secured. Each day apart from Isabel had torn a piece away from Wallace's soul, proven by his secret visits to Lord Caelin, when in fact he'd come to see his daughter.

Duncan shook his head, awed by the sacrifices of both men.

He stared at Isabel, her hair the color of aged

whisky fanning over the bed, how her chest rose and fell peacefully with each breath, her face soft with the innocence of those who slept. Did she truly not know?

Duncan flipped madly, scouring pages that detailed Wallace and Lord Caelin's protective scheme. Nay, it would appear that she did not, as the men had skillfully shielded the knowledge from her throughout her life.

The name scrawled atop the next document had Duncan catching his breath.

Frasyer's name. What was this?

The parchment made a crinkling sound as he pulled it closer. His mind reeled at Lord Caelin's next admittance.

Sir William Wallace and Lord Caelin had set up Lord Frasyer.

Since King Edward had stepped up his search to find and kill Wallace, fearful a tie between Isabel and Wallace would be discovered, Lord Caelin and Wallace had agreed on a plan. Lord Caelin had pretended to be drunk and, on a bet, had purposely lost an enormous amount of money on that fateful night three years past to Frasyer.

Aware of Frasyer's hatred of Duncan, of the earl's impotence due to a battle wound, Lord Caelin had deliberately offered Isabel as Frasyer's mistress instead of payment, in keeping with the well-planned tactics.

Confident, cocky, and believing he'd won a great victory by claiming Duncan's betrothed as his whore, Frasyer had greedily accepted. Now, even if King Edward learned that Wallace had a daughter, they'd hidden Isabel in the one place English troops would never search.

By pretending to sacrifice Isabel, her father and Lord Caelin had actually saved her from greater danger. The lengths both men had gone to in keeping Isabel safe, their bravery, left Duncan humbled.

Aware of Isabel's love for Duncan, ink written by a trembling hand as Lord Caelin had penned the entry revealed his agony in the decision to trick Isabel into moving in with Frasyer. With deep regret, he had used her big heart to sway her decision to become Frasyer's mistress. In addition, though he wanted to lessen Duncan's heartache, Lord Caelin had worried Duncan would confront Frasyer if he learned the truth, a risk he, nor Wallace, could take.

Emotion tightened Duncan's throat as he carefully folded the pages of parchment. His fingers trembled as he slid them inside the secret compartment and secured it. He closed his eyes, the magnitude of the knowledge held within the Bible storming him.

Lord Caelin had suffered along with his daughter. No, not his real daughter. Isabel was of William Wallace's blood.

If anyone would have told Duncan prior, he would have dismissed the telling as a poor joke made. He stroked his thumb along the worn leather. Truth of the fact lay hidden within, knowledge that must never fall into the wrong hands.

He released a harsh breath. If King Edward ever learned of Isabel's connection to Wallace, he would use her to lure Wallace to his death. Without a strong warrior to lead the rebel forces, Scotland's fragile hold on freedom would lay in jeopardy.

What would Isabel think once she knew? Should he tell her? He studied her as she lay peacefully within the straw bed. Wisps of whisky-colored hair curled around her cheek, her mouth caught in an innocent pout as she slept. She looked as if she was a wayward faerie who'd found peace.

No, until the ledger was in safe hands, he must shield her from the truth. If by chance they were caught, and if she knew of her birthright, Frasyer might torture information from her that could seal Wallace's fate, as well as her own.

What should he do with the Bible? Lord Caelin had asked that the Bible be delivered to Lord Monceaux. His reasoning now made even more sense. With Lord Caelin's close bond with Wallace, Lord Caelin must be aware that Lord Monceaux is a spy for Scotland—only known as Wulfe.

The pieces fell into place in Duncan's mind. With Lord Caelin's capture, unable to protect the Bible's secret, he had let Isabel believe his innocence was hidden within.

A lie.

A lie to protect Isabel.

A lie that would inspire her to recover the Bible from Frasyer's hands and deliver the secret of her parentage to safety.

A wry smile played on Duncan's lips before falling away. If indeed Lord Caelin knew of Lord Monceaux's secret life, Duncan also found it intriguing that the English lord's sister, Nichola, had married Duncan's brother Alexander. An unexpected mix to be sure.

With Lord Monceaux's sister having married Duncan's brother, Duncan had come to know the

English lord well. Though King Edward's adviser for the Scots, Griffin upheld what he believed right, the reason he'd become a spy for Scotland.

Aye, he would honor Lord Caelin's request that the Bible be delivered to Lord Monceaux. He'd trust Griffin with his life.

Duncan turned toward Isabel, aching at what she had endured, some of it unknowingly at the hands of two well-meaning fathers.

The soft glow of flames caressed the gentle curve of her face, illuminating her soft lips parted in sleep.

God, how he loved her.

An innocent in so many ways still. He wanted to teach her the pleasures of the flesh. He wanted to love her, body and soul until they lay in each other's arms exhausted. No, more than that.

He wanted her in his life.

Forever.

Except William Wallace being her father changed everything. Assuming the mess with Frasyer ever was resolved, how could he, a mere knight, marry a woman who was the daughter of Scotland's true leader?

His fragile hope of creating a life with her shattered.

Last night's anger at finding her a virgin paled in comparison to the challenges they now faced. The gentle buffeting of wind against the crofter's hut, a soft, lonely sound, matched the emotions churning in his soul.

"Duncan?"

Isabel's sleepy voice had him glancing up. She'd propped herself up on the bed, her eyes groggy. As she slowly awakened, her gaze trailed over his naked body boldly and dark with need.

Desire built inside him, a fact as natural as his each breath. With her it would always be so. "Aye?"

"What is wrong?"

If she only knew. He slid the Bible into the sack. "I cannot sleep."

She frowned, her glance briefly flicking toward the sack before turning to him. "Your wound is aching?"

"Nay." Aching didn't begin to describe the intensity of what he was feeling. "Restless is all."

A tense silence fell between them.

He sighed. Was it only hours ago that they'd made love for the first time? With his mind raging in turmoil, their joining seemed ages ago.

"Will you be coming back to bed?"

The desire in her voice slashed another chink in his willpower. In but hours they would leave the crofter's hut for Rothfield Castle. Later, when he departed Griffin's home, due to Isabel's heritage, the real chance existed that they may never be this private, this open, with each other again.

Her, the secret daughter of Scotland's most powerful rebel and, as yet, trapped as his enemy's mistress.

Him, a knight with no claim save his reputation and a fool's dreams.

Aware her true father was William Wallace, and knowing the unpredictable risk that Frasyer posed, if he had any doubts about her never returning to the earl before, they ended now. Regardless of what it took, she would never go back to that bastard.

The snap of the fire crackled softly in the silence, a subtle reminder that they were alone. Whatever happened once they left, they had the rest of this night. Precious hours until they would have to face the world again.

And return to their lives.

Overwhelmed by emotion, he took her hand and pressed his brow against their entwined fingers, needing to find the right words to explain his feelings for her.

"Last night," Duncan started, then looked down.

As he struggled to find words, taking in the paleness of Duncan's face, Isabel panicked. Did he feel guilty about taking her virginity?

"I am so sorry," she whispered, "I never wanted to lie to you."

He lifted his head, his green eyes ensnaring hers. "Do not be sorry. We are both but pawns to a greater purpose."

Softness eased the worry across his brow, his gaze so intense, a look so tender, she wanted to lean against him and have him hold her forever.

They had until dawn. For the rest of her life, she must make that enough.

Isabel drew Duncan's hand to her breast, and his fingers trembled across her tender flesh. "Make love with me." At her request, angst flashed on his face, a desperation she'd never witnessed before. A chill shot through her. "What is wrong?"

"It is that I need you so much more than I had ever believed possible."

The sincerity of his words should have offered her relief, more so in light of his anger but hours ago, except she sensed something awry. What had changed between then and now? Or were her nerves spinning troubles that weren't there? They had these few precious hours until they would leave. She refused to lose them to her doubts.

On a half groan, he drew her to him, his kiss tasting of need, but tainted with a new sense of urgency. Isabel ignored her worry and gave herself completely, savoring his every touch upon her skin. She loved him, needed him, wanted this intimacy. In but hours they would arrive at Lord Monceaux's and deliver the Bible. Then her father would be freed.

After, sadly, she must return to Frasyer.

So she lost herself to sensation as Duncan made love to her, the gentle skim of his fingers upon her curves, how he used his tongue to tease, then satisfy. Beneath his skilled hands, she found her release, but as if a man driven, with slow, mind-splintering strokes, he guided her up again until the well of feelings burst, again taking her under. Only when the flames within the hearth had burned low did Duncan join her to find his own release.

After, he rolled to his side and drew her into his arms. The steady beat of his heart echoed in her mind, his even breathing comforting her further. She could lay here forever. Happier than she could have ever imagined, with her body sated and a lethargic wash thrumming through her, she gave way to the lure of sleep.

A gust of wind slammed against the crofter's hut; Isabel started. She blinked the wisps of sleep from her eyes and turned to Duncan, but where he'd lain by her side it was empty.

And cold.

She sat up. He sat before the fire. The troubled

look on his face, the way he clutched the Bible in his hands stilled the teasing words on her tongue.

"Duncan?"

He turned toward her. The strained expression on his face eased. "You are awake then."

She swallowed hard, not missing the tension within his voice. "The wind woke me."

"It is picking up again."

Again? Hadn't he gone back to sleep as she had? "Why do you have the Bible?"

His mouth tightened. He shrugged. "No reason." He stowed the bound volume within the leather sack as if unimportant, but she caught the whitening of his knuckles as he tightened his hold.

Trepidation built in her throat. "You have found something within the Bible." It wasn't a question.

Silence.

"Duncan?"

He shoved to his feet, his expression stoic. "The sun has begun to rise. We need to depart for Rothfield Castle."

She sat up. "Not without your telling me what you found."

"There is naught to be afraid of."

"I do not believe you." She looked at the Bible shielded within the sack, her heart pounding. "Tell me."

His jaw tightened in a stubborn set. "There is no time for discussion. Once we have arrived at Rothfield Castle will be soon enough."

"Soon enough? Duncan, the Bible is mine." She held out her hand. "Give it to me."

He shook his head. "I cannot."

Anger shot through her. Isabel shoved to the

edge of the bed. The slide of cool air against her bare skin had her grabbing her gown and donning it. Whatever he refused to tell her indeed had to do with the Bible. A strangled thought flickered in her mind. Her heart slammed against her chest. It couldn't be.

She stilled and prayed she was wrong. "Duncan, tell me there is proof of my father's innocence."

"Isabel—"

"Do not keep secrets between us!"

His face darkened and his mouth tightened into an ominous frown. "Secrets?" he demanded. "You have not trusted me since a week before our betrothal and have lied to me ever since. Yet you dare issue me such a dictate?"

He had a point. Yet she shook her head. "Your anger is justified, but that does not change what news of importance you are keeping from me."

"It does not." He stared at her a long moment. "You said that you loved me. Now I am asking for your trust."

She frowned. "You always had that."

"Nay, if you had trusted me, when you learned of your father's predicament, you would have turned to me for help."

"I told you my reasons."

"Aye, that you dismissed me as having any ability to have helped you or your father."

Heat stroked her cheeks, but she angled her chin. "Since my decision three years passed, you are still a knight. As much as I wish otherwise, nothing has changed."

At Isabel's words, Duncan stiffened. But he couldn't

deny them in one regard. Frasyer was still an earl, while knighthood belonged to him.

"You are wrong," he said at last. "Much has changed. We made love."

"Last night has nothing to do with this."

He rose. "Does it not? We have given ourselves to each other in the most intimate of ways, as a woman gives to a man whom they trust. Will you trust me?"

"Let me see the Bible."

He shook his head. "Once we have arrived at Rothfield Castle." Or so he hoped he could. He prayed Griffin was in residence and her father, no, not her father, Lord Caelin, was safe.

Isabel stared at him, her mouth slightly parted, her hands fisted at her sides.

She started toward the table; he stepped before her and blocked her access to the Bible. "Is the decision to offer your trust to me so difficult?" he asked, pushing her, aware that he was asking for more than the reason to continue hiding the contents of the Bible from her.

He was asking for himself.

"Damn you, Duncan."

"Say it."

Amber eyes narrowed. "I trust you."

Relief swept through him. He'd not realized how much he needed to hear the words. They were a balm to his soul, illuminating a darkness that had lingered these past three years.

The first rays of sunlight slipped through aged slits of the tarp.

"We need to leave," he said.

Her lips pressed together, but she didn't protest. She turned away.

After the past few hours of making love, he could not leave the situation between them strained. He stepped forward, caught her shoulder and drew Isabel against him.

"This will all work out." He traced a kiss along the curve of her jaw. However much he wished to linger, to make love with her one more time, they could not tarry.

Raising his head, he drew his thumb across her lower lip, still swollen from their kisses. "Finish getting dressed. By the time you are done, I will have packed everything and we can leave."

The cheerful fire blazed high as he turned away, the warmth far from touching the coldness of his soul. The arrival of the morning had severed the fantasy of his earlier thoughts. Regardless of whether they reached Griffin's home safely, the likelihood of them being separated once there was all too real.

Should he tell her he loved her? Was he wrong to wait until they reached Rothfield Castle? What would his admission bring except raise the cost of an already convoluted situation? Bedamned.

He'd lost her once, allowed his thoughts to become tainted and had been a fool to have given up on her when she'd needed him most. As a result, she had lived too many days under the thumb of his ruthless enemy. Part of him marveled at her strength in surviving, while another part couldn't help but feel niggles of resentment at how she had not trusted him enough, trusted his strength enough to protect them both.

Nay. He'd not blame her alone. They'd both made mistakes in the past.

But here, now, he silently vowed, whatever it took he would keep her.

Until he'd seen her again, he'd not allowed himself to remember all that was special and precious about her. Now, watching her graceful movements as she dressed, the pressure inside his chest was an actual physical reminder that she was forever in his heart.

"I am ready," Isabel said.

As he. He turned to retrieve the Bible. "I—"

A loud crash thundered against the door.

Isabel screamed.

Frasyer! Duncan drew his sword and caught her wrist, pulling her around to his back. "Stay behind me!"

Chapter 19

Adrenaline pumped through Duncan's veins as the hut's door shuddered against the next hard impact.

Another solid ram.

Wood splintered. Wind-whipped snow spurted through the cracks.

Isabel's face grew ashen.

Weapon in hand, Duncan stepped before her. "Whatever happens," he ordered, "stay behind me."

At the next slam against wood, the door burst open. It crashed against the interior wall. Swords drawn, knights stormed the crofter's hut.

Behind them, framed within the muted dawn, stood Frasyer.

Gray eyes narrowed on Isabel with malignant satisfaction, his normally neatly bound brown hair tugged loose by the wind and littered with shards of ice.

Isabel gasped.

"You thought to escape me," the earl seethed. His gaze skewered Duncan. "And you. You dare enter my castle and abduct my mistress?"

Eyes blazing, Duncan grunted with disgust. "Is that what you call freeing a woman imprisoned?"

Frasyer stiffened. "Bitter words from a man whose betrothed abandons him on the eve he is to wed."

"A decision forced upon her," Duncan returned.

Understanding flickered in Frayser's eyes. "She told you of our bargain."

Duncan ignored Isabel's sharp intake of breath. "Bargain? As if killing me was not your intention from the first. Now, you believe you hold just reason."

"Reason enough to suit my needs," Frasyer replied.

Rage slammed atop Duncan's mounting worry for Isabel and settled on the man who'd stolen everything he'd once loved and threatened to do so again. "I should have guessed that your twisted ways were behind Isabel's leaving me."

Frasyer lifted his sword in warning—and promise. "The reason matters not. I will enjoy watching your blood spill upon my blade."

"No!" Isabel shouted.

Frasyer shifted his attention to her. Gray eyes narrowed and curdled with violence. "You will regret your betrayal."

"Isabel will travel to Lord Monceaux's," Duncan stated. He had to ensure Griffin's intervention, but neither Isabel, nor the Bible could stay within Frasyer's hands. "His decision, not yours, will guide her fate."

"With the Bible I presume?" Frasyer drawled.

Isabel lifted her chin. "My father is innocent of your claims."

"Lord Caelin is a fool," Frasyer stated. "As are you. You knew the consequence of breaking your vow of silence, but ignored it."

Duncan gripped his sword tighter. "Consequence? Nay, a threat, an abuse of power you enjoy serving on those unable to defend themselves." He covertly scoured the hard faces of the four knights surrounding them. He was easily outnumbered. "She does not love you, nor you her. Let her go."

The thud of footsteps sounded within the small hut as yet more knights packed inside between Duncan and the doorway. A sword's wrath!

"Her feelings toward me matter not. You want her." A brutal smile slinked across Frasyer's mouth. "That is enough. Or was."

Duncan stilled. Frasyer couldn't know of Isabel's blood tie to Wallace. If so, he would have exploited it from the first.

With predatory ease, Frasyer stepped before his knights. "Are you not curious of what changed my mind?" He glanced at the Bible on the table, then toward Duncan. "Or . . . do you already know what secret lies hidden within?"

"What secret?" Isabel asked, a tremor in her voice, clearly picking up the unspoken verbal joust between the men.

Duncan fought to shield his reaction to Frasyer's taunt, but something in his expression must have given him away; evil satisfaction curled on Frasyer's mouth.

"I see you know as well," Frasyer drawled, his sword clenched ready in his hand at odds with his casual tone. "You can imagine my surprise at learning such a truth."

"What truth?" Isabel touched Duncan's sleeve. "What is he talking about?"

Frasyer gave a cold laugh. "Why, Isabel, this is

truly a pity." Sarcasm dripped from his every word. "It would seem that no one has informed you of your true birthright."

At the confusion on her face, a muscle worked in Duncan's jaw. He fought the urge to lunge forward and finish Frasyer now, consequences be damned.

"If you know," he challenged Frasyer, "why have you not handed the Bible to King Edward to earn his praise that you constantly seek?"

Anger flushed Frasyer's face. "It would seem that I, too, was ignorant of such news of importance. Until," Frasyer said with a smug look toward Isabel, "recent events brought the Bible's existence into my hands. Unfortunately, once I'd discovered the truth, you had already abducted her from my dungeon."

Fear paled Isabel's face as she inched forward to stand at Duncan's side. "What you are both talking about?"

"My dear, Isabel," Frasyer drawled, "why of course the fact that your father is William Wallace."

Her eyes widened in shock. Shaking, her hand inched toward the pendant of Wallace's colors hidden at her throat. As if realizing her error, she dropped her hand and shook her head.

"A lie," she accused, "one you have crafted for your own nefarious means."

Frasyer shot Duncan a hard look. "Tell her."

"What?" Duncan replied. "That you would craft any story, regardless of its truth, if you believed it would serve you credit in King Edward's eyes?"

Frasyer glanced toward the Bible. "Ask her the same question once she sees the proof."

Duncan damned this moment. There was only

one way Frasyer could have known; he indeed had discovered the hidden documents.

Potent silence stumbled through the room. A caustic energy that pulsed through Duncan as he watched Isabel try and decide if Frasyer's claim was true.

As understanding flickered in her amber eyes, he saw her questions but more, the terrified understanding that it was the truth.

Bedamned, he'd not meant her to learn who her father was this way! Now, 'twas too late. The deed was done. Somehow, he must get her safely to Griffin.

"Enough!" Frasyer ordered. "Now that I have Isabel as well as proof of her heritage, I will deliver both to King Edward."

Duncan braced his legs apart and raised his sword. "She will be delivered to Lord Monceaux."

With supreme confidence of a victory, Frasyer ignored Duncan and extended his hand. "Isabel, hand me the Bible."

The weight of the Bible trembled in Isabel's hand. Why hadn't Duncan denied the earl's claim? Her heart pounded. Was William Wallace indeed her father?

If it was true, it explained so much—the reason why Wallace had visited her over the years, and why he had given her the pendant bearing his arms during her youth. Also, her father's . . . no, not her father, Lord Caelin's guarded actions toward her. But not why either man had allowed her to go to Frasyer as his mistress.

That fact made little sense.

Hysteria welled up in her throat. God in heaven.

If William Wallace was her father, she could never allow such proof to fall into Frasyer's hands. Frasyer would indeed use it for his own selfish gain and harm a nation, not to mention the men she loved.

"Isabel," Frasyer commanded, "hand over the Bible. Now!"

She shook her head. "No."

"You have made your decision, Isabel. Now," he seethed, "you will watch as your lover dies."

"No!" she gasped.

Frasyer raised a dismissive brow, then backed behind the wall of his men. "Kill him."

Guards rushed them.

Isabel screamed.

Seasoned by numerous battles, Duncan fended off the first aggressor's blow with ease, then rounded to catch the second man's blade.

Isabel jumped clear of danger as honed steel screamed with each meeting of their swords, engulfing the hut with a cacophony of angry scrapes.

To give him more power in his swing, the leather-faced man to his left had widened his arc.

"Duncan!" Isabel yelled.

At her warning, he ducked and spun, slicing through the knight's shoulder. The man screamed and caught his arm where blood spurted from a bone-exposing wound.

"Behind me, Isabel," Duncan yelled, thankful when she shot behind him.

The knight to his left attacked.

Duncan met his parry. Their blades locked, their arms trembling from the demand for strength. Duncan broke the hold, but with each attack, he was forced toward the corner of the room.

Isabel shifted away from him toward the right.

"What are you doing?" Duncan yelled, "I told you to stay behind me!"

The knight on Duncan's right caught her action. The guard rushed toward her as she crouched near the fire.

"Behind you!" Duncan yelled.

She turned, a wooden bowl filled with hot coals fisted in her hand. Isabel threw the glowing embers into the guard's face.

The knight screamed as he stumbled back. The stench of burning flesh permeated the air as the warrior dropped to his knees and curled into a writhing ball.

Exploiting his aggressor's distraction, Duncan drove his blade in the knight's side, then jerked it out. Blood coated Duncan's blade, and the warrior fell, an anguished gurgle on his lips.

"Get behind me!" Duncan ordered Isabel as he regained his defensive position against the next opponent.

Footsteps padded on the dirt as she complied.

The warrior charged as Frasyer's orders boomed to his other knights.

Muscles burned as Duncan fended off his next attacker, his prior injuries and making love draining him of much needed energy.

"Fire!" Isabel yelled.

He spared a glance toward where she pointed.

Flames raced up the side of the wood. The embers she'd thrown moments before had ignited the bedding. Smoke curled and danced in a vicious stream, quickly engulfing the entire wall of the hut.

Another knight charged.

Duncan angled his sword to shield the blow, but a clever maneuver by the knight caught Duncan's left shoulder. Pain seared his arm. He gritted his teeth and grunted as he thrust his blade forward.

The seasoned fighter evaded his every lethal swing.

A sword's wrath!

Smoke billowed within the room as the stench of sweat, wood, and fear built with each second. To his right, Isabel coughed.

"We must escape!" she rasped.

"We will. Hold on, Isabel!" He shot a glance toward Frasyer between slashes, noting the earl inching toward the exit as visibility dimmed. Then four more knights entered.

"Seize Isabel before the damn hut burns down," Frasyer boomed.

The men took in the growing blaze and for a moment hesitated, then charged.

The clash of steel and grunts of men saturated the hovel.

Duncan maneuvered his blade, fury backing his each thrust, every damaging blow, but by sheer number, the guards managed to separate him and Isabel.

A scream tore from her, a combination of fear and rage, as she kicked at the guards as they ripped her from Duncan's protective circle. Amber eyes blazed as she jammed her elbow into the closest man's neck.

She gasped for breath as another man caught her.

Duncan severed half the man's arm who was holding her, again buying her freedom. Sweat poured down his face as he dragged in a deep breath, the air blistering his lungs with heat.

A blur shot to his left.

"Duncan!" Isabel called as two more knights caught her and started hauling her toward the door.

"Isabel!" Pain sliced into Duncan's leg. He glanced down. A gash slid along his right thigh, a thin line of red curdled to the surface. He ignored it as he battled his way toward where Isabel was being dragged across the room.

Framed within the doorway, Duncan caught Frasyer watching the event with morbid glee. The bastard wanted to watch him die.

Wood groaned. The building shuddered.

"Out!" Frasyer ordered, backing outside. "Everyone out. The roof is caving in!"

Guards rushed for the exit.

"Duncan!" Isabel's scream pierced the roar of the flames as guards bolted from the hut.

Abandoned, Duncan scanned his surroundings. Flames engulfed the dried reeds and grass. Caught within the rising smoke, embers broke off and streamed into several visible breaks in the roof to spiral up into the sky. Another shudder rippled through the hut. As if in slow motion, he watched the center beam tremble, then begin to fall.

He started to bolt. Before he could step forward, the beam, smothered with blazing thatch, dropped to create a fiery wall, closing off his only route of escape.

Frasyer's laughter echoed through the pungent cloud, fragments of his face cradled in the flames as he stood safe outside.

"Come," Frasyer shouted to his men. "Let him burn in Hades as he deserves."

"Duncan!" The pounding of hoofbeats smothered Isabel's scream. The rumble of men and horses slowly faded.

He was alone.

Left for dead.

Intense heat poured over him.

His blood pounded wild. He had to somehow escape and save Isabel.

Dropping to the earthen floor, he sucked in air charred by smoke, scraping his throat raw with his every breath.

He searched the flaming debris for a break in the wall, a path he could use to crawl to the door.

Cinders from the beams supporting the roof swirled to the floor, others clung to the walls like demons to ignite a second later.

Another beam directly above him shuddered. The entire hut was going to collapse!

Duncan rolled over and pressed his body against the length of the unlit wall as its charred support began to crumble.

Wood groaned, sagged, then crashed downward.

He closed his eyes and braced himself for the fiery impact.

Heat blasted him as if billowed by a smithy. A thud. The grating of wood. The crackle and pop of burning wood roared in his ears.

Heart pounding, Duncan opened his eyes. Instead of the oak beam falling to the floor, the end nearest him had wedged halfway down the wall, which now bowed out. Soon, the entire hut would collapse.

Another pop. Sparks rained down.

He shielded his face with his garb as he turned away, beating out the embers settling on his clothes in an incessant mist. Each spark burned a hole in his garment, little pinpricks of heat searing his skin.

Yet another shudder rippled through the fire-immersed building. The last of the thatched room stumbled downward, floating batches of flaming straw in the air like the wings of a mythical beast. If possible, the intensity of the heat increased.

Desperate, Duncan jammed his sword into the wedge between the wood of the walls.

Nothing gave.

Heat, raw and blistering, scraped his face. The stench of smoldering hair screamed up his nostrils. He clawed a handful of dirt and scrubbed it on his head and prayed it would be enough.

The horrors of the painful death he faced tore through him, threatening his calm, shattering his thoughts as he fought to think of a way to escape.

An unexpected rush of cool air caught his attention. Duncan glanced over. On the opposite side of the building, with the shifting of the beam above, the corner of the hut had fractured. Now, a slit cut up the wall big enough to climb through.

Duncan scraped the earthen floor to smother flames before him as he inched forward. Smoke thickened, clogging his throat until he was forced to wrap a cloth over his mouth before he continued. Coughing, he pushed forward.

It was simple.

If he quit, he died.

He reached the corner. Exhausted, charred patches marring his garb and scarring his exposed skin,

Duncan shoved himself up. His hands screamed as he caught the smoking edge.

The building started to tremble.

He glanced back. The wall to the entry door buckled, then started falling toward him.

Duncan dove toward the opening.

Chapter 20

A wave of heat exploded over his face as Duncan's back slammed against the snow. Heart pounding, he rolled away from the fire-engulfed hut. Wind-tossed cinders stabbed his exposed skin. He scooped snow into his hands, rubbing it onto his face, hands, and clothes, extinguishing the pinpricks of heat.

For a long moment he lay there, his body shaking, his breaths coming fast. On unsteady legs, he pushed to his feet and stared at the scarred remains of the crofter's hut.

Blazing wood slammed to the earth. The beam propped against the interior wall sagged beneath the onslaught, then speared through the side wall to pile atop the already roaring stack.

He sucked in a cold breath. Another moment and he would have been burned alive.

Panic welled in his throat as he looked toward where Frasyer and his men had rode off. Isabel! He refused to believe Frasyer would harm her. If the earl had meant to kill her, he would have left her behind with Duncan to die.

Instead, he'd ridden off preening of yet another personal victory. Yet Frasyer had erred in the most basic of ways. He'd not ensured his foe was dead.

A mistake, one that would cost the bastard his life.

Hours later, wind rich with the scent of pine churned around Duncan with a lazy spiral. Golden rays reflected off crystallized snow in subtle warning of the approaching night.

Exhausted, determined, Duncan blew out a deep breath and forged ahead. Purpose kept him going, dulling the sting of the nicks from his clash with Frasyer's men and the burns to his face and the back of his hands.

He'd trailed Frasyer throughout the day, but on foot, he was quickly falling behind. He scoured the hoof-hewn, windswept path ahead. If he didn't catch up with Frasyer soon, with the drifts slowly filling in the tracks, he would lose the trail.

Duncan quickened his pace, ignoring the protests of his body.

A hawk soared overhead, its screech echoing in the wind. He took in the predator, a powerful mixture of strength and grace.

He scanned the pristine woodland ahead. He needed reinforcements. As if that was an option. On foot, it would take days to reach anyone who could aid him. Not that he hadn't considered the overwhelming odds he faced should he catch Frasyer.

Muted voices in the distance had him looking northwest. Along the hillside, shadows of movement flickered through the thick wash of fir.

With stealth honed from years of war, Duncan crossed a nearby fallen log and hid behind several boulders covered with snow. As he'd followed the trail broken by Frasyer and his knights, he doubted the men would notice his tracks.

How many were in company? He hadn't counted earlier when Frasyer had stormed the crofter's hut. Likely, the earl had more reinforcements outside.

The soft thud of hooves on snow increased. A slap of leather melded with a jangle of spurs.

Frasyer's men were coming this way.

Hand wrapped around the hilt of his sword, Duncan flattened himself against the cold stone.

The scent of sweat and leather tainted the air.

He held his breath. Waited for them to pass. At least the men were traveling north, opposite the direction he needed to take.

Tense seconds slid by.

"Are you sure you saw a movement over here," a deep voice asked. "I see no sign of anyone."

"They could still be around, well hidden," another man replied, his voice unmistakably English. "They may have pulled back when they caught sight of us."

"Aye," a third man agreed. "If the English bastards are out there, we will find them."

Relief swept Duncan as he stood. A pace away, knights upon their steeds were slowly passing. "Seathan!"

Surprise creased his oldest brother's face as he turned in his saddle. He halted his mount. "Duncan! Christ's blood." Seathan's obsidian gaze scoured him from head to toe. "You are wounded."

Duncan stepped onto the trail. "A wee scratch or two."

"Wee scratch," his other brother Alexander challenged as he halted his mount beside Seathan. "You have burns on your clothes, face, and the back of your hands."

Duncan shrugged. "Which will heal."

"You are alive, thank God for that." Lord Monceaux's brow scrunched into a frown as he scanned the nearby trees.

"It is not myself that I am worried about," Duncan said. "Frasyer has Isabel."

Somber faces stared at him at the news.

Hardness encased Seathan's face. "We will find her. Here." He handed Duncan his water pouch. "Take a drink. After, tell us everything."

Water cooled his throat in a long slide. Duncan secured the leather pouch and handed it to his oldest brother. Then he explained his finding Isabel at Frasyer's, their journeying to Griffin's to deliver the Bible, omitting the fact that he and Isabel had made love.

"He has both Isabel and the Bible?" Seathan asked, dread coating his words.

"Aye, he has the Bible," Duncan replied, "but it holds naught proof of Lord Caelin's innocence."

At his words, Griffin stiffened within his saddle.

Duncan held the baron's gaze. "You know." It wasn't a question.

Griffin nodded. "Yes."

"Know?" Alexander demanded.

Seathan shot a questioning look from Griffin to Duncan. "By God, we will both be knowing the rest."

With the sun setting and refusing to waste time, in brief, Duncan explained.

"By God's steed," Seathan said as he shook his head in disbelief.

"Aye," Alexander agreed.

"You can understand why the truth of Isabel's birthright was kept secret," Griffin said.

"I can, but it does not make the learning of the fact easier to hear," Seathan said, shooting Duncan an understanding look.

With his emotions in turmoil, Duncan withheld his comments on the topic. "We will discuss Isabel and her heritage later. First, we must catch them."

Seathan blew out a harsh breath. "And will." He shouted an order to his men.

Duncan accepted a spare mount brought to him by one of Seathan's knights and swung up into the saddle.

Seathan kicked his steed forward in Frasyer's wake. Duncan, as the others, followed suit.

"If Frasyer knows about the documents within the Bible that hold proof of her blood tie to Wallace," Griffin asked as he cantered next to Duncan, "why did he not deliver them to King Edward?"

"Seems he wanted to deliver both proof of her heritage and Isabel to the king at the same time," Duncan replied.

"The bugger would," Alexander spat, the jostle of leather and hooves upon the snow a steady backdrop. "He cares naught but for himself."

"Do you think he has reached King Edward by now?" Seathan asked.

Duncan scanned the horizon, his breaths misting before him. "Nay. With the heavy snow, even on horseback, it will take him another day, mayhap two. He rides with a sizable contingent of knights. Though we have but fifteen men, we hold the element of surprise."

Alexander shot him a grim smile. "Aye, and Frasyer believes you are dead."

"There is that," Duncan agreed. "He will not be expecting me."

"Or the rest of us," Seathan said. "You made a good distance from the hut considering your injuries."

Duncan shrugged. "I have suffered worse."

Alexander grunted in acknowledgment.

Duncan looked at Griffin. "How fares Lord Caelin?"

"He is well," the baron replied, "but I regret to say he is still within my dungeon."

"Circumstance forced you to place him there," Duncan said, aware that as King Edward's Scottish adviser, Griffin could do naught that would raise suspicion.

"I have spoken with King Edward in regards to Frasyer's claims that Lord Caelin is supporting the rebels," Griffin said.

"And?" Duncan asked.

"I advised him that after speaking with my sources, I found no evidence to prove Frasyer's charge against Lord Caelin to any degree regarding the rebels."

"But King Edward is far from convinced?" Duncan asked.

Griffin nodded. "Frasyer sent a missive to the king stating that he had evidence, concrete proof of Lord Caelin being a traitor."

"He was talking about the documents within the Bible," Duncan said.

"Aye," Seathan agreed.

Alexander nodded. "We cannot allow Frasyer to reach King Edward."

"Or for the English king to gain Isabel," Duncan added.

"If we do not stop Frasyer," Griffin explained, "once King Edward learns the truth, nothing I can say will save Lord Caelin's life."

Or Griffin's, Duncan silently added. Griffin had risked his reputation to try and save Lord Caelin. If the truth were exposed, with King Edward's hatred toward Wallace and those who sheltered him, he would order Griffin's death as well. God help them then.

"If we are to catch Frasyer," Duncan said, "we need to ride faster. Nightfall will soon be upon us."

"A point well made," Seathan agreed.

Duncan kicked his mount into a gallop, as did his brothers. "Aye, we will find the bastard and save Isabel," he called. "When we do, Frasyer is mine."

Heartbroken, a tremor whipped through Isabel's body, then another as emotion again threatened to overwhelm her. After all the tears she'd shed, one would think none would be left.

Yet, images of Duncan trapped in the flames, cinders like a horrific shower falling around him, besieged her mind.

She wrapped her arms around her body, the emptiness inside her tearing through her soul. Oh,

God, if only she and Duncan had left the eve before, then he would be alive. Instead, they'd made love.

Now, he was gone.

The only man she would ever truly love.

Frasyer moved nearby, and she stiffened.

Bile rose in Isabel's throat as she stole a glance toward Frasyer, who after several hours of travel, had installed them in a crofter's hut. Terrified of his rank, the poor people living within had hurriedly followed the earl's orders to abandon their home to him. She prayed they had relatives close by.

As much as she'd longed to secretly tell the husband and wife of her plight and ask them to find help, she'd remained silent as the farmers and their children had scurried out. Frasyer had warned her if she tried to gain their help, he'd kill the entire family.

With her heart still raw from Duncan's death but hours ago, she refused to jeopardize innocent people's lives. In the fight for Scotland's freedom, many more lives would be lost, but if she could help spare even one, she would.

Exhaustion weighed heavy on her after this nightmare of a day. Duncan was dead, Lord Caelin was imprisoned and scheduled to be hung, and she'd learned William Wallace was her father. Now, Frasyer planned to hand her over to King Edward, who would use her as bait to draw Wallace in. Then the English king would kill him.

Isabel fisted her hand. She may have lost everyone who mattered to her, but her country would not lose their rebel leader—Scotland's only hope to lead them to freedom.

Repulsed, Isabel watched as Frasyer preened

within the fire-stoked chamber as if he was already before King Edward receiving yet another title. All Frasyer could see was his wealth, of what more he could gain, not the bloodshed caused by his greed or the people he destroyed.

Frasyer shot her a cold look as he shoved another chunk of seared venison into his mouth. "Do not think to escape me."

"As if guarded by your knights I could."

He slowly chewed, swallowed.

Disgusted, she turned away.

"Face me when I speak to you."

Isabel kept her back toward him.

The clank of a blade sinking into wood made her jump. Heavy steps pounded on the wooden floor. Cruel fingers bit into her shoulder and jerked her around. Gray eyes bore into her with malicious intent.

"Defy me again and I will have you whipped."

Ice chilled her veins. Before she would have held doubts, but since he'd watched Duncan trapped within the flames, something had broken inside him. Now, he would enjoy watching her suffer.

"Or," he said, "use you for the position you were bartered for."

His mistress. She stiffened. "You cannot. An injury has prevented your ability."

Nostrils flared. Hideous glee framed the anger in his eyes. "But not the abilities of my men."

She refused to give him the satisfaction of seeing the fear his taunt inspired. "I despise you."

Frasyer's laughter, deep and cruel, rumbled within his chest. "Imagine, William Wallace bound and forced to watch while his daughter is raped."

Sickened, she wanted to turn away, the pitiful amount she'd eaten threatening to purge. "My father will not cede to your demands, regardless of your twisted efforts. He will rip out your heart with his bare hands."

"In that we both agree," he replied with confidence. "Wallace's outrage will override his common sense and he will gallantly storm to your rescue."

"I was referring to Lord Caelin. Wallace will not come after me," she lied.

The earl glanced to where the Bible sat, a satisfied smile curdling along his lips. "Deny what you will. I hold proof." He caught a tendril of whisky hair between his fingers, slid it across his lips before she could jerk away. "But we both know, he will come for you, Isabel. When he does, Wallace will die."

With his brothers, Griffin, and their men nearby, Duncan scanned the brae before him. Careless tracks smeared the pristine, snow-covered hillside.

"Frasyer is sloppy in his arrogance," Duncan said, adding with disgust, "and slow."

"Aye," Seathan agreed.

"To Frasyer," Griffin said, "his glory lies before him like gold-drenched silk."

Alexander grunted. "One I would like to be cramming down his bloody throat."

"As I." Duncan pointed toward the crest of the brae where the swirl of smoke lazing from a distance crofter's hut caught his eye. "Look over there."

"The MacNaris'," Seathan said.

Duncan stilled. "The tracks lead straight toward their home."

Somber silence settled over the men.

"Do you think Frasyer ordered them slaughtered?" Griffin asked.

Seathan clenched his teeth. "Aye, along with their twin boys, Adam and Douglas."

"Mayhap he has spared them," Duncan said, not believing it for a moment. To Frasyer, eleven-year-olds were Scots, boys who would grow to men, men who would wield their blades against England's might. If he had chosen to kill their parents, neither would the lads be spared. Muscles bunched with tension as he made to stand. "We will find out."

Seathan's hand settled on his shoulder. "It is foolhardy to storm in," he said as if reading Duncan's mind. "Whatever the fate of the MacNarisses is long past. If we expose ourselves due to carelessness, our edge of surprise and any chance of freeing them and Isabel is lost."

Duncan exhaled a frustrated breath and glanced up at the fading sun. "Aye. It is time to move into place."

Seathan glanced skyward and nodded. "So it is."

Anticipation slid through Duncan as his oldest brother waved to several of his men he'd selected to go with him after planning their approach to Frasyer's encampment.

Five knights, led by Alexander, slipped off to the west.

Griffin, followed by four other men, worked their way east.

"Duncan, wait until we are in place," Seathan

said. "Once I give the signal, then go in and bring out Isabel."

"I will." Duncan watched as Seathan and the two remaining knights made their way down the knoll to circle around. Countless moments passed as he waited, the pounding of his heart echoing the passage of time. Finally, from the brae directly across from him, he saw Seathan waving.

With his every sense on alert, Duncan stole forward. He used the cloak of trees, large drifts of snow, or anything else that nature provided to shield his presence from Frasyer's men.

By the time he reached within a stone's throw of the MacNaris' home, long shadows echoing the arrival of night greeted him. In place, he, as everyone in their band, would wait for Seathan's signal, then they would make their move.

A profile of Frasyer's knight outside the doorway had Duncan pressing behind a large oak. Catching his breath, he searched the surrounding forest to where his brothers, Griffin, and their troops hid in wait.

Smoke continued to swirl from the chimney and wavering light seeped from slits in the heavily covered windows.

No signs of a struggle or the telltale sign of bodies being hauled from within existed. With Frasyer's mood high from this day's victory, he prayed the earl had spared the family's life.

Breaks in the fresh snow leading to the nearby shelter caught Duncan's attention. The trail headed east. Had the MacNarisses left? Or had they departed to go hunting with his sons and knew not of Frasyer's arrival?

Hoping they'd left, Duncan turned his focus back to his brothers and their planned attack. He scanned the nearby woods, then glanced toward the hut. Three knights stood posted outside. One near the front entry, the other two scattered deeper into the woods to watch for any intruders. Groups of men were camped farther away.

The odds were definitely in Frasyer's favor, but he and his brothers held the element of surprise. One they'd use to give them an edge.

For Isabel's life and Scotland's freedom, he prayed it would be enough.

The crackle of burning wood echoed in the somber silence as Isabel rubbed the bruises on her arm, her body still aching—painful reminders of Frasyer's warning if she again tried to escape.

Earlier, she'd made it to the door before his men had caught her. Furious she'd dare defy him after everything, for the first time ever, Frasyer had beaten her for her attempt to flee and bruises riddled her body. After, he'd assured her this was but a warning of things to come should she again try to escape.

His abuse confirmed her earlier suspicions that he'd lost his mental balance. That he'd turned to physical brutality didn't worry her as much as his insanity. His self-serving decisions of the past would compare naught to those made with a twisted mind.

Isabel drew her blanket closer and, numbly, peered at the fire blazing in the hearth. The scent of herbed stew filling the hut made her nauseous. With her thoughts scarred from this day's horrors, she couldn't eat. And with horrific visions haunting her of Duncan trapped in the flames and left to die, she doubted she'd find sleep this night.

Somehow, she must stop Frasyer from delivering her to King Edward. If only she could get word to Duncan's brother Seathan, or any of the rebels.

The brush of a limb against the side of the hut startled her. She ignored the sound. 'Twas nothing. What did it matter anyway? Duncan was dead.

Grief swamped her, but with sheer determination, she battled it back. If she succumbed to it now, she would never have the strength to look for help let alone an opportunity to escape.

The limb again scraped against the hut.

She frowned. The wind was blowing, but not enough to bend the limb to where it would brush against the home. On edge, she glanced at the home's exit, then the two guards who talked in quite tones nearby as they ate.

Nothing was out of the ordinary, unless one considered her fate. If only she had herbs to drug the guards and Frasyer, then she could slip out while they slept.

Another swish of the tree limb against the side of the hut had her looking toward the far wall.

The sound wasn't coming from the wall, but near the far window.

Heart pounding, she stared at the crafted panes. Had someone witnessed Frasyer's abduction of her and was trying to covertly alert her to their presence? Or had the people who lived here informed the rebels of Frasyer's actions?

Her shoulders drooped. Neither explanation made sense. Besides, the earl's cruelty was known far and wide, as was the fact she was his mistress.

Only Duncan knew the truth and of the earl's destination. Now, he was dead. Emotion built in her throat.

She started to turn away.

A shadow at the window caught her attention.

The outline of a man came into view.

In the cover of night, she couldn't make out his face, but she embraced the fact that someone knew of her plight.

She looked at Frasyer.

Unaware of the stranger outside, the earl sat before the roaring fire, his thumb absently rubbing the worn leather of the Bible.

Again she glanced toward the window.

The inky outline of a face lay shadowed against the glass.

She nodded.

The shadow mimicked her action.

He'd seen her! She stole another look toward Frasyer. The earl hadn't moved.

One of the guards stood. "I will go and relieve Robert."

The other guard nodded. "I as well."

No, she had to divert their attention. Isabel stood.

"Did you need something, Lady Isabel?" the closest guard asked, his tone curious.

Frasyer turned toward her. Frowned. "She needs nothing." His curt tone assured her neither man would be allowed to aid her regardless of her request.

"I have need to relieve myself," she said.

"You will not be allowed outside until morning, when we depart." Frasyer gestured to the corner. "Use the chamber pot."

Heat stroked her face. "It would be improper with you and the men in my presence."

Frasyer shrugged. "If you choose to suffer, so be it." He turned away. "Sit down, Isabel."

Frasyer's cold voice crawled through her. Tension seeped in the room like a wash of foreboding.

She didn't move.

"Do not make me regret allowing you to remain untied." His warning held a lethal threat.

She swallowed hard and sat. After ensuring Frasyer and his knights were not looking at her, she peeked toward the window. The outline of the man was gone!

No, he was again moving into her view, but just the edge of his face. The shadowed outline of his hand made a sweeping motion. What was he telling her to do? She scanned the others in the room, then looked toward the stranger.

He repeated the murky gesture.

Isabel followed the direction he indicated. He was gesturing to the Bible. Why? She stilled. The only person who knew about the Bible and its significance to her plight was Duncan.

Duncan?

Hope rose swift and keen. What if by some miracle, Duncan had escaped?

"Isabel?"

At Frasyer's harsh tone, she jumped. Composing herself, she turned toward him. Goose bumps crawled across her skin as gray eyes watched her with suspicion.

"You seem preoccupied," he drawled.

She fought to remain calm.

"Do not do anything as foolish as to try and escape."

"As if I could overpower you as well as five knights."

Frasyer grunted, but he seemed far from convinced she wouldn't try. He watched her a second longer, then turned away.

Isabel exhaled, her body a mass of nerves. Could it be Duncan? But how? She'd seen him trapped in the blaze.

Please, God, let Duncan have lived.

"Did you need us to remain here, my lord?" one of the knights asked Frasyer.

He waved them toward the door. "Relieve the men."

No, she had to stall the guards! If indeed it was Duncan, she couldn't allow him to be caught. "Wait!"

Frasyer's eyes narrowed as he stood. "Silence."

"Why? What else could you possibly do?" she taunted, needing to buy time.

The veins streaming Frasyer's brow bulged into dark, ominous lines. "Go!" As the knights exited, Frasyer turned toward her, slow, with intent. He raised his hand. "I warned you not to cross me."

Chapter 21

Fury poured through Duncan's veins as, from the window, he watched Frasyer stalking toward Isabel with malice. His muscles strained against the urge to storm the cabin and tear Frasyer apart. At the shove of the door, his gaze shifted to the two knights exiting the home, then back toward Frasyer.

The door thudded as the knights departed, barely penetrating Duncan's focus.

Frasyer had almost reached Isabel.

Signal, he silently willed his brother, withdrawing his sword in anticipation.

Fear dredged Isabel's brow. She shielded her face with her arms, the recent bruises from an earlier beating shoving Duncan's anger up a notch. The devil take it. He'd not stand here to watch her be beaten! Duncan bolted from the shadows and rounded the corner.

A knight stood several paces away. "You there!" The guard strode toward him.

Duncan raised his sword, never missing his stride. By God, he'd reach Isabel.

Steel hissed as the knight withdrew his weapon. Stunned shock creased his face as he recognized Duncan, then anger. "This time you will die!"

Keeping his eyes on his foe, Duncan edged toward the door. "Nay, it will be the men who have chosen to serve an earl driven by evil."

An owl hooted—his brother's signal.

A war cry rose up into the night.

Caught in the sporadic torchlight, a blur of men stormed down the brae like an avalanche of fury.

The knight before him whirled toward the slope.

The advantage Duncan needed. He sprang forward and drove his sword deep into the man's side.

A muffled cry of pain fell against his palm. The man's struggles faded with the shudders of his body. The knight went limp.

Duncan had barely shoved the man away when another knight rushed him. He angled his sword. Honed steel screamed as it clashed against his aggressor's sword. Gritting his teeth, he drove forward, heedless of the roar of battle around him, thrusting like a madman, with the soul purpose of reaching Isabel.

His attacker stumbled, ducked, then swung.

Duncan's arm trembled beneath the impact of the blade. He gritted his teeth and shoved.

The warrior twisted his sword. Steel scraped, broke free. He angled his blade and charged forward.

Duncan used the man's momentum, catching his arm and pulling him forward as he turned to his side.

The knight grunted as he landed face-first into the snow.

Before the man could move, Duncan slid his dagger into his heart.

Snow muffled the man's scream.

Duncan withdrew his sword. As he shoved to his feet, he scanned the tangle of men engaged in battle with his brothers. Seathan had a knight backed up against the side of the stall. Alexander was cursing as he dodged his aggressor's blade, then he lunged forward in a surprise move sealing his attacker's fate. On the edge of the forest, Griffin was skillfully battling his opponent, forcing him back.

Seathan finished off the warrior, and Duncan caught his attention. "I am going for Isabel!"

His oldest brother nodded, then angled his blade to meet his next attacker.

Heart pounding, Duncan bolted for the door, then froze.

The entry to the hut stood open. Firelight outlined the outrage carved on Frasyer's face as he held Isabel pinned against him, his other hand clutching a dagger against her neck. Fear churned in her eyes, but he saw the courage as well.

"Drop your sword or she dies," Frasyer snarled.

Duncan glanced at the swelling upon her cheek from Frasyer's abuse. Drop his sword? Nay, he'd slay the bastard.

As if reading Duncan's deadly intent, Frasyer's grip on Isabel tightened. Blood trickled down her throat. She bit her lips, yet a cry of pain escaped.

Hands trembling with fury, Duncan dropped his weapon. Snow puffed around the blood-stained blade.

"Now your dagger."

"Your knights are surrounded," Duncan said. "You cannot escape."

Frasyer's gaze swept the melee around them outside, and his jaw tightened. "Now."

With a muttered curse, Duncan complied.

The earl nodded. "Join us," he mocked, stepping back with serene calm, dragging Isabel with him.

Duncan glanced back. Several of the earl's knights had fallen. Though his brothers, Griffin, and their men were gaining ground, they wouldn't reach them in time.

To buy precious seconds, he walked with slow steps toward the hut as Frasyer backed deeper inside. Firelight, along with a wall of warmth, enveloped him. He scanned the interior. As he'd believed, no other guards remained. Except for the knife at Isabel's neck, even odds.

"Let her go," Duncan demanded. "She is an innocent, a pawn you are using in the jealousy you hold for me."

A deep laugh rumbled in his enemy's chest. "Ah, you never cease to amaze me with your bravado. I have Isabel. Admit it, the best man has won."

To the devil with his demands.

At Duncan's silence, the earl's mouth thinned. "Bar the door."

"Afraid your men won't be able to hold off my brothers and their men?" The glimmer of worry on Frasyer's face gave Duncan the answer he needed. "Your men are falling at a fast rate. English knights poorly trained."

Outrage drove Frasyer's face a deep red, then methodically, the earl neatly stowed it beneath a facade of menace. "Kneel," Frasyer ordered.

"Even if your men win, which they will not," Duncan pushed, "Wallace will not come."

A muscle worked in Frasyer's jaw. "He will, but you will never live to see his demisc."

Cries and screams from the battle outside increased.

The earl nodded. "On your knees!"

Despising his defenselessness, Duncan knelt.

The earl twisted one of Isabel's hands behind her back; she gasped in pain.

Duncan surged to his feet. "Let her go!"

"Unless you wish your lover further harm," Frasyer warned, "back on your knees."

Battling the urge to lunge for his enemy's throat, against his every instinct, Duncan complied.

After a long moment, Frasyer lowered the blade. With one hand, he reached over to where a ball of twine lay in a wicker basket. He tossed it to Duncan. "Bind your hands."

"Do not!" Isabel yelled. Frasyer jerked her arm up; she screamed in pain.

Duncan shoved to his feet.

In the same instant, Isabel twisted and broke away from Frasyer's hold.

Frasyer grabbed one of her arms.

"You will never have the Bible!" With her free hand, Isabel grabbed the holy book from the table. Regret tore through her face as she threw it toward the roaring fire.

The Bible slapped the earthen floor a hand's length from the hearth as Frasyer recaptured both of Isabel's hands.

At the panic in her eyes, violence erupted in Duncan. He stepped forward.

Frasyer pressed the blade to Isabel's neck. "Halt!" Duncan stopped, his entire body shaking with fury. "Give me the Bible," Frasyer demanded.

The Bible. Of course. "You have Isabel," Duncan said with slow precision that belied his internal outrage. "But even if you and your men succeed this night, without proof of her heritage, you have naught but an unwanted mistress." He didn't guard his words. From Isabel's attempt to destroy the Bible, she had accepted the truth of her parentage.

"Do not give it to him," Isabel said, her voice desperate. "Throw it in the fire!"

Frasyer slammed her against his chest, his arm tight around her neck. He glared at the window. Sounds of battle grew closer. "Hand the Bible over or she dies."

Duncan gritted his teeth. He wanted to call the earl's bluff, but how could he risk Isabel's life or allow proof of Isabel's lineage to fall into the earl's grasp? If they could hold off Frasyer awhile more and give his brothers a chance to reach them, they could save the Bible as well.

He picked up the Bible and cast it a hand's length away from the earl.

Satisfaction curved Frasyer's mouth.

A man's scream tore through the night nearby. A thud of a body slammed against the aged exterior.

God in heaven, were the men his brothers' or Frasyer's men? What if Frasyer's knights were winning?

As the earl loosened his grip and leaned forward to pick up the Bible, Isabel sank her teeth into his arm. On a curse, Frasyer released her.

Isabel dove for the leather-bound pages. "You will never have the Bible!"

"Damn you!" Frasyer caught her leg.

Isabel fell hard.

Frasyer shoved her aside and bolted for the Bible.

Duncan beat him there. He couldn't risk Frasyer regaining control of the Bible. With regret, Duncan heaved the thick-bound book with proof of Isabel's heritage into the flames.

"No!" Frasyer reached out instinctively.

With the earl distracted, Duncan drove his body into Frasyer's. They both went down. The fury restrained within Duncan unleashed.

"This is for Isabel!" Duncan drove his fist into the earl's jaw. Bone gave with a satisfying crack. He backed the punch with another.

A growl erupted from the earl as blood spurted from his nose. He went down hard.

Duncan landed on top of him. "And this is for all those unfortunates you have harmed!" His swing connected on the other side of the earl's nose, which was swelling at a heart-warming pace. He caught the blur of Isabel at his side.

"He has a knife!" she yelled.

Too late, he caught the glint of Frasyer's blade as he aimed it toward Duncan's healing side. Duncan grabbed the earl's wrist. His arm trembled as he held his hand back, the blade inches from his face.

Isabel caught Frasyer's hair, jerked hard.

Frasyer's grip loosened; Duncan jammed his knee into Frasyer's groin.

The earl screamed and collapsed.

Fists flying, they rolled toward the fire. Sparks erupted into the swirl of smoke as Duncan's foot knocked against an outer log.

"Duncan, you are too close to the fire," Isabel yelled.

The earl wedged his foot against the hearth and shoved in an attempt to flip Duncan into the flames.

Using the momentum, Duncan rolled with Frasyer, shifted and pinned him against the hearth. "And this," Duncan rasped between breaths, "is for me." Ignoring the painful burns, he again slammed his fist into the earl's face.

Blood spattered against already swollen flesh. Frasyer's glare turned venomous. "You will die for this!"

Before he could wield his dagger, Duncan caught his hand, twisted.

Bone cracked. Agony sliced Frasyer's face. The dagger slipped from his hand.

Duncan wrapped his hands around Frasyer's neck. Tightened.

The earl's face transformed, twisting into an expression of panic and fear.

"Duncan," Isabel screamed, "you are killing him!"

Her voice barely registered through Duncan's blind rage. Frasyer's struggles were satisfying, feeding a primitive urge inside him to destroy the enemy, to protect his own. This man had torn thousands of lives apart, slaughtered innocent lives with careless regard. All for his own gain, the lure of wealth. Duncan tightened his grip, heedless of Frasyer's purpling face.

How satisfying that he could end the merciless bastard's life. Do it. He deserved it for how he'd abused Isabel, and the torment he'd served her, an inner voice goaded, stoking the furor inside him. God knew that with the malice Frasyer had delivered over the years, no one would shed a tear when he spewed his last breath.

On a curse and with his hands shaking with fury, Duncan shoved him away. "As much as it would bring me pleasure to watch you die," he said between harsh breaths, "I will let Lord Monceaux decide your fate." As Duncan grasped the dagger, a flash of steel to his left caught his attention.

"He has another weapon!" Isabel warned.

Before the earl could drive his blade, Duncan sank the dagger into Frasyer's chest.

Disbelief widened Frasyer's eyes as he stared at his lifeblood streaming over honed steel. Frasyer looked up. Pain, hard and deep, darkened his gaze. He made to speak but his words smothered within the gurgle of blood.

Emotion scarred Duncan's throat. "You will never harm Isabel again." He tore the dagger free. Blood smeared Frasyer's chest, then slowly worked its way to the earthen floor. Gradually, the disbelief in the earl's eyes dwindled to emptiness and then the light faded until he stared straight ahead, unseeing.

Duncan knelt on one knee, sucking in deep breaths, his head dizzy. Frasyer was dead. They'd won. Nay, the battle still raged outside.

Isabel.

He stood. She ran to him, and it was a fierce slice of heaven holding her in his arms. "I have made a mess of things," he said, never wanting to let her go. He drew his fingers through her silken hair, avoiding the bruise on her cheek. "There is so much I need to tell you." He glanced toward the door where the sounds of battle raged. "First, I must help my brothers."

Her lower lip trembled. "Of course you must."

"Stay here. Bar the door behind me." Duncan gave her a hard kiss, wanting so much more. He broke away and strode to the door.

"Duncan!" Isabel called.

He turned.

She stood before him, tears in her eyes, her face cast with worry and fear, the flames in the hearth crafting a haloed backdrop. His heart shifted. She looked as if a cross between a woman and a faerie set on the earth for him alone.

"I love you. I always have." Tears shimmered in her eyes. "I never stopped loving you."

The ferocity of his emotions nearly drove him to his knees. Instead of answering, he crossed and swept her against him. "I love you as well, Isabel. Never forget that." He kissed her hard and released her. He started to leave, stopped to grab a sheet to cover Frasyer's body, then ran to the door. He looked back one last time. "Stay until I return."

She nodded.

He lifted the wood. With his sword readied, he yanked open the door.

A large shadow bolted toward him.

Duncan shoved the door closed behind him, screamed a war cry and charged.

"Hold!" Seathan yelled, barely avoiding Duncan's swing. "By my sword, are you trying to kill me?" The glow of the moonlight caught the bruises, cuts, and swelling on the side of his oldest brother's battle-worn face.

"I thought . . ." At the fading sounds of battle, Duncan looked around. Only distant pockets of resistance remained, with Frasyer's knights quickly falling to the rebel's.

They'd won.

He turned to his brother, hiding his relief behind a scowl. "I almost gutted you."

"Aye, but then, you were always slow," Seathan teased.

Duncan gave a rough laugh. "We did it."

"A few knights escaped, but I have sent men to trail them. They will not be getting away." Seathan glanced toward the front door. "Isabel?"

"Is safe, but I had to kill Frasyer."

Seathan frowned. "Just consequence for a man so evil."

"Aye, but I would have liked to have allowed Griffin to decide the earl's punishment. It will put a burr under Longshank's arse when he learns of Frasyer's death."

"Aye," Seathan agreed, "but it cannot be helped now."

"You think Frasyer's death will sway the English king's decision in deciding Lord Caelin's fate?"

"I do not know."

Duncan met his older brother's gaze. "The Bible is gone."

Seathan tensed. "What?"

"During the fight, I threw it into the fire. Unsure who was winning the battle, I could not take the risk of it being used against Wallace."

His mouth grim, Seathan nodded. "A decision I would have made as well."

On an exhale, Duncan walked with his brother to the door, pounded on it. "Isabel! Open up, we have won."

Wood clattered as she removed the bar.

The door jerked open and Isabel flew into his arms.

Duncan drew her into a hungry kiss, needing her, never wanting to let her go. But other matters must be dealt with first. With regret, he broke the kiss.

Tears misted in her amber eyes. "When you left, I was so afraid." Her body trembled against his. "Look at your face," she said softly. "When you first walked into the hut . . . Mary's will, you have burns atop your cheek, another across your brow. And look at the back of your hands."

"They are naught." He drew her close, the bruise swelling on her cheek stirring his anger. But Frasyer was dead. He would never hurt her again. Duncan softly pressed his mouth over her lips, a kiss meant to sooth, to calm, and to convey how much he loved her.

The clearing of a throat behind him had Duncan setting Isabel to the floor, drawing away. "My brother is with me."

Her cheeks warmed to a furious red as she gazed past Duncan. "I did not know you were there."

Dry humor sparked on Seathan's face. "Obviously. I came to ensure you were safe."

"I am," she replied. "My thanks."

"Duncan told us the truth of why you broke the betrothal," Seathan said. "Having known you since a child, I should have offered you more faith. Please accept my apology."

"If you will accept mine. I should have trusted not only Duncan, but your family."

Seathan nodded. "He also informed us of your heritage. Knowing you, your determined and stubborn manner, I am not surprised." The dry teasing on his face fell away. He glanced over at Frasyer's covered body. "I will remove him and apprise Griffin of the situation."

She frowned. "Griffin?"

"Alexander's brother-in-law," Duncan replied.

By the confusion on her face, his comment far from explained why an English baron would be with Scottish rebels. An explanation he would give, but now, he needed time with her—alone.

Duncan closed the door behind Seathan as he departed with Frasyer's covered body. He caught Isabel and drew her to him. He brushed wisps of hair away from her amber eyes. Catching her chin with his thumb, he tilted her face toward him and pressed a kiss upon her soft lips.

"I love you, Isabel. You are my heart, my every breath. I allowed jealousy to smother common sense. I was a fool to ever doubt you. A mistake I swear to you, I will never make again."

She shook her head. "I love you as well, Duncan. Never again will I hesitate to seek your advice. You are the man I will always turn to, the man who holds my heart, and the man with whom I look forward to spending the rest of my life."

He caught her mouth in a hungry kiss, loving her, wanting her forever.

She pulled away. "With the burns on your face, I am hurting you."

"I barely feel them." At her silence, he stroked her cheek. "I am sorry about the Bible."

The anguish creasing Duncan's face tore at Isabel's heart. "Do not be. We are alive. That is what counts. Besides, we could not risk the Bible falling into King Edward's hands."

A knock sounded on the door.

"It will be my brothers." Duncan gave her one final kiss, hot and filled with promise. "We will be alone later, that I swear to you."

His sultry words invited erotic images that churned heat through her body. She wished the time was upon them so she could touch him, make love with him again.

Duncan opened the door, and Alexander entered.

Alexander turned to Isabel. He stared at her for a long moment. "Please forgive me for doubting you. Had I known of Frasyer's treacherous plan, I would have ridden to slay the bastard with my own hands."

"My thanks," she replied with appreciation. A tremulous smile touched her mouth. "But I believe you would have been too late, for Duncan would have already finished the task."

Alexander shot his younger brother a hard look. "Aye, I believe so as well." He paused. "The news of your heritage shocked me."

"It surprised us all," Isabel said.

Boots slapped against the dirt floor as a tall, well-muscled man she didn't recognize entered. Shoulder length brown hair paid a complement to his hazel eyes. At odds with Seathan's devil's black hair and obsidian eyes, neither did he resemble Alexander or Duncan.

"Isabel," Duncan said, "may I introduce to you my brother-in-law, the Baron of Monceaux, or as he is known to the rebels, Wulfe."

The intimidating man took her hand, bowed. "It would be my pleasure if you would call me Griffin."

Mind whirling, she stared at him in disbelief as she worked to absorb the revelation. "Wulfe? The English lord who helps the rebels? And your sister, Nichola, is married to Duncan's brother Alexander?"

A smile twinkled in Griffin's eyes. "Yes, my lady, one and the same."

His comment, laced with charm, had heat stroking Isabel's cheeks. "I am sorry. I am being rude. It is that I did not know of your rebel tie."

"Most people do not," Griffin said. "It is safer that way."

That she could believe. "King Edward—"

"Does not approve of my sister's marriage," Griffin finished.

An understatement. God forbid if the English king should learn his Scottish adviser was supporting the rebels.

"We must leave," Seathan said. "For your protection, you will travel to Rothfield Castle. Duncan and Alexander will ride with you."

She glanced from Seathan to Griffin. "What of Lord Caelin?"

"He is doing well, my lady," Griffin replied. "Though he remains locked within my dungeon, rest assured he is well cared for."

"The charges against him?" she asked, fear roughening her voice.

"Are serious," Griffin agreed. "But with Frasyer dead, there is no one to contest my findings to King Edward that Frasyer's claim of Lord Caelin supporting the rebels are unfounded."

"He will be freed then?" Her voice wavered with hope.

"With as moody as King Edward has become," Griffin said, "nothing is assured. I swear to you, I will do all within my power to ensure he is released."

"My thanks." Isabel worked to regain her composure. "And again my thanks, to all of you."

Duncan squeezed her hand, understanding her worry for Lord Caelin, the same concern he harbored as well. At least Isabel was safe. His heart swelled with love. Once they were alone, he would ask her to be his wife.

The hiss and crackle of a spark caught his attention.

Duncan turned toward the hearth. Given the passage of time, the flames had receded to glowing embers. Standing on end, wedged against the blackened wall of the hearth, lay the charred outline of the Bible. He stilled.

Had the Bible survived?

Isabel clasped her hand on Duncan's arm. "What is it?"

"The Bible." Duncan whispered the words, as if to speak them aloud would cause the miracle to disappear.

Everyone turned toward the hearth.

"I see it," Isabel said, her voice shaking with excitement, "but it is blackened."

"Blackened for sure, but it is not destroyed." Ignoring the pain the burns caused, Duncan crossed to the hearth and bent before the glowing embers.

Isabel knelt beside him.

On an exhale, he removed his sword. He pushed the blade against the blackened Bible.

It didn't move. More important, the holy book didn't deteriorate into a pile of blackened ashes.

"I will catch it on the side and push it toward the right." Duncan gestured to Seathan. "Use your sword to ensure it does not fall into the embers."

His eldest brother positioned his blade to hold the Bible secure. "Ready."

Isabel held her breath.

"Now," Duncan said. Together they pushed.

The Bible slid onto the earthen floor with a heavy plop. The pages sprawled open with an erratic flair—pages he could read.

Tears of relief streamed down Isabel's cheeks. "The Bible is intact!"

"Aye," Duncan agreed, his relief matching hers. "The leather binding protected it from the heat of the flames. That and the Bible sliding to wedge itself against the back of the hearth."

"Thank God." Overwhelmed with joy, Isabel lifted the volume into her hands. It did not hold the evidence for Lord Caelin's freedom. Instead, it held proof of her tie to a man whose sheer name was synonymous with Scotland's freedom. A man who she'd long revered.

William Wallace.

Her father.

Isabel's fingers trembled as she withdrew the yellowed parchment from the secret compartment. It mattered not that the edges were scarred by smears of yellow where the flames had heated them, or that the pages carried the scent of smoke. Within was documentation that Frasyer had intended to wield for his own gain. Proof of how much Wallace had sacrificed for his daughter. A child he had always loved.

She turned to Duncan, and he drew her into his arms, her tears warm on his neck. His body throbbed with pain at his every movement, but nothing would keep him from celebrating the fact that proof of Isabel's heritage was safe.

A woman he was blessed to hold.

A woman he would always love.

Epilogue

Morning sun spilled through the hand-crafted windows in golden rays. Isabel smiled, welcoming the warmth of the new day.

Duncan's fingers grazed her cheek in a soft caress. "You are awake then?"

She turned. Green eyes rich with desire watched her, and warmth cascaded through her body. She leaned forward to meet his kiss, accepting, savoring his rich male taste, how he seduced her with his mouth as his hands caressed her with knowing intent.

"Good morning, my wife," he said, pulling the sheets down and exposing her to his heated gaze. She watched as his hands explored her every curve. Her groan of pleasure as he cupped her most sensitive place had him lingering, touching her with infinite tenderness, until he lay his body over hers and filled her, taking her again to a shattering bliss. After, he held her. Content, Isabel snuggled against his chest.

"My wife," he repeated reverently. "Three years past, I never would have believed this day would exist."

Her heart melted. "Aye, it is a dream come true that yesterday we wed. Or that almost a moon has passed since we discovered the Bible had not burned."

Warmth filled her soul. "But wonderfully true."

Duncan lifted the halved sapphire hanging on the chain around her neck, shared with her pendant bearing Wallace's arms. "My other half." As he joined the gem to bond with its mate, a shiver of energy washed through her. He smiled. "Magic."

"Magic," she whispered, having no doubt that indeed faeries intervened in their union.

"Aye. Compliments of my grandmother."

"That makes no sense," she replied.

Green eyes danced with mischief. "Aye, it does if you talk to Alexander and Nichola. They, too, were touched by the magic of the stones left in the bowl within my grandmother's chamber. It would seem that whenever a gem within the bowl glows and warms to a woman's touch, the brother who wears its mate will end up with her as his wife."

Stunned, she shook her head. "You never told me."

"It was more a fable Seathan and I made up to tease Alexander. Now, one I believe."

She settled into his arms. "I am thankful for your grandmother's hand, however magically bestowed."

"As I."

"But there is still one halved gem within the bowl," Isabel added thoughtfully. "Its exterior is rough and the color of crushed gold, but inside it is green with what appears to be moss."

A playful smile curved Duncan's mouth. "It is a moss agate. It is said to hold the ability to make warriors powerful and shield them from those who would bring them harm. Seathan wears the other half around his neck."

"Then the halved gemstone in the bowl is for Seathan's mate to find?"

"So it appears," Duncan said. "With all the events since our battle against Frasyer, I doubt my brother has considered the woman who will be his match."

At the mention of Frasyer, the lightness of the moment fled. "I am thankful that Griffin finally convinced King Edward to drop the charges against Lord Caelin."

Duncan skimmed his fingers along the soft column of her neck. "Aye, more so with King Edward's fury at learning of Frasyer's death."

"The English king will keep his vow to find Frasyer's murderer."

"He also plans to claim Scotland as his own, both goals he will lose," Duncan said with confidence.

Pride filled her as she remembered meeting Wallace, but this time aware he was her father. She'd cherished his embrace, their long, heartfelt discussion after. As she had when Griffin had allowed her to see Lord Caelin. Though not her true father, he would always hold a place deep in her heart. Her joy more so when but two days later, Lord Caelin had been freed.

"Aye," Isabel said. "King Edward will learn that greed can never compare with the passion of the Scots, nor our desire for freedom."

Duncan laid his hand upon the flat of her stomach. "Our son will grow up knowing only freedom."

She smiled, amazed they could talk of their future, the children they would one day have, and of all the happiness before them. Only weeks before, she'd played the part of Frasyer's mistress. Now, because of Duncan, a life promising untold happiness lay before her.

The embroidery framed on the wall caught her attention, and sadness washed through her. "I miss Symon."

Duncan nodded somberly. "He was a great man, a fierce warrior, and a stalwart friend. His courage will always be remembered."

"When our child is born, I would like to name him after Symon."

"And if it is a girl?"

Warmth touched her. "Do you think we would have a lass who could bear such a stubborn name?"

Duncan's laughter filled the room. "With you as her mother, aye." He rolled over and captured her beneath him. "It is our first morning wed. Time for discussing the names of babes will come. Now, it is my wish to again make love to my wife."

His mouth covered hers and she returned his searing kiss, wanting him, needing him, cherishing his love.

Once she was so foolish to doubt him. But Duncan had taught her that he was a man to turn to, a man she could love, a man she could trust forever.

Discover the Romances of
Hannah Howell

Put a Little Romance in Your Life With
Georgina Gentry

Cheyenne Song
0-8217-5844-6   **$5.99**US/**$7.99**CAN

Apache Tears
0-8217-6435-7   **$5.99**US/**$7.99**CAN

Warrior's Heart
0-8217-7076-4   **$5.99**US/**$7.99**CAN

To Tame a Savage
0-8217-7077-2   **$5.99**US/**$7.99**CAN

To Tame a Texan
0-8217-7402-6   **$5.99**US/**$7.99**CAN

To Tame a Rebel
0-8217-7403-4   **$5.99**US/**$7.99**CAN

To Tempt a Texan
0-8217-7705-X   **$5.99**US/**$7.99**CAN

Available Wherever Books Are Sold!

Visit our website at **www.kensingtonbooks.com**.